# A DARK AND STORMY KNIT

Wilfred joined the young man on the lawn, and the young man immediately turned back the way he had come, with Wilfred following. Pamela and Bettina followed along too, and when the small procession reached the spot where the two young women were standing, they fell in line as well. Clouds still veiled the moon, but light from the streetlamp allowed them to make their way across the sodden grass, which was squishy underfoot. The chilly air smelled of damp earth.

Their destination was the porch of the Frasers' neighbor.

"It's real!" The young man repeated the words as they got closer to the porch of the neighboring house.

The porch light illuminated the scene, a scene that from a distance could be taken as a typical scary Halloween display. A figure with short dark hair was sprawled in a chair with its head lolling forward. The figure's white cotton shirt, a simple button-up style suited to a man or a woman—though the figure appeared to be female—was blotted with large bloodstains, and there was a puddle of blood on the porch floor.

"Oh, my goodness!" Bettina reached for Wilfred's arm. "That's a real person, a dead person!"

**Books by Peggy Ehrhart**

*Knit & Nibble Mysteries*
MURDER, SHE KNIT
DIED IN THE WOOL
KNIT ONE, DIE TWO
SILENT KNIT, DEADLY KNIT
A FATAL YARN
KNIT OF THE LIVING DEAD
KNITTY GRITTY MURDER
DEATH OF A KNIT WIT
IRISH KNIT MURDER
KNITMARE ON BEECH STREET
A DARK AND STORMY KNIT

*Anthologies*
CHRISTMAS CARD MURDER
(with Leslie Meier and Lee Hollis)

CHRISTMAS SCARF MURDER
(with Carlene O'Connor and Maddie Day)

IRISH MILKSHAKE MURDER
(with Carlene O'Connor and Liz Ireland)

**Published by Kensington Publishing Corp.**

# A DARK and STORMY KNIT

## PEGGY EHRHART

Kensington Publishing Corp.
www.kensingtonbooks.com

KENSINGTON BOOKS are published by

Kensington Publishing Corp.
900 Third Avenue
New York, NY 10022

All Kensington titles, imprints, and distributed lines are available at special quantity discounts for bulk purchases for sales promotion, premiums, fund-raising, educational, or institutional use.

Special book excerpts or customized printings can also be created to fit specific needs. For details, write or phone the office of the Kensington Sales Manager: Attn.: Sales Department. Kensington Publishing Corp., 900 Third Avenue, New York, NY 10022. Phone: 1-800-221-2647.

KENSINGTON and the KENSINGTON COZIES teapot logo Reg US Pat. & TM Off.

First Printing: September 2024
ISBN: 978-1-4967-4957-4

ISBN: 978-1-4967-4958-1 (ebook)

10 9 8 7 6 5 4 3 2 1

Printed in the United States of America

For my sister, Ann Uemura.

# ACKNOWLEDGMENTS

Abundant thanks to my agent, Evan Marshall, and to my editor at Kensington Books, John Scognamiglio.

# CHAPTER 1

Still holding the rubbery snout that had completed his wolf costume, Wilfred Fraser stood in the middle of the Frasers' comfortable living room blinking in the sudden light.

"That's certainly an improvement," he commented to his wife, Bettina, and their neighbor, Pamela Paterson. "I was about to feel my way to the dining room sideboard and fetch some candles."

Lightning flashed beyond the windows that looked out on Orchard Street, and a sharp crack of thunder followed almost immediately.

"The storm is right overhead," Wilfred added, and just then the lights flickered.

"I'll get the candles," Bettina said. "Then we'll be ready if the power goes out again."

Without shedding the charming red cape that had transformed her into Little Red Riding Hood, she headed for the arch that separated the Frasers' living room from the dining room. In a few moments, she was back, carrying a set of pewter candleholders furnished with partially burned-down candles.

"We're home earlier than we expected," Wilfred said. "Arborville's Halloween parade and bonfire are always so festive—too bad they were cut short by the storm."

Another lightning flash and a rumble of thunder made it clear that the storm hadn't yet moved on its way, despite the fact that it had featured gale-like winds. Bettina hugged her red cape around her and even pulled the hood up over her hair, which was a shade of scarlet that vied with the cape in brightness.

"That hot spiced cider we planned will certainly be welcome," she said, "and maybe a fire in the fireplace."

"Your big bad wolf is happy to oblige, dear wife." Wilfred stepped toward the hearth. "The fire is already laid and it will be but a moment's work to set it alight."

Wilfred lowered himself to his knees before the hearth, a stout figure in the furry hooded jumpsuit, complete with ears, that made up his wolf costume. He struck a match, and soon a tiny flame grew larger and engulfed the crunched-up newspaper he had tucked beneath the kindling. As the kindling began to crackle, he pushed himself to his feet and headed for the kitchen.

Knowing that Wilfred enjoyed the role of attentive host, Pamela stayed behind, as did Bettina.

"Sit down, sit down!" Bettina said, and waved Pamela toward a comfy armchair, the one closest to the fire. A pillow covered in a bright handwoven fabric contrasted with the chair's peach-colored upholstery. Bettina herself took a seat on the sofa, which was also furnished with decorative pillows.

"There were certainly some clever costumes tonight"—Bettina interrupted herself to chuckle—"especially that mermaid. I wasn't sure how she managed to walk."

"I thought you and Wilfred were among the cleverest," Pamela said. "Little Red Riding Hood and the Big Bad Wolf. And you were both dressed for a chilly night too, though not for a storm. I thought the mermaid looked cold."

Pamela wasn't surprised that her costume hadn't elicited a reciprocal compliment from Bettina. It wasn't, in fact, even much of a costume, just a headband featuring cat ears worn with black slacks and a black sweater warm enough to stand up to a late-October evening.

A comforting aroma was drifting in from the kitchen, spicy, with cinnamon and nutmeg predominating. No sooner had Pamela noticed it than Wilfred stepped through the arch that led to the dining room bearing one of Bettina's sage-green pottery platters. It was heaped high with plump golden-brown cookies whose texture suggested they involved oatmeal. He set the platter on the coffee table and returned the way he had come.

A few moments later, he was back, carrying a wooden tray that held three of Bettina's sage-green pottery mugs. He set the tray on the coffee table and lowered his bulk, still in the furry jumpsuit, onto the sofa next to his wife. As he settled into place, a sudden flash of lightning illuminated the yard beyond the front window and an ominous grumble of thunder followed.

Bettina shivered and leaned close to her husband. "I'm certainly glad we're in here and not out there," she said, "and this"—she paused to accept a steaming mug from Wilfred—"is a perfect treat."

Wilfred had already handed Pamela her mug of spiced cider, and she lifted it to her lips. The apple flavor, mellowed by the slight fermentation that turned juice into cider, provided a rich and fruity backdrop for the interplay of cinnamon, nutmeg, and cloves—all enhanced by the welcome warmth of the mug's contents. Lowering the mug after her first taste, Pamela noticed the source of one other elusive taste she'd noted: A curl of orange peel bobbed in the amber liquid.

"Have a cookie," Wilfred urged as he nudged the cookie platter toward Pamela's side of the coffee table.

Pamela chose a cookie and bit into it, pleased to discover that Wilfred had included raisins in his classic oatmeal cookie recipe. She leaned back in her armchair, mug of spiced cider in one hand and cookie in the other, enjoying the presence of her best friends and the warmth provided by the fire, with its bright ribbons of flame.

Wilfred and Bettina seemed equally content, and a few moments passed in quiet enjoyment. Woofus the shelter dog had joined his master and mistress on the sofa, curling his shaggy bulk to fit compactly on the one unoccupied sofa cushion. His gentle snores only added to the sense of comfort and security.

But then he stirred, raising his head and twisting toward the windows. The angle of his ears shifted, as if he was straining to make sense of a sound not audible to the humans in the room.

"What is it, boy?" Wilfred asked, resting a hand on the dog's flank.

Woofus, of course, was incapable of articulating an answer. There was no need, however. A scream, clear and high, cut through the silence. Woofus responded with a sharp growl and jumped to the floor as Wilfred pushed himself to his feet.

The scream came again, louder.

Wilfred was at the door in a moment. Bettina watched from the sofa, alarm evident even in profile, as he opened it and cautiously peered out. From her armchair, which faced the sofa and the door, Pamela could see that the rain had stopped and a few dark-clad figures were visible.

"Trick-or-treaters, maybe?" Pamela said. "It's awfully late though."

"The older kids come out late sometimes," Bettina responded, turning to face Pamela. "It's more fun for them in the dark."

But these trick-or-treaters, if they were trick-or-treaters, were evidently not having fun.

"It's real! It's a real person!" a voice shouted as one of the figures moved across the Frasers' lawn. "And she's dead!"

Wilfred pulled the door open further and stepped out onto the porch. Bettina was on her feet then, and Pamela too, and both hurried toward the doorway.

The closest of the figures was a young man, perhaps in his late teens. Following him were two more people, both young women. The expressions on the faces of all three were so extreme that they could have served as models for the latest horror-movie promotion: brows corrugated, eyes wide, mouths agape.

"She's dead!" the young man repeated. He was now

just a few yards from where Wilfred stood, and he gestured to his left. "On the porch," he added. "I didn't know what to do."

Wilfred joined the young man on the lawn, and the young man immediately turned back the way he had come, with Wilfred following. Pamela and Bettina followed along too, and when the small procession reached the spot where the two young women were standing, they fell in line as well. Clouds still veiled the moon, but light from the streetlamp allowed them to make their way across the sodden grass, which was squishy underfoot. The chilly air smelled of damp earth.

Their destination was the porch of the Frasers' neighbor.

"It's real!" The young man repeated the words as they got closer to the porch of the neighboring house.

The porch light illuminated the scene, a scene that from a distance could be taken as a typical scary Halloween display. A figure with short dark hair was sprawled in a chair with its head lolling forward. The figure's white cotton shirt, a simple button-up style suited to a man or a woman—though the figure appeared to be female—was blotted with large bloodstains, and there was a puddle of blood on the porch floor.

"Oh, my goodness!" Bettina reached for Wilfred's arm. "That's a real person, a dead person!"

"It's like someone stabbed her." One of the young women spoke up in a tremulous voice, followed by a desperate sob.

Bettina, sensing someone more in need of comfort than she was, released Wilfred's arm and pulled the young woman into a hug. Pamela stepped a bit closer, though the scene was too grisly to contemplate at length.

"I don't think it's the woman who lives here," she observed. Pamela's house faced the Frasers' house from the opposite side of Orchard Street and she was familiar with the comings and goings of her neighbors, though she was not as determinedly social as Bettina.

"No"—Bettina ventured a quick glance at the occupant of the chair—"it's not Adrienne."

Pamela's gaze, meanwhile, had strayed to another curious aspect of the scene: the fact that the house's front door was ajar, revealing that lights were on inside. With Bettina occupied murmuring to the young woman, who she held in a gentle hug, and Wilfred offering words of comfort to the young man and the other young woman, Pamela edged toward the step that led up to the low cement porch.

A moment later, she was on the porch. She nudged the door open further and slipped into the brightly lit living room. She did not remain there long, however. An assertive hand seized her arm and tugged her backward, almost causing her to stumble. A voice squealed, "What on earth are you doing?"

Pamela turned to discover Bettina staring at her, an unaccustomed frown disturbing features more suited to cheer.

"The killer could still be here," she squeaked, "in this house. Have you lost your mind?"

She backed toward the open door, pulling Pamela along with her. When they emerged onto the porch, Wilfred was nowhere to be seen.

"He's gone back to your house to call the police," explained one of the young women, the one who hadn't availed herself of a hug. "Do you think the killer could be in there?" She nodded toward the porch, where light from the living room could be seen through the open door.

"Maybe we shouldn't be standing out here," the young man said, as if the thought had just occurred to him.

But the sound of sirens looping through the night air announced that the police were near. Wilfred stepped out of the Frasers' house and started across the lawn, joining the small group awaiting the police just as a police car pulled up along the curb, the bright lights edging its roof popping off like flashbulbs. Its siren cut off abruptly with a sound like a hiccup, the lights went dark, the doors opened, and two uniformed officers emerged.

With just the streetlamp and veiled moon illuminating the scene, it was still possible to recognize the two officers as they neared the group—Officer Anders, boyish and slender, and Officer Keenan, older and burlier.

"You reported a dead body?" Officer Anders said, after introducing himself and Officer Keenan—though both were familiar from more mundane assignments, like handling traffic flow at school dismissal or routing drivers around road repair crews. Officer Anders's boyishness was hard to mask, despite the creased forehead and stern manner.

"On the porch," Wilfred said. "It's not a Halloween decoration."

Officer Anders nodded at Officer Keenan, who took off toward the porch.

"The door was ajar when we got here," Bettina said. "There are lights on inside. The . . . body . . . isn't the woman who lives here."

"Check inside the house," Officer Anders called to Officer Keenan.

Officer Keenan was now inspecting the figure in the chair, but he called back, "Sure thing."

Officer Anders had taken out a small notepad and a pen. He opened the notepad and then stared at the fresh page, as if suddenly realizing that taking notes would be difficult with limited light.

"We could all go next door," Wilfred said, nodding toward the Frasers' house. "Bettina and I live right there."

"How did you happen to be here?" Officer Anders ignored the suggestion.

"*We* found it." One of the young women spoke up, the braver one, who hadn't cried. "We went up to the door, trick-or-treating, and then we noticed the . . . decoration . . . wasn't a decoration."

"And I screamed," added the other young woman, "and he"—she indicated Wilfred—"came out."

Officer Keenan rejoined them then, panting slightly. "Nobody in the house," he reported. "I checked all over, attic, basement. The body on the porch has been stabbed, no weapon left behind."

"Call Clayborn." Officer Anders looked up from the notepad page where he was evidently managing to write something. "Names?" he asked, focusing again on the three trick-or-treaters.

Once he had recorded their basic details, he turned his attention to Wilfred, Bettina, and Pamela. "Once again," he said, "how did you happen to be here?"

"We—Bettina and I—live next door," Wilfred explained, "and Pamela lives across the street, and we were all sitting in Bettina's and my living room when we heard screams."

"And that was the first sign that anything out of the ordinary had happened?" Officer Anders glanced first at Wilfred, then at Bettina, then at Pamela. "No earlier sounds of people arguing, or . . ."

Bettina answered. "We were at the parade and bonfire. We'd only been home about ten minutes when we heard the screams."

Wilfred gestured at the furry jumpsuit. "I don't normally dress like this."

"And I'm not really Little Red Riding Hood." Bettina couldn't resist a flirtatious giggle.

Two arrivals, one expected and one unexpected, increased the cluster of people on the lawn to ten. A second police car nosed into the cone of light cast by the streetlamp, making it easy to identify the man who emerged as Lucas Clayborn, Arborville's sole police detective. Detective Clayborn had barely taken two steps when headlights flashed as a second car turned into the driveway of the house that was now the focus of police attention.

The door of that car was flung open and a blond woman wearing a long flouncy dress topped by a little fur jacket jumped out onto the asphalt.

"What on earth is going on?" she exclaimed, advancing toward where the two officers stood a little ways apart from the rest of the group.

Detective Clayborn was advancing from another direction, and she turned to him as he got closer. "What on earth is going on?" she repeated. "Why are police standing on my lawn?"

Noticing Wilfred, Bettina, and Pamela, she added, "And why are you here?"

"Adrienne—" Bettina's voice overlapped with Wilfred's, but Officer Anders interrupted them both.

"Are you the homeowner?" he inquired, edging forward.

Meanwhile, Officer Keenan beckoned to Detective Clayborn and led him toward the porch. Pamela watched their progress and observed as Detective Clayborn, stolid and imperturbable as always, negotiated the step leading to the porch and bent over the figure in the chair.

When she turned her attention back to the other new arrival, who she now recognized as the Frasers' neighbor, Adrienne Haskell, it was to discover that Adrienne was staring at the porch.

"What's happened to my sister?" she whispered, swaying slightly. "That's my sister. She was fine when I left."

Bettina propped her up when she began to sway more violently.

"I left her at home to handle the trick-or-treaters." Adrienne was still whispering. "We were both invited to a party, but she didn't want to go. She isn't . . . *wasn't* . . . very sociable."

Detective Clayborn had completed his inspection of the figure in the chair. As he stepped off the bright porch and started back across the shadowy lawn, Pamela heard him tell Officer Keenan to summon the county's crime scene unit.

Officer Anders asked Adrienne once again if she was the homeowner, and Detective Clayborn echoed the question as he drew near.

"Yes," Adrienne said, speaking a bit louder and pulling free of Bettina's support. "I'm Adrienne Haskell and the—" She paused as a sharp intake of breath interrupted her words.

"The . . . body . . . is her sister," Wilfred explained in a quiet murmur.

"Mel Wordwoman," Adrienne added, whispering again.

"And you are?" Detective Clayborn turned to the three trick-or-treaters, who had been hovering uncertainly nearby.

"We were trick-or-treating." It was the braver young woman who spoke, and she held up a bulging tote bag as if to prove her point. "We were out before the storm started, and when it blew over, we thought we'd do a few more houses."

"The . . . uh . . . *that* . . ." The young man's voice trailed off, and he nodded toward the porch. "It just looked like a scary decoration until we got right up close to it."

Detective Clayborn turned back to Officer Anders. "There's no point in trying to get detailed statements out here in the dark. I'll drive Ms. Haskell to the station and you can follow along with the trick-or-treaters.

Before you leave, tell Keenan to stay behind and wait for the crime scene unit. And the house is a crime scene now."

Officer Anders tipped his head in assent, then he glanced toward where Pamela, Bettina, and Wilfred stood. "What about them?" he inquired.

Detective Clayborn sighed. The current crime scene was not the first at which Pamela had crossed paths with Lucas Clayborn. For such a pleasant suburban town, Arborville had seen an outsized number of murders, murders carried out in curious circumstances and by curious means. Pamela had often been on the scene when a body was discovered—or even discovered it herself—and the insights provided by the curious circumstances and curious means had resulted in her identifying the killer while Arborville's finest were still distracted by red herrings.

Detective Clayborn sighed again. Addressing Pamela, Bettina, and Wilfred directly, he said, "Go home. Just go home. But don't leave town. I know where you live."

Woofus required a full accounting of the adventure that had taken away his master and mistress and their guest so precipitously. He satisfied his curiosity by sniffing vigorously at their shoes and gazing raptly into Wilfred's face. Smiling gently and murmuring sounds of comfort, Wilfred stooped to stroke the animal's shaggy head. Once Woofus seemed content that his household was back to normal, Wilfred proceeded to the kitchen.

"I'm going to heat up the rest of the cider," he called over his shoulder as he disappeared around the corner.

Bettina picked up the mugs that had been hers and Wilfred's and headed for the kitchen, and Pamela followed along bearing her own mug.

A few minutes later, the three friends had resumed their places around the coffee table, mugs replenished with steaming cider, and oatmeal cookies at hand. Wilfred had detoured to the fireplace before taking his seat next to Bettina, and the fire had been coaxed back to crackling life with another log and a bit of strategic poking.

"A crime scene next door . . ." Bettina shook her head slowly and her lips tightened into a mournful line. "And poor Adrienne. I knew she'd had a guest for the past week or so, but I didn't know the guest was her sister."

"I guess there's someone in town she can stay with?" Pamela had raised a cookie to her lips but paused before taking a bite. "If her house is a crime scene, she can't spend the night there, can she?"

Bettina shuddered and the tendrils of her scarlet hair quivered. "I can't imagine she'd want to. I certainly wouldn't."

"She mentioned a few times that she grew up in Arborville," Wilfred said. "There must be friends who will take her in for a bit."

"Or she can stay here . . . I'm sure she knows that." Bettina snuggled closer to Wilfred as if to acknowledge the comfort offered by his bulky presence.

Conversation faltered then, replaced by wordless sociability. The fire, the cider, the cookies, even the faint snores emanating from Woofus, who was stretched out below the hearth—all aided in soothing the shock of the evening's grim discovery.

Sounds of doors slamming and people calling to one another indicated that vehicles from the county sheriff's office had arrived. Time passed. Finally, an hour or more after the crime scene unit had done its work and the remains of Mel Wordwoman had been dispatched to the county morgue, Pamela rose from the comfy armchair.

"You don't have to leave!" Bettina was on her feet as well. "We have the spare bedroom . . ."

"I'll be fine at home," Pamela said. "The cats will be wondering where I am. And I'll make sure all my doors and windows are locked."

"We'll walk you across the street, at least." Bettina grasped one of Wilfred's hands as he pushed himself up from the sofa with the other.

# CHAPTER 2

Pamela's house was large—very large for just one person, though she shared it with three cats. Wilfred and Bettina insisted on accompanying her all the way into the entry and waiting while she turned on enough lights to make things, as Bettina said, "cheerful."

Pamela hadn't always lived alone in her large house. When they were newly married, she and her architect husband had chosen Arborville because it reminded them of the Midwestern college town where they met and fell in love. And they had chosen their fixer-upper of a house, which was over a hundred years old even then, because as penurious but energetic newlyweds, they recognized its potential.

Now, with its potential realized, Pamela lived in it alone. Michael Paterson had been killed in a tragic accident on a construction site when their daughter, an only child, was still in grammar school. Pamela had stayed on in the house, unwilling to disrupt their daughter's life any more than it had already been disrupted. Fifteen years later, that daughter was all grown up and living across the Hudson in Manhattan.

Two of the cats, Catrina and Ginger, had crept out to greet their mistress and investigate Wilfred and Bettina. The third cat, an elegant Siamese named Precious, merely glanced over from the top platform of the cat climber in the living room.

Once Wilfred and Bettina had gone on their way, Pamela climbed the stairs to her bedroom, accompanied by Catrina and Ginger. Discovering the body, and the police activity that followed, had been alarming. But the subsequent few hours spent in the Frasers' living room with spiced cider, oatmeal cookies, and the comforting fire had soothed, and sleep came easily.

Despite the fact that she was still wearing her robe and slippers, Pamela paused at the end of her front walk for several long moments the next morning. As was her habit, she had hurried outside before breakfast to collect the *County Register*, but instead of hurrying back inside, she stood staring at the house that had been the scene of the previous night's drama.

The day was bright. The storm that had provided such a suitable backdrop for that drama had left its evidence only in the dampness of the earth and the droplets of water still glinting on shrubbery and grass. But evidence of the drama remained—in the form of crime-scene tape, bright yellow, furled across the front porch of the house next to the Frasers'.

It was a pretty red-brick house, different in style

from Pamela's wood-frame house, sheathed in clapboard siding, and the Frasers' Dutch Colonial, which was the oldest house on Orchard Street. In the summer, climbing roses crisscrossed the house's brick façade, their blooms soft against the angular brick.

Resisting the impulse to slip the *Register* from its plastic sleeve prematurely, Pamela turned and headed back the way she had come.

The kettle was hooting frantically as Pamela stepped into her kitchen, so frantically that Catrina and Ginger had interrupted their breakfast to stare at the stove and Precious had fled the room. She deposited the *Register* on the kitchen table and turned off the flame under the kettle. Before dashing out to collect the newspaper, she had ground fresh beans for her morning coffee and slipped a paper filter into the plastic filter cone atop her carafe. Now she tipped the kettle over the carafe, inhaling the dark and spicy aroma that was released as the steaming water swirled over the fine grounds.

She was just about to slip a slice of whole-grain bread into the toaster when the doorbell's chime summoned her to the entry. As she walked toward the door, Precious darted past her and disappeared through the doorway that led to the kitchen, no doubt intending to finish her breakfast.

A figure, partly obscured by the lace curtain, was visible through the oval window in the front door. The figure was recognizable by its size and shape, and especially by its bright scarlet coiffure. Pamela opened the door to greet Bettina, dressed for this pleasant fall day in an olive-green corduroy pantsuit enlivened by an orange silk shirt featuring a floppy bow at the neck.

Teardrop-shaped nuggets of green jade dangled from her earlobes.

"Marcy Brewer has been busy," Bettina said, in response to Pamela's greeting. "I suppose you've seen the *Register*'s headline." In a non sequitur, she added, as she handed over a white bakery box secured with string, "I hope you haven't had your toast yet."

Pamela gestured toward the kitchen doorway and replied, "Coffee's just ready—and there's plenty for two."

In the kitchen, Pamela set the bakery box on the table, picked up the *Register*, and extracted it from its flimsy plastic sleeve.

"No point in actually reading the article," Bettina said. "There's nothing in it that we don't already know."

"Marcy must have shown up at the police station last night." Pamela unfolded the paper and spread it out on the table. A dramatic headline spanning two columns read, HALLOWEEN MURDER SHOCKS ARBORVILLE. Smaller letters below added, TRICK-OR-TREATERS STUMBLE UPON REAL CORPSE.

"She does have ways of getting Clayborn to talk," Bettina commented as she removed a carton of heavy cream from the refrigerator. "And I'm surprised she wasn't ringing our doorbells last night."

Pamela transferred her cut-glass cream pitcher and sugar bowl to the table and then opened the cupboard where she kept her wedding china. The china was precious and beautiful, with its gold rims and garlands of pink roses, but she used it every day, enjoying it as she did her other treasures, though most of those were tag-sale and thrift-shop finds.

"It's the pumpkin spice crumb cake," Bettina said as she loosened the string on the bakery box and folded back the top flap. She had already poured a goodly dollop of cream into the cream pitcher.

Once plates and cups and saucers had been arranged on the little table, with napkins and silverware at hand, Pamela tipped the carafe over each cup. The dark liquid swirled against the cups' pale interiors, and steam bore the coffee's seductive aroma upward.

Bettina was just transporting a square of crumb cake to Pamela's plate when the doorbell's chime startled her and her hand trembled. The crumb cake reached its destination safely, but Bettina was on her feet the next moment.

"It's Marcy Brewer," she announced. "I'm sure of it, working on *Arborville Neighbors Horrified by Halloween Night Killing.*"

She edged stealthily toward the doorway leading to the entry and peeked around the corner.

"I was right," she reported when she returned to the chair that faced Pamela across the little table. "But we have better things to do than talk to her."

As if to demonstrate what those better things might be, she served herself a square of crumb cake and added two heaping spoonfuls of sugar to her coffee. Once the sugar had dissolved, she reached for the cream pitcher and began to dribble in cream, stirring gently as the liquid in the cup was transformed into the pale mocha concoction she preferred.

"Did you sleep well?" she inquired, transferring her gaze from the cup to Pamela's face. "You look rested."

"I did, actually," Pamela said. "Thanks to you and Wilfred, I felt quite comforted by the time I climbed into bed."

"It's shocking to see crime-scene tape right here on Orchard Street," Bettina murmured. "I suppose Clayborn will want to give Adrienne's house a more thorough going-over than he was able to do last night. Who knows where the actual stabbing took place? Maybe inside. Or did Mel answer the door, step outside, and then sink down into the chair after she was stabbed? The chair is always on the porch."

She nudged a morsel of crumb cake free with her fork and conveyed it to her mouth.

"I called him first thing this morning to ask if there was anything he'd like readers of the *Advocate* to know about the Halloween murder," she said after she'd followed up the bite of crumb cake with a swallow of coffee.

"And . . . ?" Pamela offered an encouraging smile. Bettina was the chief reporter for Arborville's weekly newspaper.

"He has plenty of time for Marcy Brewer, but not for me." Bettina's lips twisted into an annoyed grimace. "He said there was no reason to meet in advance of our usual Monday meeting because there won't be another issue of the *Advocate* till next Friday."

"He might have more information for you by Monday." Pamela's smile took on a comforting edge. Bettina often complained that, as a reporter for a weekly newspaper, she had no chance to beat the *Register*'s Marcy Brewer to a scoop.

"You haven't tried your crumb cake yet." Bettina looked as concerned as if more was at stake than sampling the Co-Op Grocery's most popular bakery item.

Happy that Bettina had been distracted from one of her perennial laments, Pamela seized her fork. She carved off a bite of crumb cake that included both a portion of the moist golden cake and a crumbly nugget of the rich and buttery topping.

"Even better than usual, don't you think?" Bettina said after studying Pamela's reaction.

The Co-Op's crumb cake never disappointed, and the substitution of the more complex pumpkin spice for the usual hint of cinnamon in the topping was an autumn tradition.

"Very good, yes." Pamela nodded and reached for her coffee cup. She preferred her coffee black, and enjoyed the way its bitterness set off the sweet treats that she and Bettina often shared.

They ate in silence for a bit, sipping coffee on and off as the squares of crumb cake on the wedding-china plates dwindled to slivers and then vanished, leaving only crumbs.

"Have you heard anything from Adrienne?" Pamela inquired when the time seemed right to replace eating with talking.

Bettina looked up startled, as if the shift to conversational mode was unexpected. She opened her mouth, but before any words came out, the doorbell chimed. She scooted her chair back and jumped to her feet.

"Marcy Brewer does not give up!" she exclaimed as she darted toward the entry. "This time I'll make sure she doesn't come back."

Pamela listened, picturing the combative set of jaw and the resolute stare that would greet Marcy Brewer as the door swung back to reveal Bettina. But instead of the curt announcement she had expected—something on the order of *Pamela Paterson and Bettina Fraser are not granting interviews this morning*—the words that came from Bettina's mouth were welcoming, and her tone was cordial.

The mystery was solved a few moments later, as Holly Perkins entered Pamela's kitchen. Holly was a fellow resident of Arborville, and a member of the knitting club that Pamela had founded long ago. She and her best friend, Karen Dowling, were its youngest members, in their thirties, but as devoted to the craft as any knitters could be.

"I'm just on my way to the salon," Holly said. Holly and her husband owned a hair salon in a nearby town. "And I stopped by to see if you were okay. What a shock to see that headline in the *Register* this morning!"

"It was a shocking event." Bettina waved Holly toward the seat that she herself had vacated, while Pamela stepped into the dining room to fetch an extra chair. "But we're fine—and there's pumpkin spice crumb cake."

Pamela arranged the extra chair at the end of the little table and quickly set about grinding beans for a fresh carafe of coffee.

"I can't stay too long," Holly said as she perched on the chair that had been Bettina's. She was slim and quite lovely, with waves of dark hair that set off her glowing complexion. Her smile revealed perfect teeth and brought a dimple into play.

She lifted the flap on the bakery box and added, "It's hard to say no to the Co-Op's crumb cake. Half a piece is plenty for me, though."

Bettina set a plate and napkin and fork in front of her.

"Take a whole one." Pamela spoke from the counter. She had just set water to boil and was slipping a fresh filter into the carafe's filter cone. "I've already had my share."

"You're sure you don't want more?" Holly twisted her head to address Pamela.

"She doesn't." Bettina laughed, and transferred one piece of crumb cake to Holly's plate and the other to her own. "And I always do. That's why she's thin and I'm not."

Soon the kettle's whistle signaled that the water within had reached a boil. Very soon after that, Bettina's and Pamela's cups had been refilled and Holly had been provided with her own cup of the fragrant brew.

"Quite a thorough article in the *Register* already," Holly commented after she had sampled her crumb cake and followed the taste with a swallow of coffee. "I guess Marcy Brewer doesn't sleep."

"She doesn't," Bettina agreed, "and she's been ringing doorbells on Orchard Street this morning."

"I guess the . . . victim . . . wasn't actually a resident of Arborville?" Holly glanced from Bettina to Pamela and back to Bettina. "Mel Wordwoman her name was?"

"Just staying with her sister for a bit." Bettina nodded. "She lived in Manhattan—at least according to the article in the *Register*."

"A professor"—Holly nodded too—"at Fulham, in the Bronx. Did you get to the part about her most recent book?"

Pamela suspected Bettina hadn't read that far, given her annoyance at Marcy Brewer's tendency to swoop in and monopolize Detective Clayborn every time anything newsworthy happened in Arborville. She herself had just glanced at the headline.

"TOWARD A NEW WAVE FEMINISM," Holly clarified. "A *Womanifesto* she called it." Holly smiled, but not broadly enough to activate her dimple. "I thought that was clever, like *manifesto*, but for women. Like *herstory* instead of *history*."

She paused for another sip of coffee and then went on. "I was curious about the Womanifesto and so I Googled it. I had time to dawdle because Desmond opened the salon this morning and I don't have a client until ten. Anyway, based on the internet summary, the Womanifesto is pretty intense."

"Feminism has had several waves already," Pamela murmured.

"And thank goodness," Holly said. "Nell reminds us all the time how much better women's lives are than when she was young."

Nell Bascomb, in her eighties, was the oldest member of the knitting club.

"And so, yes," Holly continued, "it sounds like I'd agree with lots of the arguments in the Womanifesto, but not with—" She set down her cup as if to focus her energies on what she was about to say. Her dark eyes widened and she stared straight ahead, speaking in portentous tones. "You weave the web that is your prison . . ."

"What?" Pamela's voice overlapped with Bettina's.

"One of her themes is that a true feminist must renounce domesticity of all kinds."

"No knitting?" Bettina looked as distressed as if the prohibition expressed in the Womanifesto was aimed at her personally. "I'm certainly happy that my Wilfred has taken over all the cooking now that he's retired, but knitting is a different story . . ."

"A society without men," Holly said. "That was Mel's ideal."

Then who would do those domestic things, Pamela wondered, if women were supposed to renounce them and there were no men around? But Holly seemed focused on her crumb cake now, and Bettina was tackling her second piece. Perhaps enough discussion had been devoted to the Womanifesto for the moment.

Ten minutes later, Holly's plate and cup were empty, as were Bettina's, and Holly was climbing to her feet. Those feet were shod in a dashing pair of black patent boots that reached nearly to her knees. A slouchy black mohair sweater and black leggings completed the outfit.

"Knit and Nibble at your house Tuesday, Bettina?" she inquired.

Bettina smiled and nodded. The knitting club members took turns hosting the group, and the host served dessert midway through—thus the Knit and Nibble nickname.

"I know Wilfred will come up with a delicious treat

for us," Holly said, and the three of them headed for the entry.

Once Holly had been sent on her way, Pamela and Bettina returned to the kitchen. The carafe was empty, but Bettina seemed disinclined to leave quite yet.

"There was a point Marcy didn't bring up in her article," she observed as she lowered herself back into her chair.

"Um?" Pamela had cleared the table and was slipping the breakfast things into the dishwasher.

"Was Mel targeted specifically, or is there a killer on the loose?"

"She usually likes those sensational angles," Pamela said. "What do you think?"

"It sounds like Mel had ideas that people could object to." Bettina had twisted in her chair so she could face Pamela.

"Male people?" Pamela settled the last saucer into place in one of the slots designed for smaller plates on the dishwasher's lower rack.

"Yes," Bettina said. "I hope it would be a male person and not a woman, like a resentful knitter . . . or weaver . . . or whatever."

"Oh, Bettina!" Pamela turned away from the counter. "Devotees of the domestic arts are a peaceful lot. They wouldn't kill a person for saying, *You weave the web that is your prison*, would they?"

"I hope not!" Bettina thumped on the table to emphasize her point.

Pamela closed the dishwasher. Work awaited in her office upstairs, but she settled back into her chair. As associate editor of *Fiber Craft* magazine, she had always worked from home, even before so many people realized that if they sat in front of a computer all day for their job, there was no reason for the computer to be in a downtown office that required a demanding commute to and fro.

Now, however, there was time to linger and chat for a bit, especially about more cheerful topics than the Halloween night murder—though the first topic Bettina introduced was tangential to that event.

"Have you heard from Pete?" she inquired. Her manner was offhand, but her probing glance betrayed an interest beyond the casual.

"Not today," Pamela said.

"Last night, maybe?" The glance became more probing. "Though he wouldn't have known yet about the . . . uh . . ."

"He still might not know about *the . . . uh . . .*"

"He reads the *Register*, doesn't he?" Bettina leaned forward. "And I'd think, given the nature of your relationship with him, he'd want to check in and make sure you're okay."

"Marcy's article didn't mention me—or you or Wilfred, for that matter."

"But she was very specific about the house where the body was found, and the house's owner." Bettina nodded slowly as she spoke. "Anyone familiar with this stretch of Orchard Street would know that Adrienne's house is next to mine and right across from yours."

Pamela let a few moments pass before she spoke again. Then, in her own version of an offhand manner, she asked, "What is the nature of my relationship with Pete?"

Bettina sighed, uttered the word "Well" as if it was itself a sigh, and then sighed again.

A few more moments passed before she went on. When she spoke, it was to say, "I know it's not serious, on his part either. You've made that plain—and you passed up your chance for serious a long time ago, with someone who wanted to be serious . . ."

Pamela had been watching Bettina closely. She felt her brows contract in a scowl, and a low rumble emerged from her throat. Had she been a cat, her tail would have been flicking ominously back and forth.

"All right, all right!" Bettina made a patting motion, as if restraining something unruly. "Not another word, ever, about Richard Larkin. I promise."

"You've said that many times before." Bettina looked so contrite that Pamela reached across the table and squeezed one of her hands.

Half an hour later, Bettina had gone on her way and Pamela had climbed the stairs to her bedroom, where she dressed for the day. Bettina lamented the fact that her friend had no interest in the fashionable outfits that her tall and slim figure would display to such advantage, but Pamela was content with her wardrobe of jeans and hand-knit sweaters, or casual blouses in the summer. Standing before the bathroom mirror, she combed the dark hair that hung straight to her shoulders and declared herself ready to face the day.

Pamela's work for *Fiber Craft* involved evaluating manuscripts, copyediting those chosen for publication, and reviewing occasional books. Today, a deadline loomed for an article that had been a last-minute choice for the next issue of the magazine, and Pamela crossed the hall to her office, removed Ginger from her desk chair, and settled down in front of her computer monitor. Once the computer had come to life, with its familiar beeps and chirps, and the monitor screen had brightened, she opened Word and clicked on the file labeled "Smocks."

The article's full title was "Looks Aren't Everything: The Practical Function of Smocking in the Traditional Garb of British Agricultural Workers." She had skimmed it when it arrived the previous morning, and had been fascinated by the way the author used a discussion of the needlework technique known as smocking to illuminate country life in nineteenth-century Britain.

Smocks were the long linen shirts worn with leggings by farmers in England and Wales. Smocking—tiny pleats in the fabric, anchored with embroidery thread—was used to make the garment fit smoothly through the chest and shoulders. It could be highly decorative, with patterns linked to particular regions. But it was also useful. Smocks were expensive, costing as much as a week's wages, so they were designed for hard wear and expected to last a long time. The smocking, which compressed the fabric, reinforced it so that it could stand up to hard use.

She set to work. The article's author was British, and so there were minor adjustments to be made in spelling—

*colour* changed to *color*, for example—and punctuation, with *Fiber Craft* favoring more commas than in typical British usage.

After about an hour of work, she closed her eyes, pushed her chair back from her desk, and raised her arms over her head in a prolonged stretch. She was enjoying the respite from the monitor's glare and the shoulder hunch that keyboard work entailed, when a faint beep alerted her to the arrival of a new email.

She clicked on the icon for her email program and discovered a message from Celine Bramley, her boss at *Fiber Craft*. A stylized paper clip indicated that the message brought with it attachments.

The message itself was brief. "Please let me know by Wednesday at 5:00 p.m. which of these, if any, are suitable for *Fiber Craft*," Celine Bramley had written. "Don't forget, I need the smock article by 5:00 p.m. today." Across the top of the message, short titles accompanied by the Word logo gave a preview of the content in the three attached files: "Victorian Hair," "Dark Arts," and "New Black."

"Yes, I know you need the smock article by five today," Pamela murmured to herself as she minimized the email program and returned to her copyediting work.

Only a few minutes had passed, however, before she was distracted by the telephone's ring, the landline, on the phone in her office. She swiveled her desk chair to reach it and picked up the handset. The voice that responded to her "Hello" was a pleasant masculine voice.

"Hey, Pamela," the voice said. "Pete Paterson here."

Pete Paterson was the Pete Bettina had inquired about. The coincidence of his last name and first initial being the same as Pamela's had led to their acquaintance when a person who was looking for him called her number by mistake.

As he spoke, she pictured him. He was fit and athletic, with the wholesome good looks of a model in an L.L.Bean catalog—though as far as she knew, despite the surprising turn his career had taken in midlife, it had never included modeling.

"Are you and the Frasers doing okay," he asked, "after last night?"

"We're fine," she replied. "It's those poor kids who found the body that might still be on edge."

"I saw the article in the *Register* first thing," he said, "and I would have called sooner, but I got a frantic message at seven a.m. from somebody whose porch roof got caved in by a tree that fell over in the storm."

"I hope nobody was on the porch."

"Fortunately not, but the tree has to be removed—and I doubt it's the only tree that went over last night, so the tree service contractors are going to be busy. Then, when the tree's gone, I'll be rebuilding the porch."

"'No job too big or too small,'" Pamela quoted the motto featured on Pete's estimate pad.

"I should be able to get it done while we've still got some nice fall weather," Pete said. "Anyway, I'm glad to hear you're okay—and I'll see you tomorrow night. I hope we're still on for dinner."

"Of course." Pamela smiled, though Pete wasn't physically present to see it. "Till tomorrow night, then."

Still smiling, Pamela returned to work on the smock article. An hour later, she'd finished going through it once and her stomach was reminding her that a breakfast of pumpkin spice crumb cake, tasty as it was, did not sustain a person much past noon.

Back at her desk after a grilled cheese sandwich, she double-checked her copyedits on the smock article and sent it off to Celine Bramley. Three more articles awaited her attention, to evaluate for publication, not to copyedit, and she clicked on the short title for the first file listed at the top of Celine Bramley's email message: "Victorian Hair."

The article's full title proved to be "Something to Remember Them By: Victorian Hair Art," and, skimming the first few paragraphs, she realized that it was about the Victorian custom of clipping the hair of the deceased and displaying it in various ways. A few years ago, she had evaluated an article called "Memorializing the Departed: The (Hair) Art of Victorian Mourning Brooches."

That concept, wearing the hair of a departed loved one as jewelry, had struck her as macabre. So did the custom described in this article: twisting and knotting the hair into flowerlike shapes to create pictures for display.

"Too soon for this," she murmured. The memory of the previous night was still too fresh to be reading about dead people, even just their hair.

She closed the file and opened the next one. Its full title was "Fiber Arts and the Dark Arts," and a glance at the first paragraph revealed that its topic too was curiously disquieting.

"Casting on, casting spells," the author had written. "Weaving tangled webs of deception. Women's mastery of fiber arts has always made them dangerous, sorceresses transmuting fragile threads into cloth . . ."

"No, no . . ." she murmured. Already the style seemed unsuited to *Fiber Craft*, but the author deserved a fair reading—just not at the moment.

She closed the file and moved on to "New Black"—which turned out not to be macabre or eerie, though it focused on the color black. "Black Is the New Black: Was the Puritans' Garb Actually a Fashion Statement?" was written by a chemistry professor who described herself in a brief bio as having a long-standing love for clothes.

When we think of the Puritans in their black clothing, she pointed out, we often see their choice of that color as a sign that they had renounced earthly vanities—in the same way that members of modern-day religious orders dress in black. In earlier times, however, black clothing was associated with luxury rather than simple living. With premodern dyestuffs, a true black was very hard to achieve and thus rare and valued.

"Fun," Pamela commented to herself. "Who would have thought that?" And she wrote an enthusiastic recommendation that the article be published.

Copyediting the smock article and evaluating one of the three new articles was enough accomplishment for the day, Pamela decided. The sky was still light behind the shades at her office windows. A walk would be welcome after so many hours at her desk, and a visit to the Co-Op Grocery was overdue. Fish would be nice for dinner that night, and a pot roast for later, and cheese and whole-grain bread and cat food, of course. She saved her work, closed her evaluations file, and exited Word.

Ten minutes later, she was stepping onto her porch, trying not to glance at the crime-scene tape marking off the porch of the tidy brick house across the way. There were plenty of other, pleasanter, things to look at: trees with leaves that glowed amber and ruby against the fading sky.

# CHAPTER 3

"Quite an interesting development." Wilfred leaned back with a relaxed sigh.

The *interesting development* had been noted earlier, but there had been cheese omelets to prepare, as well as sausages and toast, and coffee to brew, and orange juice to portion out into Bettina's Swedish crystal juice glasses. Now Pamela, Bettina, and Wilfred regarded one another contentedly from chairs ranged around the Frasers' dining room table.

The table held the remains of the Saturday-morning brunch that Wilfred had cooked and served, and he still wore the apron that he tied over his postretirement uniform of bib overalls when he assumed chef duty. The pretty peach-colored linen napkins were crumpled, and the sage-green pottery plates were streaked with melted cheese and pork sausage grease. Coffee mugs had been refilled, however, and the fresh coffee seemed an invitation to chat.

"I never knew we had one of those surveillance

cameras here on Orchard Street," Bettina commented. "They're quite the thing now, and people do install them."

"I've always felt safe in my house without one," Pamela said, taking a sip of her coffee. Wilfred and Bettina enjoyed good coffee as much as Pamela did, and their coffee of choice was a variety from Guatemala.

"Convenient for the police, in this case, though the article in the *Register* wasn't all that clear on how the footage came into their hands." Wilfred thought for a moment and then went on. "I suppose the homeowner is one of our very close neighbors and, after the news of the murder came out, he decided to check whether his camera had captured anything interesting."

"The church could have a surveillance camera," Bettina said, "and the church is almost directly across from Adrienne's house."

Wilfred chuckled. "In any event, police now know that the killer was dressed in black, wearing a mask, and could have been either a tall woman or a medium-sized man. And the victim was stabbed right in the doorway."

"Better than nothing," Pamela murmured, "but not much better. And no murder weapon has been found. That was in today's article too. Some kind of knife, based on the injuries, but fingerprints could be helpful."

A gruff bark drew their attention to the living room where Woofus, visible through the arch that separated the living room from the dining room, was sprawled out on the sofa. He had raised his shaggy head and was gazing in the direction of the front door. A moment later, the doorbell rang.

Bettina started to get up, but Wilfred was on his feet first, leaning on the table as he rose. "Dear wife," he said. "Don't disturb yourself. I'll get it." He headed toward the arch.

A moment later, they heard the front door open and a coquettish voice cooed, "Good morning, handsome!"

Since the front door was not visible from the dining room table, Pamela directed a questioning glance at Bettina. "It sounds like she's recovered from the shock of Thursday night," Bettina said with a laugh.

"Who?" Pamela asked.

"Adrienne." Bettina laughed again. "She's always flirting with Wilfred. Silly, really, at her age."

Pamela forbore pointing out that Bettina herself was known to flirt on occasion and was possibly even a bit older than Adrienne.

Wilfred appeared in the arch with Adrienne at his side. He pulled out a chair for her at the table and inquired whether she'd like a cup of coffee.

Pamela knew Adrienne as a neighbor, of course, though Adrienne hadn't lived on Orchard Street as long as Pamela herself, or the Frasers. They had waved in passing and even had the occasional chat when they met at the Co-Op or around town. Adrienne was indeed Bettina's age or older, in her mid-fifties, but slim. Her wardrobe, like Bettina's, was extensive, and her blond hair fell in careful waves to her shoulders.

"I'd love a cup of your delicious coffee, if I'm not intruding." She aimed a flattering glance at Wilfred and lowered herself into the chair.

"Not intruding at all," Wilfred responded. "We finished brunch some time ago."

He hurried off to fetch the coffee as Pamela and Bettina gathered up the plates and flatware and followed him to the kitchen.

"I came here for a reason," Adrienne said, when they were all back and settled around the table, and she had a mug of coffee before her.

"You've been okay, I hope," Bettina cut in. "We were concerned you might need a place to stay while your house was . . . while the police were . . ." Her voice trailed off.

"Fine, fine." Adrienne waved a graceful hand. "I have a lot of friends in town. Mel and I grew up here, you know. I was the big sister, but I don't want to tell you by how many years." She giggled.

Mel, Pamela recalled from the article in the *Register*, had been forty-two.

Adrienne went on. "Our last name wasn't really Wordwoman. Mel didn't like our last name—she thought it was a relic of a patriarchal society—so she made up her own last name. And she didn't like her given name, Melissa, either. She thought it was too girly. I thought our last name was okay, but I kept my married name when I got divorced. It was okay too, and it would have been a hassle to change it back.

"I'm still the big sister—or *was*, I should say." Adrienne paused to adjust her expression, seemingly in response to the need for the past tense in the statement she had just made. "And Mel still comes—*came*—back to Arborville when she needed rest and a little cheering up."

"Mel needed cheering up?" Bettina bent her head toward Adrienne and gave her an intent look.

The question seemed natural, given Bettina's sympathetic nature, but Pamela suspected an ulterior motive. As a reporter for the *Advocate*, Bettina was always alert to hints that a story was more complex than it first appeared.

"Mel was troubled." Adrienne sighed, and her expression became more genuinely mournful. "Very troubled—it was almost like some kind of a breakdown, perhaps in connection with her job, or that group of feminists she associated with in the city, the bicycle fish people."

"Bicycle fish?" Bettina straightened up and blinked.

"Something to do with a woman without a man being like a fish without a bicycle?" Pamela suggested before Adrienne could answer.

Adrienne nodded. "One of those feminist sayings from ages and ages ago." She fingered a strand of her carefully arranged hair. "Before my time, of course."

Not to be outdone, Bettina added, "Before mine too."

Wilfred, meanwhile, had half-risen to check the coffee mugs for possible refills.

"No more for me." Adrienne waved a hand over her cup.

"Pamela? Dear wife?" He aimed a questioning glance at each.

No one wanted more coffee, but Adrienne lingered at the table. "I came here for a reason," she repeated, "and then I got sidetracked." She reached for the handbag resting beside her chair. It was made of fine smooth leather in a burgundy shade that matched her sweater and slacks, and from it she pulled a folded sheet of paper.

"I found a strange note on the floor in my front hallway. The police brought me back from the police station and let me pack a few things on Halloween night, before I went to my friend's house. I picked it up and stuck it in my pocket, and there was so much going on that I forgot about it till this morning."

She unfolded the paper, laid it on the table, and oriented it so the message could be read by Bettina. "This is a copy," she said. "I thought the note might be important, so I gave the original to the police before I came here."

Pamela could see the words clearly, though from an angle. They were printed in a very large font, as if by a computer, on an ordinary sheet of white paper.

"'When shall we . . . three . . .'" Bettina read slowly. She pulled the sheet of paper closer. "'When shall we three meet again?'"

Adrienne nodded. "'When shall we three meet again?' And the original note wasn't folded." She stroked the copy as if to smooth out the fold marks. "It was like a flyer someone might hand you on the street."

"Did the police think it was important?" Bettina inquired.

Adrienne wrinkled her nose. "Clayborn? Is that his name? The detective?"

"I talk to him frequently," Bettina said, "for the *Advocate*."

"Does he listen when you tell him things?"

A muffled laugh came from Wilfred's end of the table.

"Not really, no." Bettina shook her head, and her earrings, jade teardrops that echoed the rich green of her leggings-and-tunic ensemble, swayed.

"Clayborn is focusing on the logical things, because he's a man . . ." Adrienne paused for a coquettish half smile and a glance at Wilfred, then she added, parenthetically, "Of course, I don't mean to be critical of men. Where would we be without them?"

"I suppose he's studying that surveillance video," Pamela offered.

"Canvassing the neighbors too," Adrienne said. "A few people from Orchard Street have gotten in touch to ask how I'm doing, and they mentioned that the police had been around."

"How about her colleagues at Fulham, and her friends in the city?" Wilfred asked. "That seems *logical*." A genial smile made it clear that he was teasing.

"I gave him the names of some of her friends." Adrienne nodded. "And the police searched her apartment and carried off her computer—as well as her phone, from my house. I had to sign a receipt for both of them."

"Clayborn should be able to come up with some leads." Bettina laid a comforting hand on Adrienne's arm.

"The thing is, though"—Adrienne swiveled to face Bettina—"he doesn't really listen."

Appearing at the Frasers' door in a carefully chosen outfit, and with her hair and makeup perfect, had made it seem she'd recovered from the initial shock of her sister's murder. She'd even managed to flirt with Wilfred. But now her eyes were woebegone, and the lips that shaped her words trembled.

"I tried to tell him about Mel's state of mind," she moaned. "Something was going on, something that wasn't good, but she wouldn't talk to me about it." She seized Bettina's hand in both of hers. "I want to look around in her apartment. I have a key."

"The police looked, you said . . ." Bettina added her other hand to the cluster of hands.

"But how would they know what to look for?"

"Do you know what to look for?" Bettina's voice was soft but probing.

"I *knew* her," Adrienne whispered. "I was her sister. I don't want to go alone, though. Will you come with me? I can tell from your articles in the *Advocate* that you're good at making sense of things."

It was decided, then, that Bettina would accompany Adrienne into the city the next day. When Bettina suggested that Pamela be included in the adventure, Adrienne was happy to agree.

She started to rise from her chair, considerably cheered up. Wilfred, ever the gentleman, rose too. Before he stepped away from the table, he picked up the note Adrienne had brought.

"You'll want to keep this." He held it toward her, but before he relinquished it, he studied it for a moment. "Shakespeare, I think," he said. "The witches in *Macbeth*."

Adrienne's eyes opened wide and she inhaled deeply. "Of course! Why didn't I recognize it?" She exhaled.

"Mel was a Shakespeare scholar. The explanation for her death lies across the Hudson, I'm sure. Something to do with Fulham, or those friends of hers."

It was early afternoon when Pamela crossed the street to her own house. The brunch had been a late-morning affair to start with, and leisurely, and then Adrienne had arrived, and there had been so many things to talk about. She climbed the steps to her porch, collected her mail, and unlocked her door.

Once inside, Pamela lowered herself into the chair that was the entry's main piece of furniture. A coupon-laden flyer from the big supermarket in Meadowside went into the paper-recycling basket, along with a card offering 25 percent off on replacement windows, installation included. She stood up again and headed for the kitchen to tuck the bill from the water company away with the other bills.

Work for the magazine waited upstairs, but not very much work, and it wasn't due until Wednesday at five. And Saturday wasn't traditionally a workday, except for shopping and housework. Tomorrow was the outing to Mel's apartment in the city, which would be a change of pace, if nothing else.

Just as she stepped through the kitchen doorway, the phone rang, the landline on the wall by the kitchen table. A familiar voice greeted her as she spoke into the handset, familiar but strangely subdued.

"Hey, Pamela . . . hello," Pete said.

"Hello." Pamela had already said it once, but she repeated it and waited for Pete to go on.

"I've had a . . . something's come up . . . and I can't . . ."

"It's okay," Pamela said, intuiting what was to come. "I don't imagine the people with the damaged porch roof are the only Arborvillians in need of handyman services after that storm."

"That's . . . uh . . . not exactly what's going on . . ."

When Pete wasn't smiling, his eyes took on a melancholy cast. Pamela pictured him now, not smiling, and she wished, just for a moment, that he was there in person so she could do more than merely speak words of comfort.

"Whatever it is," she said, "I really do understand, and it's perfectly okay about tonight." She paused and then blurted out, "I have a pot roast."

"A pot roast." Pete laughed, more like a muffled cough, really, and then added, "I do like you, Pamela. You've been . . . it's been . . . great."

Pamela wasn't sure how to respond, so she didn't say anything. After a long moment of awkward silence, Pete said, "I'll call you . . . soon," and bid her goodbye.

She realized she was still holding the bill from the water company. Somehow she was grateful for the distraction of a small task: opening the drawer that held bills waiting to be paid and filing it away.

Housework suddenly seemed like the best use for the rest of the afternoon.


A few hours later, sheets had been changed, two loads of laundry washed and dried, kitchen and bathroom scrubbed, carpets vacuumed, and every dust-collecting object or piece of furniture thoroughly dusted. As a last touch, Pamela arranged the needlepoint pillows that decorated her sofa in a neat row, making sure the needlepoint cat was not standing on its head.

She had launched the pot roast midway through her washing and cleaning spree. The aroma coming from the kitchen now, meaty and comforting with a hint of bay leaf and thyme, promised that dinner would offer a suitable recompense for her domestic labors.

# CHAPTER 4

As a dedicated fashionista, Bettina dressed for her life in Arborville—no matter how casual the occasion—with noteworthy flair. But today's activity involved a trip across the Hudson to New York City—Manhattan specifically, and the Village even more specifically. Accordingly, she had styled her ensemble with special care. She wore a skirt suit in a bouclé tweed reminiscent of Chanel. The rust and brown tones, a nod to the autumn day, were enlivened by a silky top in vivid salmon. Chunky gold chains accented the neckline, and the chain motif was repeated in matching earrings. On her feet were rust suede pumps. A rust suede handbag completed the look.

"Adrienne's going to drive," she said after pausing to stoop and offer Catrina, who was dozing in the sunny spot on the entry carpet, a head-scratch. "She's back in her house, and very grateful for that. I suppose you noticed that the crime-scene tape is gone."

"I did." In acknowledgment of the fact that their outing would be taking them into the city, Pamela had set aside her usual jeans in favor of black slacks, paired with one of her recent knitting projects—a crewneck pullover in tawny brown with a large black cat cleverly worked into the front. "Nothing in today's *Register* about the murder, though. I wonder if Detective Clayborn will have anything new to tell you when you meet with him tomorrow."

Bettina made a dismissive sound that resembled a cat sneezing and commented, "I'm not holding my breath." She lifted her wrist to consult her pretty watch. "We've got a few minutes before Adrienne's expecting us. How was your date with Pete?"

"It wasn't." Pamela raised one shoulder in a half shrug. "He called to say something had come up . . . so I made a pot roast."

Bettina stared. For a few moments, her face was expressionless, then a vertical line appeared between her carefully shaped brows.

"That's not like him," she murmured after another few moments. "He's always seemed so . . . gentlemanly. Did he say what had *come up*?"

"It's really okay." Pamela stepped toward the closet, opened the door, and took out a light jacket. "We should probably get going now."

But Bettina remained right where she was. "How did he sound?' she asked. "Just matter-of-fact, or like the something that had come up was bothering him?"

"It's really okay," Pamela repeated. "I'm sure he'll get back in touch after he takes care of whatever he has to take care of."

Maybe he wouldn't, though. His voice on the phone

echoed in her brain, saying, *You've been . . . it's been . . . great*. Was that a goodbye? Would she mind? Her feelings for him weren't serious, as she'd told Bettina often enough.

No matter. Bettina was moving now, toward the door. Soon the two friends were crossing Orchard Street heading for Adrienne's porch, now bare of anything that might call to mind the events of Halloween night.

Adrienne, too, had dressed for the adventure in the city with care, though not as formally as to involve a skirt suit. She was wearing slacks and a sweater in a buttery-yellow wool that nearly echoed her wavy hair. Over the sweater, she wore a supple jacket made of smooth leather the color of cream.

Pamela hid a smile as Adrienne and Bettina looked each other up and down before speaking, clearly interested in each other's fashion choices. The evaluation resolved itself in a hug, and Adrienne thanked Bettina—and Pamela—effusively for joining her on the visit to Mel's apartment.

Adrienne's car was a BMW, not the latest model but sleek and luxurious for all that. Soon they were en route to the city, heading east out of Arborville, navigating the on-ramp to the George Washington Bridge, and then merging with the many lanes of traffic flowing toward the toll booths and the towering bridge beyond.

Pamela had ended up in the back seat of the BMW, by choice—though being much taller than Bettina, she had been offered the passenger seat in front. As Bettina and Adrienne chatted quietly, she enjoyed focusing on the passing scene. The fall day was bright and clear, and from the upper level of the bridge, the view south was of the Hudson, nearly as blue as the sky it reflected and skimmed with little whitecaps like shreds of lace. The jagged Manhattan shoreline was marked by angular buildings jutting upward, while on the New Jersey side, docks stretched like fingers from a shore softened in spots by autumn foliage.

As they approached the east end of the bridge, Adrienne steered the BMW into the lane that veered onto the West Side Highway. Soon they were speeding south, along the Hudson's shore, with the river's broad expanse on the right and a view of New Jersey beyond. After about twenty minutes, the exit for Fourteenth Street came into view, and Adrienne swung left, leaving the highway behind.

They bumped over the cobblestones of Fourteenth Street for a few blocks, made a turn, and entered a world of narrow streets lined with narrow buildings, flat-roofed, four stories tall, and each with a half flight of stone steps leading to a pair of ornate wooden doors.

Rows of narrow windows, some furnished with window boxes trailing ivy, looked down from red-brick façades

"Parking, parking, parking," Adrienne murmured from the front seat. "Always a problem in the Village. Mel never bothered with a car, but in the suburbs . . ."

Her voice trailed off as she braked abruptly. With a lurch, the BMW reversed direction.

"We're in luck," Adrienne exclaimed as she pulled forward.

She eased the BMW into position alongside a small sedan and, with a skillful maneuver that Bettina greeted with a hand clap, backed it into the only empty spot in the whole block.

Once out on the sidewalk, they joined the throng of well-dressed people hurrying about their business. Adrienne explained that Mel's building was a few streets away, but that the parking space had been too good to pass up. The street they were on was residential, one narrow brick building after another, but after a block they turned onto a cross street that featured shops and restaurants.

At the corner, a florist's wares had spread out to the sidewalk, pots of musky-smelling chrysanthemums in shades of amber and maroon, with gourds and pumpkins crowded among them. Next to the florist, a few tables and chairs sheltered by an awning flanked the door of a small café. The autumn morning was warm enough that people were enjoying their coffee and croissants alfresco.

Pamela and Bettina had lagged behind Adrienne to contemplate the wares on view in the window of a vintage clothing shop, when Pamela heard a voice behind her say, "Mom?"

Bettina responded first, though she wasn't the mom being addressed, and when Pamela turned, it was to see her daughter Penny's back and her dark curls, as Bettina pulled her close in a hug. Penny was not alone. Nearby stood another young woman, taller than Penny and with tousled blond hair that fell below her shoulders.

Adrienne had backtracked, and now she stepped forth with eager curiosity as Bettina, always at ease in social situations, launched into introductions. The other young woman, already known to Pamela and Bettina, was Sybil Larkin, the daughter of Pamela's neighbor, Richard Larkin.

Penny and Sybil had been friends for some years and were now sharing an apartment in the city. They had bonded over a mutual love of vintage fashion, and so a Sunday spent browsing for new—but old—treasures made perfect sense.

As Adrienne chatted with Bettina and Sybil, Penny edged close to Pamela.

"What are you and Bettina doing in the city?" she inquired. "And why didn't you let me know you were coming?"

"Um . . . oh . . ." Pamela thought she detected a note of suspicion in Penny's voice, and she wasn't sure how to answer.

She knew that her daughter feared for her and Bettina's safety when they engaged in their sleuthing adventures—though agreeing to accompany Adrienne to look around in her sister's apartment didn't exactly qualify as sleuthing. And she had no idea what Adrienne and Bettina were telling Sybil about their agenda for the day. Still . . .

"It was such a nice fall day," she said. "And Adrienne hasn't lived on Orchard Street all that long. Bettina and I are just getting to know her, so when she invited us . . . and it's always fun to stroll around in the Village . . ."

Penny leaned close and tilted her head to peer up into Pamela's face. Michael Paterson had been short for a man, not much taller than Pamela, and Penny had taken after her father, whose genes were the source of her curly hair too. It had been hard for Pamela to see this small person off to college and then to realize that, yes, it was time for her to be independent and make her own way.

"You're sure, Mom?" Penny's stare was intense. "You're just here for a stroll around the Village?"

"Strolling, yes." Pamela nodded. "We're going to do some strolling, and . . ." She glanced toward where Bettina and Adrienne appeared to be taking leave of Sybil. "It looks like they're just about ready to stroll on."

Penny mustered a smile and reached out for a hug. "Have a good stroll," she murmured as Pamela pulled her close.

"Come out to Arborville next weekend if you want," Pamela said as she loosened her arms and stepped back.

"Okay," Penny responded with a wider smile. "I will."

Adrienne led the way past more shops and restaurants as they dodged among people hurrying here and there on the crowded sidewalk. After a few blocks, she turned to the right, and they found themselves on a residential street that paralleled the one where they had parked. Mel's building was halfway down the block, narrow red brick like its neighbors. Perhaps it had once been someone's spacious townhouse, but the three doorbells with accompanying nameplates revealed that within its walls there were now three apartments.

They climbed the six stone steps that led to the impressive double doors, and Adrienne produced a pair of keys. She unlocked the door and they entered a short hallway. A steep flight of stairs stretched before them.

"Mel had the second-floor apartment," Adrienne explained. She glanced at Bettina and said, "That means lots more steps. Will you be okay?"

"Will you?" Bettina responded with a good-natured smile.

Once Adrienne was en route up the stairs, leading the way, Bettina nudged Pamela. Pamela turned to see an expression of comic disbelief on her friend's face—brows raised, eyes wide, and lips compressed as if trying to stifle an explosive laugh.

Adrienne unlocked Mel's apartment door and pushed it open to reveal a living room much longer than it was wide, with two tall windows at one end and a fireplace with a marble mantel on the wall that faced the door. A carpet covered most of the floor, with only a small rim of worn parquet visible around the edge. The carpet was modern in feel, olive-green with random swirls of bright orange. Flanking the fireplace, two rust-colored love seats faced each other, with a glass-topped coffee table between them. The walls of the apartment were white, but the many framed posters and prints added a lively note.

A large desk and a pair of beige metal filing cabinets dominated the opposite end of the room. Papers and books were piled on the desk, but a large empty spot in their midst suggested that the desk's furnishings had also included a computer. Pamela was about to raise that possibility when Adrienne spoke.

"That's where the computer was, but the police have taken it," she said. "Perhaps they'll find some clues among Mel's digital files."

"It looks like she stored hard copies of . . . whatever . . . too." Bettina had stepped over to one of the filing cabinets and was tugging on the handle of the topmost drawer. It opened with a metallic screech and she peered inside.

Pamela, meanwhile, had gone exploring. The apartment wasn't large, but a few yards down from the front door, another door in the same wall led to a tiny hallway from which doors opened into a bedroom and a bathroom. The bedroom was as tidy and attractively furnished as the living room with, Pamela noted, a single bed—though the room could have accommodated a double bed or larger. She herself, though she slept alone, still slept in the double bed that she and her husband had shared.

The phrase *bicycle fish* popped into her mind. According to Adrienne, Mel's feminist friends were the bicycle fish people, an allusion to the notion that a woman without a man is like a fish without a bicycle. As an editor, Pamela was perhaps more interested in linguistic precision than most people, and the phrase had struck her as odd at the time.

Wouldn't calling themselves bicycle fish imply the opposite of what they wished to imply? Fish with bicycles would be like women *with* men, not without. Or maybe they thought of themselves as fish without bicycles, and happy that way, and Adrienne had simply garbled the expression. In any event, Mel's single bed seemed a statement—almost a defiant statement—that she had no intentions of inviting company into her bed any time soon.

Bettina's voice reached her from the next room as she was peeking into the tiny bathroom, which featured a shower but no tub.

"Pamela!" she called. "Come and see what we found!"

Pamela ducked back through the doorway to see a manila file folder open in the empty spot on the desk. Several sheets of paper were spread out around it, computer printouts containing brief single-spaced paragraphs separated by double spaces.

"They're like some kind of surveillance reports," Bettina said.

She picked up the nearest one and quoted, "ZZ was seen in the company of a *m*— on 9-17 in Washington Square Park. I followed and observed them enter Tortilla Flats together at 6 p.m."

She handed the sheet of paper to Pamela, who skimmed further down the page, murmuring to herself, "ZZ . . . the same *m*— . . . kissing in the alley between Cheshire Cat Cheese and Dolly's Bakery . . . 8:17 p.m. 9-21 . . ."

"M, dash?" Pamela looked up.

Adrienne laughed. "It means *man*. They don't like to spell the word out, or even say it."

Another page seemed to chronicle the forbidden adventures of "RB" over the course of a week. A stakeout in front of her apartment building had even observed a *m*— accompanying her into the building at 7 p.m. on 10-3 "carrying a parcel suspiciously shaped like a wine bottle" as well as "a bag that appeared to contain takeout from Broadway Bistro." The following paragraph, dated 10-4, noted that the same *m*— was observed leaving the building "THE NEXT MORNING" at 8:19 a.m. A parenthetical note added the detail that the $m$— was believed to be one "GT."

"She was spying on people!" Bettina had been holding a clutch of pages fastened together with a paper clip, poring over the top one, but now she flung them to the table. "What a busybody! And who cares if RB is sharing a takeout dinner and a bottle of wine with GT—or even if he spends the night? They're grown-ups, and single, I assume."

"How do we know it was Mel who was spying?" Pamela asked.

Her voice overlapped with Adrienne's, who then repeated the comment that had been interrupted by Pamela's question.

"The group's ideal world is a world without men," she said, shaking her head and clicking her tongue in disapproval. "I can't see it myself." She lifted a hand to fondle one of the blond waves that strayed over the supple leather of her jacket.

"Maybe it was a group effort—the spying," Pamela suggested. She displayed the page she'd been studying and pointed to a small handwritten notation at the bottom. It read, "Submitted by LK."

"And look here"—she picked up one of the pages scattered across the table—"this one says, 'Submitted by RU' . . . and here's 'Submitted by TL.'"

"Mel was responsible for some of them, though," Bettina said, picking up another page at random, "at least if she's MW."

Adrienne had been rummaging through another manila folder. "Probably," she murmured, "Mel Word-woman."

She extracted a few pages from the folder and spread them out, exclaiming, "Photos!"

Indeed, interspersed among the lines of text, which resembled the brief paragraphs on the other pages they had inspected, were photos, obviously not posed. They showed men and women hugging, kissing discreetly in out-of-the-way spots, even just sitting together on park benches.

"There's probably more from this spying project on Mel's computer and phone," Pamela suggested. "I wonder what the police think of it if they've found it."

"I'm seeing Clayborn tomorrow morning, though he never tells me anything." Bettina shuffled through a few more pages. "He saves all the good tidbits for Marcy Brewer."

"I wonder if they even opened these filing cabinets," Pamela said. "Maybe not—much easier to just collect the victim's phone and computer."

"Most people don't keep paper records like they used to," Adrienne commented, "and if there's a question of some kind of threatening correspondence that could lead to a killer, I suppose mostly it would be email or a text or phone message."

Pamela stepped over to the filing cabinet they hadn't explored yet and opened the top drawer. Labels on the tabs of the manila folders indicated the folders contained syllabi for various courses, like Shakespeare's History Plays or Women in Elizabethan England. A check of the other file drawers revealed nothing out of the ordinary—manila folders filled with articles Mel had written, course materials for classes she had taught, printouts and Xeroxed copies of texts perhaps assembled while doing research.

Bettina and Adrienne, meanwhile, had been gathering up the curious evidence of the spying project and slipping the pages back into the folders from which they had come. Now Adrienne slipped the folders back into the space that had been vacated when they were removed. She pushed on the drawer, and it closed with a metallic screech that made Pamela shiver.

"I guess there's a kitchen . . . somewhere?" Bettina looked around.

"Somewhere," Adrienne replied. "These city apartment kitchens aren't big, and anyway, Mel didn't cook. She thought kitchen work was a form of servitude, and that the bicycle fish people should declare themselves liberated from it."

She led the way past the desk to where a door opened in the back wall. The kitchen was indeed small, hardly more than a narrow hallway with a stove, sink, and refrigerator lined up along one side and barely any counter space. The group entered in single file, and Pamela and Bettina watched as Adrienne opened the oven to reveal shoes neatly arranged on the two racks. One cupboard held books and another held piles of magazines. Adrienne pulled one out to display the cover, which featured a comic drawing of a fish riding a bicycle. The refrigerator contained half a bottle of white wine and a cardboard carton with smudges of sauce on the flaps that sealed the top.

They left the apartment then and made their way down the stairs to the first floor. As they approached the door that led to the street, another door opened, a door off to the side. At first it opened only a crack, but an eye was visible peering through the crack. After a moment, it opened wider to reveal a woman. She was small and gray-haired, but dressed in a chic ensemble consisting of black boots, a flared black skirt, and a black pullover belted at the waist.

"Is it true?" she whispered, pulling the door open wider still. "About Mel?"

# CHAPTER 5

"I'm afraid so." Adrienne stepped forward. "I'm her sister. I've been here before, but I don't think we've met."

After introductions all around—the woman's name was Gisele Dupree—Adrienne explained what had happened to Mel.

"So sad, sad, sad . . ." Gisele shook her head. "Someone she knew? Or was it just random?"

"No one knows yet." Adrienne echoed the mournful head shake.

"I suspected something," Gisele said, "because there were no flowers this morning."

"Flowers?" Adrienne, Bettina, and Pamela all spoke in unison.

"She always gave me flowers." As if responding to the continued puzzlement, Gisele went on. "They were, you might say, hand-me-down flowers." Gisele's lips twitched in a slight, sad smile. "Every Sunday morning for the past year or more, a florist delivered flowers for Mel, like a standing order, beautiful flowers—roses one week, peonies, tulips, orchids, gorgeous arrangements . . . but she always refused to accept them. She told me I should take them, so I did."

"Did you ever get any idea who sent them?" Bettina asked.

"No." Gisele shook her head again. "I didn't want to pry, but look—" She stepped back from the doorway and beckoned them to come in.

The layout of her apartment was similar to the layout of Mel's, with the two long and narrow windows looking out onto the street and the fireplace with the marble mantel in the wall facing the door. But Gisele's décor was, one might say, more feminine—featuring a pink velvet sofa like something from the Victorian era, flowered chintz curtains, and a few graceful wooden pieces including a glass-doored cabinet with crystal and china visible within.

A hand gesture had accompanied her request to look. The hand's fingers were pointing at the remains of a flower arrangement on a table near the windows.

"There isn't much left," she said. "It's been sitting here for a week. Right after it came, Mel left for Arborville." She stepped closer to the table and touched the vase. "At the beginning it had freesias and some lilies too, but they got very sad and I picked them out and tossed them."

Several roses remained, deep ruby-red and open so wide that the pollen-encrusted filaments at their centers were on display. Most were drooping and a few had even shed petals onto the surface of the table.

"Usually there was no card—or Mel took the card

off before she brought the flowers to me," Gisele said. "But this last time—I guess she was distracted or in a hurry . . ."

Something had been tucked under the vase that held the flowers—just a large clear-glass vase of the sort that florists use. A corner of the something was visible, and Gisele tilted the vase slightly and pulled out an envelope.

"I peeked," she confessed and handed the envelope to Adrienne, who was standing closest to her.

Adrienne drew from the envelope a card with "Metropolitan Florals" engraved across the top in a flowing script and a few handwritten lines added below.

"Not very informative," she murmured, and handed the card to Pamela.

As Bettina edged closer and bent toward the card, Pamela read its message aloud: "'You know I'll always feel this way.'" She looked up and commented, "But no signature, so we don't know who will always feel this way."

"I don't think we need to ask what way he—or she?—feels, though." Bettina laughed. "Red roses have a pretty universal meaning." She paused a moment and then addressed Gisele specifically. "I guess the police spoke to you? Because you said you had a sense something had happened . . ."

Gisele nodded. "Someone from the Arborville police—Clayborn?—was here Friday, asking if I knew Mel, if she'd said anything about threats, if I'd noticed visitors . . . but he didn't tell me why he was asking."

"Did you tell him about the flowers?" Bettina asked.

"No." Gisele tightened her lips, raised an eyebrow, and shrugged—as if she now wondered whether that had been a mistake. "But the flowers didn't seem to be a threat," she added as if to convince herself, "and someone from the florist always delivered them—nobody who she actually knew. I could hear the voices in the hall when the flowers arrived."

"No reason to tell him," Bettina assured her with a satisfied glance at Pamela, who suppressed a laugh. She knew Bettina liked nothing better than feeling she had an inside track on a puzzling Arborville crime.

"Bettina knows Detective Clayborn," Adrienne explained, "because she's a reporter."

"Oh, my!" Gisele focused on Bettina, her eyes widening. "I'm impressed."

"It's just the Arborville town paper," Adrienne hastened to add, "a weekly."

Bettina glanced at Pamela again, this time with less satisfaction.

"All the same . . . impressive." Gisele gave Bettina an encouraging smile. "And I hope I did the right thing." She modulated her expression and turned to Adrienne. "I'm so sorry about your sister . . ."

Her voice trailed off, and a silence descended on the little group. When it seemed no one else, not even Bettina—with her deep reserves of sociability—was inclined to prolong the conversation, Pamela spoke up.

"We'll let you get back to . . . whatever you were doing, unless . . ." She surveyed the faces now focused on her. "It's getting on toward lunchtime, and I was going to suggest we suburbanites treat ourselves to lunch in the city." She nodded toward Gisele. "Would you like to join us?"

"I would," Gisele said, cheerful again, "but I have a lunch date lined up already."

"Attractive woman," Adrienne commented when they were back out on the sidewalk, "but she'd be so much more attractive if she did something about that gray hair. It's so easy now to maintain a very youthful color, even if it isn't your own."

"Whatever." Bettina raised a hand to the tousled scarlet waves that framed her face. "Some people prefer a more natural look." She checked her watch and added, "It's definitely lunchtime. Where shall we eat?"

"Follow me," Adrienne commanded, and she pivoted to head back the way they had come.

At the corner, she turned, and they zigzagged among other strollers on the busy sidewalk, passing shops and restaurants. After about five minutes, she slowed and then stopped. They had reached their destination, a narrow storefront. An awning sheltered the window that, along with the door, took up almost the whole façade. Across the window, delicate script spelled out the restaurant's name: Dominique's.

"I came here with Mel once," Adrienne said, reaching for the brass door handle and pushing the door open. "She liked it because it's owned and run by women."

Overlapping voices filled the small room with a low hubbub, and most of the tables that crowded the floor were occupied.

"No reservations," Adrienne replied to the hostess's query, but nonetheless a table was found and they were soon seated. The table was elegantly set, with a white linen tablecloth and napkins, and silverware, stemmed water glasses, and wineglasses at the ready. But it was so small as to arouse curiosity about how it would accommodate plates once the meal was served.

All around them were well-dressed, well-groomed people projecting a kind of urban intensity focused at the moment on wresting the utmost enjoyment from a Sunday afternoon's leisure. Floating above the hubbub a voice that could have been Édith Piaf's sang something in French.

A server appeared, a young woman all in black, offering menus and inquiring whether they would care for drinks.

"Just water, I think," Adrienne responded after a glance at Bettina and then Pamela.

"Calves brains in brown butter sauce," Bettina commented after she had opened her menu, which resembled a leather-covered booklet. "I don't believe I've ever seen calves brains on Hyler's menu."

"Everything sounds very French," Pamela murmured.

"I think I had the sole when I came here with Mel." Adrienne looked up from her menu.

The server delivered a bottle of mineral water featuring an elaborate label, poured a sparkling draft into each water glass, and announced the specials for the day. One of those specials was lamb chops with rice pilaf and braised spinach—so appealing that Pamela,

Bettina, and Adrienne all ordered it, as well as the goat cheese in puff pastry to start.

"So . . ." Adrienne surveyed Pamela and Bettina as the server turned away. "Do you think we found anything in Mel's apartment that could explain why someone wanted to kill her?"

Bettina took a sip of water and set down the delicate stemmed glass before she spoke. Her bright lipstick left a faint imprint on its rim.

"That evidence of the bicycle fish people spying on one another and recording what they observed was"—she paused—"noteworthy. Certainly the ones being spied on could have resented it."

"And some of the reports had been submitted by 'MW.'" Pamela emphasized her point by raising a hand with the index finger extended.

Adrienne nodded. "I'd be annoyed to learn that someone had been spying on me—especially if it had to do with me and . . . men."

Pamela waved her index finger. "But, in the case of Mel's bicycle fish group, if group members knew that other group members had been up to those kinds of . . . activities, would the repercussions be so horrible as to make murder seem necessary?"

"We don't know what the repercussions would be," Bettina observed. "Expulsion from the group, or . . . ?"

"Were the bicycle fish people all academics like Mel?" Pamela directed the question at Adrienne.

Adrienne shrugged. "Would that be important?"

Pamela shrugged too, but then said, "Maybe their professional advancement depended on being in Mel's good graces."

She was about to add, *Ambition has been known to drive people to kill*, but she had lost her audience. Bettina and Adrienne were both watching their server thread her way among the tables, squeezing between chairs filled with gesturing people and holding two plates aloft.

"One more coming," she explained when she reached them and delivered two orders of goat cheese in puff pastry.

She had delivered them to Bettina and Adrienne, but very soon the third order arrived, and thoughts of Mel's apartment and the spying project were temporarily set aside. Each plate held a turnover, square in shape, golden brown and glistening with butter. A bit of melted cheese escaping through the delicate steam vents scored in the tops hinted at what the crust enclosed. A curly tangle of arugula added a pop of bright color to the plate, which was simple white china.

The puff pastry yielded easily to Pamela's fork, falling away to reveal the pale and creamy cheese within, and the taste did not disappoint. The cheese, set off to advantage by the light and flaky crust, was smooth and mild, but with a slight tart earthiness.

"Perfect," Bettina announced after her first bite.

"Yes, perfect," Adrienne chimed in.

After a few more bites, Bettina sighed a happy sigh. Gazing around the lively room and then lingering on the view of the bustling sidewalk beyond the window, she said, "There really is something special about lunch in the city."

Some minutes later, the plates that had held the goat cheese in puff pastry were empty except for a few leaves of arugula and an occasional flaky crumb. The server whisked them away, and in no time at all they had been replaced by larger plates bearing the meal's main attraction.

Pamela surveyed the plate that had been set in front of her. It held two lamb chops with their arched rib bones and plump morsels of meat. Tucked along one side of them was a mound of pilaf, each rice grain distinct and shimmering with the rich broth it had absorbed in cooking. Tucked along the other side was the spinach, braised into tenderness but still a bright fresh green.

Expressions of anticipated delight almost immediately gave way to silent appreciation as knives carved off bites of lamb to reveal a perfect moist pinkness and forks conveyed those bites to eager mouths. Pamela detected a hint of garlic in the lamb, just enough to enhance the delicate flavor. The spinach was the perfect complement, buttery and slightly bitter but not so assertive as to distract from the lamb, and the pilaf offered a contrast in both texture and in taste. The rice was firm but tender, and savory with broth.

At length, the silence was broken, but with sighs and hums of pleasure rather than with words. By the time anyone spoke in a complete sentence, the plates held only the rib bones from which all the meat had been carved away, accompanied by stray grains of rice and strands of spinach.

"That was perfectly heavenly!" Bettina exclaimed. "I can hardly wait to see the dessert menu."

Adrienne smiled a smile that struck Pamela as tinged with pity. "I, for one, intend to pass on dessert," she said as she discreetly patted her stomach. "One can't always eat everything one wants . . . or"—her gaze traveled from Bettina's face downward and then back up—"one can, but then . . ."

"I like my desserts," Bettina responded, "and my husband likes me just the way I am. So go ahead and skip dessert, but I'm not planning to."

Adrienne turned to Pamela, but the server arrived before she could speak, and the busyness of clearing the table provided an interruption that Pamela found quite welcome. As the server, laden with plates and silverware, turned away, she recalled an idea that had popped into her mind as the goat cheese in puff pastry was being served. She'd been distracted, then, by the food and the discussion of the food, but now . . .

"Let's suppose," she said, "that a man was responsible for the flowers Mel received every week."

"She had boyfriends when we were growing up." Adrienne nodded. "That doesn't mean a woman couldn't be sending her flowers, of course . . ."

Bettina opened her eyes wide and took a deep breath that sounded like a hiccup. "But—why would she give the flowers away if they weren't from a man?"

"Yes! Yes!" Pamela nodded too, but more vigorously. "So, let's suppose a man was responsible for the flowers . . ."

"I'm supposing," Bettina said. "What next?"

She glanced up at the server, who had reappeared carrying menus.

"Dessert, it looks like." Pamela extended a hand to receive a menu, but Adrienne waved hers away, saying, "Nothing else for me except coffee, black."

The server directed a questioning look at Bettina, who reached up to accept her menu, and said, "Coffee, yes, and dessert for sure."

She opened the menu, turned to the last page, and bent toward the list of offerings. Pamela did likewise, after requesting coffee, and the server departed.

"Chocolate mousse," Bettina murmured, half to herself. "Definitely the chocolate mousse."

Chocolate mousse sounded good to Pamela too, though the dessert list also featured pastries and tarts and cakes and crème brûlée. The lunch had started with a pastry of sorts, and the main course had been so bountiful and filling—like a full dinner in the middle of the day. Chocolate mousse wasn't exactly *light*, but with coffee she thought it would supply the perfect conclusion to the meal.

After two orders had been placed for the chocolate mousse and the server had departed, silence descended on the table, with Adrienne seeming to bask in the virtue exhibited by renouncing dessert. A few long minutes passed, and then, focusing only on Pamela, Bettina spoke.

"Let's suppose a man was responsible for the flowers . . ." She paused. "What do I suppose after that?"

"Someone could have been spying on Mel too, writing up reports like the ones we saw."

"Someone could have," Bettina agreed, with a nod that set her earrings in motion, "but we didn't see any about MW. We only saw a few signed by MW."

"The ones *about* her wouldn't come into her hands," Pamela said. "For one thing, how could she be trusted to preserve evidence that she herself was . . . consorting with the enemy." She prefaced the last few words with a shrug, as if to question whether the bicycle fish people would go as far as that in their suspicion of men.

"She gave the flowers away," Bettina pointed out.

"But a spying person might not know that." Pamela felt her lips shaping a regretful smile.

"Was one of the bicycle fish people so angry at Mel's apparent hypocrisy that she murdered her— thinking, *Mel expects us to renounce men but won't do it herself*?"

"I'd certainly be angry." Adrienne joined the conversation. "I could never understand why Mel thought she couldn't do her writing and research and all that and still have men in her life—though they can be distracting . . ." She paused to direct a flirty glance toward a nice-looking man at a nearby table. "But, yes, if I was one of the bicycle fish people and thought Mel was carrying on with a member of the opposite sex, I wouldn't like it at all."

Three cups of coffee arrived then, followed by two servings of chocolate mousse in porcelain ramekins. Conversation paused, though Adrienne had only coffee to focus on. Bettina tasted her mousse even before adding sugar and cream to the dark and bitter liquid in her cup, pronouncing the mousse to be perfect.

Pamela too sampled her mousse first, expecting that a follow-up sip of coffee in the natural state she preferred would complement the dark sweetness the mousse promised. She was not disappointed. The mousse was sweet, yes, but the flavor was deep and complex, hinting at cacao's exotic origins, but smoothed by the whipped cream, and the lingering sweetness from the mousse enhanced the coffee's own bitter complexity.

The infusion of sugar and caffeine had evidently stimulated Bettina's mental processes. No sooner had she set down her spoon next to her empty ramekin than she reintroduced the topic they'd been discussing before the dessert and coffee arrived.

"It would be most useful," she said, "to know who was sending those flowers."

"How could we ever find that out?" Adrienne seemed genuinely puzzled.

Bettina raised her brows, flashed an amused glance at Pamela, and uttered a single syllable: *"Duh!"*

Adrienne's lips parted, but no sound came out.

"There was a card with the flowers," Pamela explained. "It didn't give the name of the person who ordered the weekly flowers to be sent—presumably Mel would know that—but it did give the name of the florist."

"Metropolitan Florals," Bettina chimed in, aiming her comment at Adrienne. "I was looking over Pamela's shoulder. We reporters *always* keep our eyes—and ears—open." She picked up her handbag, opened the flap, and took out her phone. "It's probably right in the neighborhood."

Metropolitan Florals *was* right in the neighborhood. It turned out to be the florist they had passed en route to Mel's apartment. They made their way back until they reached the shop, with its autumnal bounty spilling onto the sidewalk.

A transaction was in progress at the counter when they stepped inside, a customer paying for a potted chrysanthemum, which she then gently lowered into a tote bag. Once she had moved aside, the woman who had been serving her focused on the new arrivals.

"Good afternoon," she said cordially. She was a pleasant-looking woman, not young but not old, wearing a crisp linen shirt tucked into artistically faded jeans. The sleeves of the shirt were rolled up to reveal a few delicately etched tattoos.

"Are you in the market for anything in particular?" she added.

Bettina took the lead. "Maybe you can help us," she said, though her confident expression implied there was no *maybe* about it. "We're wondering who's responsible for the flowers delivered every week to Mel Wordwoman, around the corner." She gave the specific address.

"I don't know," the woman said, pursing her lips.

Undaunted, Bettina persisted, "Would anyone know?"

The woman shook her head. "He pays in cash, up front, a month at a time, and never gives his name."

"I take it he's a he, though." Bettina glanced back at Pamela and tipped her head in a meaningful nod.

"Most definitely a he!" The woman's face was suddenly transformed by a jolly smile.

"Could you describe him?"

"Describe him?" She thought for a moment. "In a word . . . *hot*! Mel Wordwoman is lucky, lucky, lucky."

"*Hot* is a broad description . . ." Bettina's voice trailed off, but her inquisitive expression completed the thought.

"Tall, taller than usual, slender but not skinny, jet-black hair, and dreamy blue eyes . . ." She paused and frowned. "He's overdue this month. We didn't deliver any flowers today because he hasn't come by to renew the order." Her eyes widened. "I hope that doesn't mean they've broken up!"

Pamela held her breath. Apparently the neighborhood grapevine was taking its time with the news of Mel's murder—otherwise the woman they were speaking with would have said something the moment Bettina mentioned Mel's name. And apparently neither Bettina nor Adrienne thought it was her place to explain why Mel would no longer know that the flower delivery had ceased. It occurred to Pamela that the man might have made the flower delivery anonymous in order not to get Mel into trouble with the bicycle fish people.

"She was helpful," Bettina commented after they had left the shop.

"What would you have done if she hadn't been?" Adrienne inquired.

"Told her I was a private investigator, of course!" Bettina laughed. "Working on a divorce case."

The sidewalk was too crowded for three people to walk abreast, so Adrienne took the lead as they made their way back to her car. Pamela and Bettina followed her, walking side by side. The autumn afternoon had reached the stage of mellow sunlight slanting from the west, a reminder that the days were growing ever shorter.

Pamela was enjoying the slanting sunlight, the urban bustle, even the traffic noises, her mind momentarily at rest. But then a thought intruded, and she grabbed Bettina's arm. A scurrying man sporting a jaunty scarf dodged around them.

"What do you think it means," she asked, leaning close to Bettina to make herself heard, "that the man sending the flowers didn't renew the order when October ended?"

# CHAPTER 6

At ten a.m. on Monday, Bettina stepped across Pamela's threshold bearing a plate. It was covered with foil, and she held it at arm's length as if to distance herself as far as possible from its hidden contents.

"I cannot believe this!" she exclaimed once both her feet were planted firmly on Pamela's thrift-shop carpet. She thrust the plate at Pamela. Catrina, napping in the patch of sun that set the carpet's rich colors aglow every morning, looked up in alarm.

"Do you know what I discovered when I got back home after my meeting with Clayborn?" she inquired. Pamela, of course, had no way of knowing, and Bettina quickly answered her own question.

"I discovered Adrienne sitting in my kitchen with my husband. They were drinking coffee from my mugs and eating . . . *this*!"

She leaned forward and, with a dramatic gesture, peeled the foil from the plate. Centered on the plate was half a loaf of what looked to be chocolate chip pound cake.

"*Oh*, she simpered, with the most fake smile I have ever seen, *I expected you to be here too, and I just dropped by to ask what you learned from Detective Clayborn*. Then she gestured at . . . *this*"—Bettina pointed a finger tipped with a red-painted nail at the pound cake—"and said, *I did a little baking this morning*."

Bettina made a snorting sound that once again attracted Catrina's attention. "So"—her voice took on a high-pitched, singsong tone—"Ms. I Don't Eat Dessert changes her tune when she has a chance to ply my husband with goodies. How she can imagine that fake blond hair of hers looks natural is beyond me! And first thing in the morning, to pay a call on her next-door neighbor, she's all dressed up like she's going to a . . . to a . . . whatever."

Never mind that, beneath the wine-colored coat she was now removing, Bettina was wearing a close-fitting jersey sheath in the same deep shade. She had accented its neckline with a lustrous silk scarf that blended reds, blues, and purples in an abstract print, and clusters of pearls dangled from her earlobes.

Had her own wardrobe choice been questioned, she would have pointed out that she'd been meeting with Arborville's lone police detective in her professional capacity as a reporter for the town newspaper. (In fact, she was responsible for nearly all its content.)

"What did you learn from Detective Clayborn?" Pamela asked, still holding the plate. The foil had been patted back into place and the offending pound cake was hidden again. She began to edge toward the kitchen doorway.

"Do I smell coffee?" Bettina made a show of sniffing the air. "I didn't drink any from the pot Wilfred made for Adrienne."

"It's all gone," Pamela said. "But I can make more." She turned and stepped into the kitchen.

"I'd like that." Bettina followed her.

As Pamela carried out the ritual of arranging the paper filter in the carafe's filter cone, heating water, and grinding beans, Bettina set out wedding-china cups, saucers, and little plates. From the refrigerator she took the carton of heavy cream that Pamela kept on hand especially for her and poured a generous amount into the cut-glass cream pitcher that matched the cut-glass sugar bowl.

Soon the kettle began to whistle, and soon after that, the aroma of brewing coffee filled the small kitchen. When they were both seated with coffee at hand, Bettina had one more task to complete before conversation could take place. She pulled the sugar and cream closer and commenced the process of transforming the dark and bitter liquid in her cup into the pale and sweet libation she favored.

"What *did* you learn from Detective Clayborn?" Pamela asked again, after Bettina had tasted her coffee and smiled in approval.

Pamela had set the plate with its foil-covered cargo on the table when she entered the kitchen, and there it had remained. Now Bettina picked up one corner of the foil and peered beneath.

"It did look kind of good," she murmured, "but I

couldn't give Adrienne the satisfaction of eating any in front of her."

"You know where I keep my knives," Pamela said, "and I see you already put plates on the table."

"Just in case." Bettina climbed to her feet. "But we'll need forks too."

A few moments later, she was back in her chair, slicing generous portions from the partial loaf of pound cake and easing them onto the small rose-garlanded plates.

Pamela picked up one of the forks Bettina had delivered and tasted her serving. Yes, the dark tidbits that she had suspected were chocolate chips proved to be chocolate chips. Their firm texture and bittersweet flavor contrasted pleasingly with the tender buttery crumb of the cake in which they were embedded.

"Not bad," Bettina announced after sampling a few bites. "Not as good as the Co-Op bakery's pound cake, even though theirs doesn't have chocolate chips." She nudged off another bite and raised her fork to her mouth. After she had chewed and swallowed, she added, "Anyone could mix up a batch of pound cake and throw in some chocolate chips. It's an obvious idea."

Pamela surveyed her friend with a fond smile. Bettina's fork was en route to her mouth, but it paused halfway there.

"What?" Bettina said, staring across the table. "You look like you're thinking something."

"I am thinking something." Pamela continued to smile. "I'm wondering if you're ever going to tell me about your meeting with Detective Clayborn."

"Of course, of course." Bettina took one last bite of

cake and then set down her fork. After a long swallow of coffee, she returned her cup to its saucer with a clink and murmured, "Let's see . . .

"First of all," she began, "the Arborville police have interviewed neighbors all up and down Orchard Street. That's how they found the surveillance footage showing the attacker, though the figure was all in black and was wearing a mask and it wasn't even clear whether it was male or female. But most of the neighbors said they were at the bonfire when it happened."

"Did you ask him about the computer from Mel's apartment, and whether they found anything helpful on her phone?"

"He wasn't happy to hear that I'd been inside Mel's apartment, though I pointed out that it wasn't a crime scene and that Mel's sister had a key and had a perfect right to go there and bring whoever she wanted." Bettina took a sip of coffee. "Then he harrumphed and said investigations were ongoing."

"I suppose you didn't get any sense that he knew the women in Mel's group had been spying on each other . . ."

Bettina shook her head, setting in motion the pearls dangling from her earlobes. "The sense I got is that he doesn't think the solution to the mystery is to be found across the river. He asked me why a killer who lived in the city and wanted to kill someone who lived in the city would wait until that person was visiting the suburbs to do it."

"Kind of sensible." Pamela frowned and then massaged the wrinkle she felt forming between her eyebrows. "If the killer was a city person, wouldn't it be easier to cover your tracks in the city? And why wait till Halloween?"

"That seemed to be his reasoning." Bettina nodded. "The murder happened in Arborville because the killer lives in Arborville."

"But did you point out . . ." Pamela raised a finger and shook it to emphasize what she was about to say. "Did you point out that New York City police detectives undoubtedly have more experience solving murders, so a killer from the city might have thought he—or she—would have less chance of being caught if he tracked his victim to Arborville?"

"I didn't point that out." Bettina laughed. "Clayborn wouldn't have liked that at all." Her eyes strayed toward the portion of cake that remained on the serving plate.

"Go ahead," Pamela urged. "Adrienne doesn't ever have to know that you liked it."

Bettina picked up the knife, but before she put it to use she turned her gaze to Pamela. "Adrienne's hosting a memorial reception, Wednesday, at some place in the Village. She's invited all Mel's friends and colleagues—the bicycle fish people, I presume—and we're invited too."

"I'd go . . ." Pamela said.

"Really?" The knife Bettina wielded ceased its motion and she stared at Pamela. "I wouldn't. If Adrienne thinks I still have any interest in what happened to her sister, she's sadly mistaken. I didn't know her well before because she hadn't been living next door all that long, but now that I *do* know her . . . no thanks!"

Pamela nodded. "Makes sense . . . and Detective

Clayborn is probably right. Mel's murder had nothing at all to do with anything east of the Hudson. He'll just focus on Arborville and in no time at all . . . tomorrow even . . . he'll announce to Marcy Brewer that he's solved the case and that will be that, and there will be a big headline in the *Register*."

Bettina continued to stare. "Do you really believe that?"

Pamela struggled with the urge to smile.

"You don't, do you?" Bettina's mobile features shifted from amazed to amused. "You've gotten caught up in this mystery now and you want to meet these bicycle fish people . . ."

"We could see if any of the names match the initials in the spying reports—both the people being spied on and the people doing the spying."

"Did you write down any of the initials?" Bettina inquired.

"No," Pamela admitted. "But if we mingle at the reception, we might hear things . . ."

"Okay," Bettina said. "We'll go. It's at two, a place called Rodeo. Adrienne is going into the city early, to make sure things are set up nicely for the event. So we'll just go on our own—and I wouldn't want to ride with her anyway."

That settled, Bettina finished serving herself a fresh slice of pound cake, and Pamela warmed up what was left of the coffee. Coffee at hand, as well as cake in Bettina's case, they turned their attention to topics more domestic. A Knit and Nibble meeting was coming up, with Bettina hosting, and she reported that Wilfred had been studying his cookbooks in search of a dessert appropriate to the season. Pamela confided that she needed a new knitting project and was still at a loss as to what that would be.

Half an hour later, Bettina returned her empty coffee cup to its saucer and sighed. "I've got to get to work," she said as she rested both hands on the table, scooted her chair back, and pushed herself to her feet. "Clayborn didn't have much to say that I can use, but my editor expects something about police doings for this week's *Advocate*."

Pamela rose too, and together they made their way to the entry, where Bettina slipped back into her stylish wine-colored coat.

Pamela opened the door and saw Bettina off with a hug. She was just about to close the door when an idea that had been lurking, unformed, in a corner of her mind suddenly took shape.

"Bettina!" she exclaimed. Bettina halted, teetering as she pulled back from launching herself down the steps. "The man responsible for the flowers . . . did he not renew the order because he knew Mel would be leaving for New Jersey right after the last October delivery?" Bettina turned and Pamela went on. "Or was there some other reason?"

"The Sunday before Halloween," Bettina murmured. "That was the arrangement Gisele showed us—or at least what was left of it." She closed her eyes and frowned, miming serious thought in a way that was almost comic. "Are you thinking what I'm thinking?" she whispered after she opened her eyes.

"That he knew she'd be dead . . . because . . ."

". . . he's the killer . . ." Bettina's voice faltered.

"Oh, Pamela! How could he do such a thing! After being so sweet with the flowers!" Her expression was as woebegone as if she'd just learned that Wilfred was not the person she'd taken him to be.

Pamela nodded. "He'd tried and tried to win her love, but finally he just gave up."

"And the thought of her continuing to exist, forever out of reach, was more than he could bear." Bettina sighed.

She went on her way then, and Pamela closed the door and returned to her kitchen. Perhaps the flower man, as she had come to think of him, was a suspect. What to do with that information she wasn't sure. Work waited upstairs for the magazine, however, and the kitchen table was in need of tidying.

She transferred the wedding china and silverware to the counter by the sink and pondered the remains of the chocolate chip pound cake. The plate that held it was unfamiliar, not part of Bettina's pottery set but a sunny shade of yellow. Most likely the plate, like the cake itself, had come from Adrienne's kitchen. She slipped the bit of cake, barely a few slices' worth, into a ziplock bag and turned toward the counter with the plate in hand.

Pamela's kitchen sink was centered under a large window that looked out at Richard Larkin's house, specifically at the window over Richard Larkin's kitchen sink. Sometimes, especially in the evening while preparing dinner, Pamela noticed Richard Larkin in his kitchen, bending over his sink.

In fact, a figure was bending over Richard Larkin's sink at this very moment, not tall enough to be Richard

Larkin, however. When the figure raised its head, Pamela heard herself inhale sharply—simply because the sight was unexpected. She found herself looking at a woman looking back at her through Richard Larkin's kitchen window. But then she reflected that maybe one of his daughters was visiting. She hadn't gotten that good a look before the woman moved away.

The next thing Pamela knew, the door that led from the kitchen onto a small side porch opened and the woman stepped out carrying a bag of garbage. It was clear now that she was not one of Richard Larkin's daughters. She was older, perhaps as old as Pamela. Could she be someone he had hired to come in and clean for him? Pamela had never noticed cleaning help next door in the past, but perhaps he'd become so taken up with work that he no longer had time to look after his own house.

Surely that was the explanation. Thinking no more about it, Pamela unloaded the clean dishes from her dishwasher and replaced them with the dishes and silverware she had cleared from the table. Once the kitchen was tidy she climbed the stairs to her office.

Ginger looked up from her languid sprawl across Pamela's computer keyboard and allowed herself to be transferred to Pamela's lap. The push of a button brought the computer to life with its usual beeps and chirps, and as soon as the monitor's screen brightened, Pamela clicked on the Word icon. Two articles remained to be evaluated, "Something to Remember Them By: Victorian Hair Art" and "Fiber Arts and the Dark Arts."

She'd postponed looking at either, finding the topics unsettling after Halloween night's adventure. But time had passed now, and she felt able to ponder the notion of people desiring to keep their departed loved ones close, in a sense, by creating art objects from locks of hair clipped after death.

As was often the case with articles submitted to *Fiber Craft*, this article was accompanied by illustrations—photographs of items from museums like the Victoria and Albert, as well as items in the author's own collection. *People will collect anything*, she mused to herself as she began to scroll through the illustrations, though Victorian hair art was certainly a niche.

She had to admit, though, that the examples of hair art illustrating the article were charming, if one could suppress a shiver at the recognition that the delicate filaments composing them had been collected from the scalps of dead people. But maybe that was the point, in a curious way—to ease the pain of grief by transforming a souvenir of the deceased into art.

The hair art took the form of framed arrangements—often wreaths—not unlike the arrangements of dried flowers preserved under glass that Pamela had occasionally seen in antique shops. In this case, the "flowers" were composed of hair, shaped into blossoms and furnished with stems and leaves also made of hair. Elaborate frames completed the creations.

The article was interesting and well-written, and the illustrations were certainly arresting. Enough time had passed, she thought, since the article on mourning brooches made from hair had appeared, so hopefully readers would not have a sense of déjà vu—and anyway, Celine Bramley would make the decision on when to run this most recent hair art article.

Pamela minimized the file, rolled her chair back from her desk, and closed her eyes, enjoying the soothing darkness after the glare of the monitor screen. The article had been absorbing, but based on the message her stomach was sending her brain, she suspected that lunchtime had come and gone. An evaluation of "Something to Remember Them By: Victorian Hair Art" had yet to be written, and a break for a cheese omelet would provide sustenance for that task.

Half an hour later, Pamela was back at her computer. In a few paragraphs she summarized the hair art article, alluded to the author's credentials—she was a history professor at a small college in New England—and recommended that the article be published. Then she opened the file for "Fiber Arts and the Dark Arts."

Reading the first paragraph, which mentioned knitting along with other methods of transforming fibers into fabric, reminded Pamela that Knit and Nibble was meeting the following night. As she had confided to Bettina, she was somewhat at loose ends—was that a fiber metaphor?—about what her next knitting project would be.

She continued to read, but her mind was determinedly elsewhere—specifically, it was in her attic. Yes, she could buy some new yarn, though a recent project, now complete, had involved a huge splurge at the fancy yarn shop in Timberley: eight skeins of natural cream-colored wool imported from the Shetland Islands.

Souvenirs of Pamela's many knitting projects resided in two large plastic bins in her attic. They were leftovers, partial skeins of this yarn or that yarn, or even whole skeins left from when she had bought too much. Pamela was by nature frugal, and the idea of using these odds and ends that she already possessed rather than buying yet more yarn suddenly seemed like the best idea in the world. Abandoning "Fiber Arts and the Dark Arts," she climbed the stairs to her attic.

Pamela's attic was unfinished, with exposed rafters and studs, lit by a single dangling light bulb and the light from the little dormer windows, which were tucked under the sloping ceilings on all four sides. It smelled of dust and old wood, and the air was warm and stuffy even on this brisk fall day.

The space served as storage—for Christmas decorations, out-of-season clothes, books that had overflowed the shelves in living room and office, piles of knitting magazines . . . all manner of odds and ends, including a trunk and a large suitcase filled with things Penny had had at college but hadn't wanted to accompany her to her new lodgings in Manhattan.

The plastic bins stuffed with yarn were stacked one on top of the other near the pile of knitting magazines. She lifted the top one to the floor, pulled up a nearby stool, and opened both bins. Seeing the jumble of contrasting colors, each a reminder of some much-enjoyed project, she had a sudden idea. Why not borrow the idea of a patchwork quilt and create a patchwork garment?

Patchwork quilts, she knew from articles she had read for *Fiber Craft*, had developed out of a frugal desire to make use of fabric scraps left from other projects or even salvaged from discarded clothes. Penny was devoted to the idea of sustainable fashion, outfitting herself mostly with vintage treasures sourced from thrift shops. Surely she'd appreciate a sweater created from odds and ends of leftover yarn.

The project would be simple and fun. Pamela would knit squares, perhaps about three inches by three inches, from a random assortment of colors. Then she would sew them together to create a boxy pullover sweater. The look would be angular and quite modish, rather like the Mondrian-inspired tunic dresses she'd once seen in an exhibit of fashion from the 1960s.

In fact, with that inspiration in mind, she set about rooting through her bins for yarn in primary colors. A partial skein of ruby-red yarn brought to mind the glamorous sweater with long sleeves but bare shoulders she still got out for festive occasions at the holidays. A pretty shade of blue recalled a gift she'd made for her mother one year.

The task of collecting the yarn for her new project was unexpectedly moving. The nostalgia was unavoidable when she came upon yarn left from garments she'd made for a very young Penny, including a tiny sweater that had been outgrown within a few months. Then, deep at the bottom of the second bin, she found a whole unused skein of kelly-green yarn, left from a pullover she'd given her beloved husband when they were first married.

She held the skein in her hand, wondering if she should use it for the sweater she envisioned. Would the memories it awakened be so painful as to distract her from the enjoyment of her frugal project? But the patchwork quilts that were her inspiration for the patchwork sweater idea had sometimes included fabric salvaged from clothing worn by the departed. Like the Victorian hair art—the parallel was startling!—they were in a sense mementos of loved ones.

She added the skein of kelly-green yarn to the pile accumulating at her side.

# CHAPTER 7

Early Tuesday, Pamela was standing at the end of her front walk. She had just picked up that morning's *Register* and she was lingering to stare, not at an alarming headline but rather at a figure bent on a similar errand in Richard Larkin's yard. The figure, who stooped down and seized the newspaper as Pamela watched, was a woman, the same woman she had glimpsed through Richard Larkin's kitchen window and then on his side porch the previous day.

She had decided then that the woman had been engaged to help with cleaning and other household chores. But here the woman was again, early in the morning, and wearing a robe and slippers—as if she had made herself quite at home next door. The woman noticed her staring and waved cheerfully. Pamela blinked and waved back, taking the opportunity to look more closely at this addition to her neighbor's household.

The woman was middle-aged, slender, and fair-haired—a natural sort of dishwater blond that went with her attractive but unremarkable features and the decidedly unglamorous effect of her plaid flannel robe and fuzzy slippers. As Pamela gazed, she waved again, slipped the newspaper from its plastic sleeve to glance at the front page, and headed back toward Richard Larkin's porch.

*No reason I should care*, Pamela murmured to herself as she retraced her steps to her own porch. Who Richard Larkin was sharing his house with was no business of hers at all. She resolved to put the matter completely out of her mind, grateful for the distraction afforded by the frantically hooting kettle, which had driven the cats from the kitchen. She'd been outside longer than she'd intended, and she switched off the burner and quickly set about grinding beans for coffee.

Two hours later, Pamela sat at her computer contemplating "Fiber Arts and the Dark Arts." She'd had breakfast and dressed, made her bed and tidied her bedroom, and read through the article carefully, twice.

The author's credentials were vague and his—or her?—name, E. K. Jordan, was ambiguous. In a rambling way, the article suggested that throughout history the seemingly magic processes by which fibers were transformed into fabric linked those adept at these processes, usually women, with sorcery.

"It's no coincidence," the author wrote, "that when knitters 'cast on,' they might as well be casting a spell, or that spiders too *weave* the tangled webs that use a secret skill to deceive their unwitting prey. Women's power to create fabric from fiber inspires fear, and their *craft* might as well be witchcraft."

Certainly, Pamela thought, other thinkers had had these thoughts, and more skilled writers had expressed them elsewhere. She'd read other articles for *Fiber Craft* that touched on the theme, but in connection with discussing a specific skill, technique, or tradition. This article merely spun—those metaphors were everywhere!—out a theory detached from any specific craft or practice.

"Not recommended for publication," she wrote on her evaluations page, and added a brief explanation.

Wilfred had been baking something sweet. That much was clear the moment Pamela stepped into the Frasers' living room that evening.

"It's a surprise," Bettina said. "He's kept it a secret, even from me. But I think it will be served with whipped cream."

Bettina had dressed for that evening's meeting of Knit and Nibble in a knitted creation that Pamela had watched take shape over many, many months. It was a stylish burnt-orange tunic, with long sleeves and a V-neck suitable for displaying the string of colorful Murano glass beads that Bettina had accessorized it with. Earrings made from similar beads dangled from her ears.

Pamela herself was wearing the same sweater she'd worn on the trip into the city, the tawny brown sweater with the large black cat on the front. She carried the yellow plate that had held the chocolate chip pound cake.

She was not the first arrival, though she lived just across the street. Nell Bascomb was seated in a comfortable armchair, and side by side on the sofa that faced the armchair and its twin were Holly Perkins and Karen Dowling. The armchairs had recently been re-upholstered in a dark peach color that coordinated nicely with the sage green of the sofa, a look enhanced by new curtains that incorporated peach and dark green in an abstract print.

The presence of the other people was welcome. Pamela had debated asking Bettina if she'd noticed the new arrival at Richard Larkin's house, but she was just as glad there was a reason not to mention the topic, at least not at the moment.

Bettina noticed the plate and laughed. "Thanks, I guess," she said. "Adrienne will probably be wanting her plate back—so she can deliver more goodies to my husband." She reached out for it, but at that moment the doorbell rang.

"You're busy," Pamela said. "I'll do something with it." She set her knitting bag on the sofa and headed for the kitchen.

There, she chatted with Wilfred for a few moments as he kept an eye on the clock. Judging by the aroma that filled the kitchen, his baking project was very near delicious completion.

She returned to the living room to greet two new arrivals. One of them, Roland DeCamp, was known to her. He had already taken his customary seat on the hearth, the elegant leather briefcase that served as his knitting bag open at his side. The other arrival was a visitor who'd gotten in touch with Bettina through the *Advocate*.

Gayle Witherspoon was tall and sturdy, with hair turning unabashedly gray and gathered into a careless ponytail. She was wearing loose-fitting jeans and a fleece pullover, also gray. She explained that she'd seen a recent *Advocate* article in which Bettina mentioned the Knit and Nibble group in connection with a local craft fair. She'd been reminded of how much she once loved knitting and resolved to recapture her skills.

"I know you all have to vote on new members," she said as she glanced around the room, "but Bettina is very kindly allowing me to be here tonight as her guest . . . and, we'll see . . ."

She looked around as if searching for a place to sit. The sofa was already occupied by Holly, Karen, and Pamela's knitting bag, and Nell was occupying one of the armchairs. Gayle seemed to sense that the other was reserved for her hostess, so she crossed the room and lowered herself onto the hearth next to Roland's briefcase.

Pamela surveyed her fellow knitters, recognizing projects that had been underway for some time. Christmas was already in the air. The lead-up seemed to start earlier and earlier each year, and much of the work dangling from the needles around her, some of them already in motion, was aimed at the celebration of that holiday.

She knew that the fat skein of maroon yarn Bettina

had just extracted from her knitting bag was slowly being transformed into the sleeve of a pullover sweater destined for Wilfred Jr. Last year's Christmas project had been a similar pullover, but in royal blue for her younger son, Warren. Karen too was at work on a pullover, powder blue with a V-neck, for her husband, Dave.

A curious shape was taking form on Nell's needles, bulbous but asymmetrical at the bottom, then narrowing into a column—like a large sock seen in profile. In fact, it was a sock, or half of one. A favorite do-good initiative of Nell's involved knitting Christmas stockings for the children at the women's shelter in Haversack, which she and the other volunteers filled with small gifts and candy, but candy only in small amounts, at Nell's insistence.

Next to Karen on the sofa, Holly was absorbed in, as she had explained at the previous meeting, a gift for herself: cable-knit leggings in a dramatic shade of chartreuse, to be created one leg at a time and then joined. Pamela suspected she'd be explaining her own project soon because the vicarious enjoyment of the other knitters' work was part of the fun of Knit and Nibble. For now, though, she focused on launching the first of the many squares that would be sewn together to make the garment she pictured. From the odds and ends of yarn she'd culled from her plastic bin, she'd tucked a partial skein of deep blue yarn in her knitting bag before crossing the street to Bettina's house. Now she cast on twelve stitches, because with medium-weight yarn four stitches equaled about an inch.

She was distracted midway through, though, by a low moan coming from the direction of the hearth. Roland continued to knit, his face serene and his fingers given over to the rhythmic motions of his task. Next to him, however, Gayle was not knitting. She was holding a knitting needle in one hand and a strand of black yarn in the other, and her forehead was puckered in confusion.

"I . . . I was so sure it would come back automatically," she squeaked. "I loved it so much when I was younger. But now . . . I just . . ." She dropped the needle, which was steel and clattered on the bricks of the hearth.

She turned an appealing gaze on Roland. "Could you . . . ? I need to cast on . . ."

Before Roland could react, Bettina propelled herself out of her armchair. "Come," she said, plucking the errant knitting needle from the hearth with one hand and tugging at Gayle's arm with the other. "This isn't a good place for you. You'll be more comfortable somewhere else."

Within a minute or two, Bettina had installed Gayle in the armchair she herself had vacated and was perched at her side on a chair fetched from the dining room. Gayle handed over the skein of yarn she'd carried as she was relocated and Bettina took hold of the loose strand that trailed from it. She demonstrated how to make a slip knot, looping the yarn and pulling the strand through the loop, then thrust the needle from the hearth through it.

"Simple," she murmured, holding out the result for Gayle to study. "Now we just keep looping," she said, suiting her actions to her words, though after a few loops she paused to aim a meaningful glance in Pamela's direction.

Once she had Pamela's attention, she nodded toward Roland, who was placidly knitting away, perhaps unaware that he had been rescued from what would certainly have been an annoying distraction. Pamela smiled to herself. Bettina was not the most expert knitter in the group, but Gayle was watching most appreciatively as a row of even loops accumulated on the needle in Bettina's hand.

The question of what Gayle actually planned to knit arose next, and she admitted her first goal was simply to refresh her memory of the process. Bettina suggested a scarf, Gayle nodded, and Bettina handed her the needle and instructed her to continue adding loops until she decided she'd reached a good width for a scarf.

Pamela returned her attention to her own work then. The little square grew quickly and involved no thought at all—she'd decided the nubby texture of the garter stitch would suit the feel of the garment she had in mind, so there was no need even to keep track of knit rows and purl rows. The repetitive motions of her fingers set her mind free to roam, and up popped the image of Richard Larkin's new housemate. She felt herself frown and willed her mind to roam elsewhere.

The other occupants of the sofa, Holly and Karen, were chatting quietly about Thanksgiving. "Coming so soon—can you believe it!" Karen exclaimed.

Holly nodded in disbelief and remarked, "The year will be over before we know it."

Pamela's frown returned. Yes, time was flying by and, just as Bettina had been predicting for years, Penny had grown up and moved out and now she was alone in her big house and Richard Larkin was seemingly no longer alone in his big house and . . . the square that had been growing so rapidly on her needles had turned into a rectangle while her mind roamed.

She ceased knitting in midrow and slipped her work off its needles. Then she gingerly unraveled a few rows to transform the rectangle back into a square and threaded one of the needles through the row of loops along the top. She was grateful that casting off required concentration, thus temporarily banishing the melancholy summoned by Karen and Holly's words.

Soon she'd cast on for her second square, using the same deep blue yarn, and embarked upon the first knitted row. Across from her, Bettina had once more set her own project aside to address a tangled clump of yarn hanging from one of Gayle's needles, murmuring encouragement as she did so.

A second tantalizing aroma had been gradually drifting in from the direction of the kitchen, joining the aroma of the mystery dessert. Its identity became clear just as Roland began to stir. He eased back the immaculate shirt cuff that extended half an inch beyond the discreet pinstripe of his jacket sleeve. He bent his carefully barbered head toward the face of his impressive watch. He counted under his breath, "Fifty-six, fifty-seven, fifty-eight, fifty-nine—"

At that moment, Wilfred appeared in the arch that separated the living room from the dining room. "I believe it's just eight o'clock," he said, glancing genially from knitter to knitter. "I've made a pot of coffee, there will be tea for the tea-drinkers, and you'll be sampling my you-think-it's-pumpkin-but-it-isn't pie."

Bettina was on her feet then, perhaps grateful for an excuse to hand Gayle's needle, with its tangled clump still intact, back to its owner. Gayle tucked the needle and its cargo into her knitting bag and rose to her feet as well.

"Please let me help," she said, and she followed Bettina toward the dining room and the kitchen beyond.

Three people in the kitchen was enough, Pamela surmised, and she remained where she was, happy to join Holly and Karen in a discussion of the chrysanthemum varieties available at the garden center. Just as pansies were eagerly sought for window boxes and planters as soon as spring arrived, Arborvillians decked their porches with chrysanthemums in the fall.

As the knitters on the sofa chatted, Bettina and Gayle began delivering plates. Each plate contained a wedge of pie, its pale golden-brown surface garnished with a drift of whipped cream. Soon the coffee table was crowded with pie and coffee and tea, and Wilfred had fetched another chair from the dining room to join the group.

Roland remained on the hearth with his coffee and pie beside him, taking the place of his briefcase, which had been moved to the floor. Everyone else was clustered around the coffee table, though the small plates that held the pie were transferred to laps once the business of eating was underway.

"It certainly looks like pumpkin pie!" Holly exclaimed, brandishing her fork before taking a bite.

"And it looks *amazing*!" She directed one of her most bewitching smiles at Wilfred, made all the more bewitching by her perfect teeth, glowing skin, and raven hair.

"It's the season for pumpkin pie," Nell observed. "Especially for the frugal people who display their Halloween pumpkins whole and then eat them."

Nell herself did this, and her waste-not, want-not ethos extended to drying the pumpkin seeds and setting them out for the birds.

"I know it's the season for pumpkin pie." Wilfred chuckled. "And I'll be gearing up for my Thanksgiving baking soon—but I thought it would be fun to try something a little different, something that still fits with the season, though." He paused and gazed around with a look that seemed an invitation to partake.

Holly had continued to brandish her fork. Now the others joined her, and forks swooped in unison toward the sage-green plates with their pie-wedge triangles. Pamela was not the first to speak, concentrating instead on simply enjoying the smooth-textured custard, rich with eggs and cream, and hinting at a familiar flavor enhanced with a bit of spice.

"It's sweet potato pie, isn't it?" Nell looked up from her plate. "An old Southern treat, but I think it made its way north some time ago."

Wilfred nodded and winked. "I make it just like my pumpkin pie, but with sweet potatoes baked or steamed and then mashed. It's perfect for autumn, when there's not much local fresh fruit, except for apples."

"Yummy, yummy," Holly said, and her opinion was echoed and elaborated upon by everyone else, even

Roland. His enthusiasm was also evident in the fact that only a tidbit of crust remained on his plate.

As pie was disappearing from other plates, leaving only pastry crumbs and dabs of whipped cream on their sage-green pottery surfaces, conversation turned to other topics. Gayle was welcomed to the group, and she talked again about how much she had loved to knit as a girl.

"Where did you grow up?" Holly inquired in her sociable way.

"Oh, here," Gayle said. "We lived on Linden, and I went away to college, but then I came back and got married and just stayed and stayed."

"Who wouldn't? Arborville is perfectly *awesome*. I don't ever want to leave!" A smile that brought Holly's dimple into play underscored her enthusiasm, and she added, "To think that you got to grow up here!"

"Arborville is a great town to raise children." Bettina joined the conversation. She nodded toward Karen, across the coffee table from her. "Your little Lily is a fortunate child, and maybe she'll stay and stay, like my Wilfred Jr., and you'll have grandchildren, maybe even a granddaughter like my little sweetie. You should have seen her Halloween costume, a fairy princess, tiny and all in pink with wings and . . ."

Bettina had become quite breathless. She paused and inhaled deeply.

"It's too bad the storm spoiled the festivities this year." Holly's smile faded. "I have such happy memories from years past."

"The storm wasn't the only thing that spoiled them." Roland spoke as if no one else in the room was aware that the evening had also featured a murder. "But what can you expect when people are out running around disguised as who-knows-what? Of course someone who's up to no good is going to take advantage."

"My sister loved Halloween," Gayle said, "but Heather's gone now, long gone." Her melancholy expression did her face no favors. Minus a smile, her mouth was a nondescript line and her eyes peered out beneath drooping eyelids.

She scanned the group from her perch in the armchair on loan from Bettina. "Does anyone know whether the police are making any progress?" She turned to Bettina, who was still sitting next to her in the chair from the dining room. "Has the *Advocate* heard anything from . . . what's his name? Clayborn?"

Bettina had no news to offer, Pamela knew well, but before her friend could even communicate that fact, Nell leaned forward in the other armchair. Pamela knew what was coming, as did everyone except Gayle. Even Roland prepared to look abashed.

"A terrible thing has happened in our little town." Nell's pale eyes were stern in their nests of wrinkles. "We do not need to turn it into fodder for gossip, and because Bettina and Pamela, as well as Wilfred, were among the first to discover the tragic scene, we especially don't need to ask them to revisit such a distressing episode."

Gayle at first seemed taken aback, then vaguely defiant, perhaps bristling at the idea that she was being scolded. Wilfred half-rose from his chair and surveyed the coffee table.

"I see some empty mugs here," he said, his ruddy

good cheer in striking contrast to Gayle's mood. "There's plenty more coffee in the kitchen, though I'm afraid we ate all the pie. Eight people, eight slices."

"And the slices were a perfect size," Nell added, as if to smooth over with a compliment any ill will caused by her earlier statement, even if the compliment was not directed at Gayle.

Murmurs of "I'm fine" and "One mug was plenty" greeted Wilfred's offer, but had anyone actually wanted a refill, the sight of Roland consulting his watch would have provoked second thoughts.

"It's a quarter after eight," he announced. "The coffee was delicious, but I, for one, have knitting to do."

"Yes, yes, of course." Gayle glanced around nervously, like a person puzzled by the etiquette of an unfamiliar situation. She picked up her work and thrust the empty needle at random into the snarled clump of yarn dangling from its mate.

Bettina and Wilfred quickly cleared the coffee table and carried mugs and plates and the rest to the kitchen, along with Roland's mug, plate, and fork from the hearth. Roland had returned to his knitting, which, judging from the four double-pointed needles he was employing, looked to be one of the sock projects he had been challenging himself with lately.

Pamela had taken a minute to hold her in-progress square against the finished one just to see how much remained to do before it too was a perfect square. She tucked the finished one back in her knitting bag and happened to glance toward Roland before launching a new row.

He had stopped knitting and was staring at Gayle,

his shoulders hunched and his lean face tense. Bettina and Wilfred were still in the kitchen, and the two extra chairs fetched from the dining room were vacant. Roland set his work aside, arranging it neatly on the brick hearth. He rose, edged past the coffee table, and perched on the dining room chair closest to the armchair where Gayle sat.

"Anything worth doing is worth doing well," he intoned, and Pamela smiled to herself, reflecting that Wilfred's fondness for old sayings had spread even to Roland.

He held out a hand. Gayle looked startled, but when he wiggled his fingers in a beckoning gesture, she relinquished her project to his grasp. He studied the sad results of Gayle's industry for a long moment, at one point turning it over to study the reverse side.

"In my opinion," he said gravely, "we have very little recourse." He might as well have been announcing to his corporate colleagues that chances of evading a threatened lawsuit were minimal. "Therefore," he went on—but instead of completing the sentence, he substituted actions for words.

He extracted from the tangled clump of yarn the needle that Gayle had plunged into it, slid the clump off the other needle, and handed both needles to Gayle. Then he seized the strand of yarn that tethered the project to the skein at Gayle's side. He tugged, and within seconds the clump of yarn had vanished. In its place was a long yarn tail, slightly crimped from having been subjected to Gayle's efforts.

"Now what?" Gayle peered into Roland's stern face.

"Now we start over." He looped a slipknot near the

end of the tail, thrust a needle through it, and looped a few more cast-on stitches. Handing the needle to Gayle, he said, "Try to make them even, and not too tight."

At this point, Bettina returned to the living room. Amusement crinkled her eyes and turned up the corners of her mouth as she contemplated the scene that greeted her. Pamela was also smiling, and she and Bettina shared a glance as Bettina lowered herself into the chair vacated by Wilfred. Holly and Karen, at Pamela's side on the sofa, had been neglecting their work as well, mesmerized by a glimpse at this unfamiliar side of Roland.

Once Gayle had cast on the number of stitches that Roland deemed enough for her project, still a scarf as she had declared earlier, he took the needles from her hands and demonstrated the basic knitting stitch. Pamela returned to her own work then, amused by the quiet murmurs coming from across the room as Roland inspected each row his pupil completed before allowing her to go on.

"I hope Gayle appreciated that," Bettina said to Pamela as she closed her front door after waving good night to the other Knit and Nibblers. "She doesn't know Roland the way we do, so maybe she just assumed he was that kind of guy."

"He does like things to be done right—" A sudden burst of laughter interrupted the thought and then Pamela went on. "Do you think he'll sit up late tonight knitting, checking his watch to make sure he's putting in exactly the amount of time he lost while helping Gayle?"

"I can see him doing that." Bettina laughed too. "We'll have to notice how much further along the current sock is when we get together next Tuesday. We never did decide if he really wears those hand-knit socks he makes, did we?"

"Maybe on weekends," Pamela said.

She'd been standing near the door too, bidding people good night. Now she leaned over to pick up her knitting bag from the sofa and prepared to make her own departure, while Bettina fetched her jacket from the closet.

"Before I leave, though"—Pamela paused in the act of buttoning her jacket—"that memorial reception is tomorrow. I think we agreed that it might be interesting to go . . ."

"You convinced me." Bettina nodded. "It's at two. Who's driving?"

"I'll drive," Pamela said. "Come over at one. Even if it takes more than an hour to get there and park, it's probably kind of a drop-in thing. We might learn more if it's already in full swing when we get there."

# CHAPTER 8

Bettina's ensemble stood out amid the crowd that had gathered to honor the memory of Mel Word-woman. Most of the attendees, who were all women, wore jeans or casual pants, and the neutral colors and simple cuts of the garments seemed more a strategy to avoid attracting male attention than an acknowledgment that the gathering had been occasioned by a death. Even Adrienne had chosen a pantsuit in an inconspicuous heathery tone.

Bettina, however, had taken from her closet her chic black crepe coatdress. A triple strand of pearls filled in the neckline and pearl earrings dangled from her earlobes. On her feet were black suede pumps with impractically high heels.

Adrienne had reserved Rodeo's party room for the event. It was reached by walking through the restaurant proper, a warren of small rooms crowded with mismatched tables and chairs. Paintings of all sorts, as if collected from many sources over many decades, decorated the low-ceilinged walls, completing the bohemian effect. At least half the tables were occupied, as people chatted over the remains of lunches served on simple cafeteria-style dinnerware.

The party room was more spacious, and it looked out on a busy Village street through narrow floor-to-ceiling windows in wooden frames. A long table held bowls of guacamole and baskets of corn chips. From a bar along the back wall a server, the only man in the room, dispensed drinks, which seemed to be limited to red or white wine, various soft drinks, and beer.

Adrienne noticed them when they walked in, waved from a post near the windows, and gestured toward the bar.

"We should get something," Pamela whispered to Bettina, "so it looks like we're here to mingle. And then we should mingle, and the only person we know is Adrienne, so . . ."

Some minutes later, glasses of soda in hand, Pamela and Bettina edged through the crowd till they reached the cluster of people who had collected around the event's hostess. The conversation underway was lively enough that acknowledging Adrienne with a nod and listening with an amiable expression on one's face seemed sufficient. Perhaps introductions would be forthcoming later. For now, it appeared that the focus of interest was a member of Mel's circle named Blair Tyler.

"I'm not saying I'm *glad* she's not here," said a dark-haired woman. "I'm just saying it's *interesting* that she's not here."

Adrienne had taken a few steps back, accosted by a

new arrival who wanted her ear. With a glance in Adrienne's direction, as if to make sure her attention was really elsewhere, another woman leaned toward the dark-haired woman.

"Maybe Blair was afraid she wouldn't be able to act sad." Her tone was mischievous.

"Now, now, now," the dark-haired woman responded, but a small smile crept across her unlipsticked lips.

"I thought Blair had a point," the other woman said. "We don't need to reject men out of hand just because they can be a distraction. They might bring a valuable perspective to the group. I mean, if we're trying to understand Shakespeare . . . he was a *man*, after all."

"Yes." The dark-haired woman nodded sharply, and a crease appeared between her untended brows. "And he excluded women from the Globe Theatre to the point that the female roles were acted by male actors. Mel believed turnabout was fair play, and I agree."

"I still think Blair had a point." The first woman spoke again. She was attractive and petite, with her blond hair styled in a no-nonsense bowl cut. "I respected Mel—she certainly was a role model for women in academia—but I wasn't opposed to admitting men, even if just as a know-the-enemy move."

"We'd have to change the name if we let them in," the dark-haired woman said. "It wouldn't make very much sense to call ourselves Shakespeare's Rib with men as members." She focused on Pamela for a moment and then turned back to the blond woman. "And what about the Womanifesto? Wasn't the whole point that it's not a *Man*ifesto?'

Without waiting for the blond woman to answer, she

addressed Pamela. "You don't look familiar." Her glance strayed to Bettina and then she focused on Pamela again. "Are you new to Shakespeare's Rib? Where do you teach? And who's your friend?"

"Bettina Fraser," Bettina said as she extended her hand, apparently not bothered by the fact that the dark-haired woman seemed to consider Pamela more worthy of her attention. "And this is Pamela Paterson and neither of us teach anywhere. We're neighbors of Adrienne's."

The dark-haired woman peered at them and said, "So you didn't actually know Mel, then?"

Almost simultaneously, the blond woman accepted Bettina's hand, smiled, and murmured, "I'm Zoe Zander."

"Natalie Gidding," the dark-haired woman added belatedly.

The many conversations going on around the room had blended individual utterances into a cheerful—curiously cheerful, given the nature of the event—hubbub. But suddenly, in a lull, one voice rose above the rest.

From near the bar came the words, "Well, well, well . . . look who's here!"

Eyes turned, not to the bar but to the doorway, and in the doorway there appeared a striking woman. She was tall and willowy, with strawberry-blond hair that cascaded past her shoulders. Her outfit, like the outfits of most of the other guests, was simple to the point of austerity, but the components looked expensive: a camel hair coat that she removed to reveal well-fitting pants and a silky shirt, both the color of rich cream.

"Who's that?" Bettina asked, addressing no one in particular. The answer was forthcoming anyway.

"So Blair came after all." It was the dark-haired woman, Natalie Gidding, who spoke.

Pamela and Bettina were forgotten then, as a few people broke off from a neighboring conversational group and clustered around Natalie and Zoe.

"Is she in charge now?" someone asked, twisting her head to aim a glance toward the new arrival.

"There were only two candidates for president," Natalie pointed out, holding up a ring-less hand with two fingers extended.

"If one of them dies before the vote is taken, does that mean the other one automatically wins?" someone else inquired, a much younger woman, bespectacled and with the manner of an earnest graduate student. "That doesn't seem exactly fair."

"May I remind you"—the dark-haired woman took a deep breath and straightened her back, as if recalling a stressful event—"that none of the other eligible people wanted to run."

"The president has to have a PhD in one of the humanities, and people who have already served can't run again," the blond woman, Zoe, whispered, seemingly for the benefit of the much younger woman. Speaking louder, she went on, "It's a ton of work, but Mel was really committed to the cause, and she was editing *Bicycle Fish* too. Who will do that now?" She shrugged and looked around.

Blair, the new arrival, had joined a group nearer the door, and that group had slowly migrated toward the table with the guacamole and corn chips, although sometime while Pamela and Bettina had been occupied overhearing conversations, more offerings had been added. Now, in occasional glimpses made possible by people edging forward and then stepping away bearing plates of food, Pamela could see long pans of enchiladas, bowls of yellow rice, bowls of deep red beans in thick sauce, and plates of sliced tomatoes and cucumbers.

Never one to pass up an interesting dining possibility, Bettina took a few steps in the direction of the long table, but Pamela lingered, curious about the fate of *Bicycle Fish.*

"Blair will probably want to take that over too." Someone spoke up from the fringes of the group, an older woman with a stern expression, wearing an ancient gray wool suit. "It will be the beginning of the end, if you ask me. Who knows what articles she'll approve for publication, given her views on . . . our oppressors? Losing Mel was a great blow to this organization."

Bettina was nearing the table. A spot opened up, making the stack of empty plates accessible, and she quickly stepped into it. After picking up a plate, she twisted around and beckoned Pamela to join her. Pamela took a plate and followed Bettina, edging along the table and helping herself to rice, beans, and an enchilada, adding a few spoonfuls of guacamole as a garnish before retreating to a relatively uncrowded corner of the room.

The enchiladas had looked particularly appealing, rolled up and tucked side by side in a long baking pan, and topped with a layer of sauce in which chunks of tomato and chiles figured prominently. Standing with a plate in one hand and a fork in the other, managing to wield the fork to carve bite-sized pieces from the enchilada was challenging but well worthwhile. Within the rolled-up tortilla was a filling that melded crumbly white cheese with slivers of chicken, a mild complement to the complex earthiness of the corn tortilla and the spicy acidic sauce.

The rice was a rich yellow, speckled with bits of green pepper and aromatic with turmeric and garlic. And the beans, deep red and glistening, tasted as if they had been simmered long and slow, to the point that they'd formed a creamy souplike sauce.

"Delicious!" was Bettina's verdict as she beamed at Pamela with a dribble of enchilada topping escaping from the corner of her mouth.

"Yes, isn't it," said a voice nearby. Pamela looked past Bettina to discover that the voice was that of Blair, standing alone, holding a half-empty plate. Blair smiled when they made eye contact. "I don't believe I know you," she said. "I guess Mel had friends who weren't members of Shakespeare's Rib too."

It seemed curious that Blair wasn't mingling with the attendees who did seem to be members of Shakespeare's Rib, at least based on the conversations she had overheard and the general look of people, but—it suddenly occurred to her—perhaps Blair was in disfavor. She'd advocated a radical change in the group's membership policy and run for president with the apparent aim of pushing for that change. Now the woman who represented the group's long-standing tradition of being women-only was dead—murdered in fact. Even the people sympathetic to Blair's ideas, like the blond woman, Zoe, might be hesitant to be seen hobnobbing with her at this particular event.

These thoughts passed through Pamela's mind so rapidly that her response to Blair's comment was delayed by only a few seconds.

"I'm Pamela Paterson," she said. Encumbered by the plate and fork, offering a handshake wasn't possible. "And this is my friend, Bettina Fraser," she added as Bettina nodded with a mouthful of food. "We're neighbors of Mel's sister, Adrienne."

"That was the house where the . . . murder . . . took place," Blair whispered. "How shocking for the whole neighborhood, and such a pretty block." She paused, frowned, and stared at her plate for a moment. Her face was long and thin, with bold features, a look to which the elegant clothes and the flowing strawberry-blond hair lent a kind of glamour. But the frown recast the look from glamorous to resolute.

She looked up as if recovering from a brief distraction and said, "I'm Blair Tyler."

After a long moment of silence, during which Pamela hesitated to continue eating lest conversation start up suddenly, Bettina surveyed the room and remarked, "Lovely event, and such a charming venue." Her glance traveled to the long windows, the street beyond, and the narrow storefronts across the way. On this autumn afternoon, the street was in shadow with the sun behind the buildings already well on its way toward the western horizon.

"Yes . . . yes, it is," Blair murmured. "So nice of

Adrienne to—" She broke off. A sudden silence, as dramatic in its way as the effect of a thunderclap, had fallen over the room.

Bettina turned back to Pamela, but that was not where her attention remained. Everyone, it seemed, was focused on the doorway, and with good reason, as Pamela realized when she too gazed in that direction.

A man had entered, a tall and very handsome man, with dark hair and strikingly blue eyes. Managing to appear unselfconscious, though quite obviously aware that he was causing a stir, he pondered the scene for a few moments, his eyes darting here and there. When they landed on Blair, he seemed to sigh. Then he strode rapidly toward the corner where Pamela, Bettina, and Blair were standing.

Blair seemed to recognize him and opened her mouth, but before any sound came out he said, "I had to come . . . foolish, I know, but I just . . . I just . . . I wanted to see the people who did this to her." He sighed again and raised a shaking hand to rub his face.

"*Did this to her*?" The question came from a woman who had been on her way to the table with an empty plate, apparently in quest of second helpings. Despite her shape, which suggested she had eaten many second helpings in her life, she was attractive, with glossy brown hair pulled into a careless updo that left tendrils to frame her pretty face.

"What about what she did to these people, me included?" the woman added. "I used to like men."

"You can still like them," Blair said. "I like them."

But the woman had already continued on her way.

Blair turned back to the man, who had become quite distraught. Sensing that they would welcome privacy, Pamela nudged Bettina and took a few steps to the side, then a few more. They concentrated on their plates in silence. The food had cooled considerably but was still quite appealing, and nothing but a few grains of rice, a bean or two, and a smudge of enchilada sauce remained when they deposited them at the end of the table where used plates had begun to accumulate.

A few people were still returning for second helpings, but servers had started to clear away the bowls and enchilada pans that had been emptied, as well as the used plates that were piling up. But there was more food to come. Dessert, it seemed, would be ice cream bars in their paper wrappers, delivered to the table on deep trays where they lay heaped on beds of crushed ice. An excited bustle greeted their arrivals and soon conversation had been replaced by contented nibbling and licking.

Pamela and Bettina found themselves once more in the company of Adrienne, the three of them standing with their backs to the long windows, ice cream bars in their hands.

"It looks like he's gone now," Adrienne said after a bit, talking almost to herself.

She was referring to the handsome man, Pamela supposed, because the only other man in the room, the server behind the bar along the back wall, was still at his post. The handsome man *was* gone, and Blair was nowhere in sight either.

"He seemed upset," Bettina commented.

"He had a reason." Adrienne accompanied the words with a secret smile of the sort that often hints at a secret.

"Oh?" Bettina responded. Pamela knew her friend well enough to know that this simple syllable really meant, *Tell me all about it.*

"Later," Adrienne whispered. "When we get outside." She stepped away from the windows. "People are starting to leave. I should go stand by the door in case anybody wants to thank me."

"Or offer condolences," Bettina suggested to Adrienne's retreating back.


"Rodeo certainly wouldn't have been my choice for an event like this," Adrienne commented as they all stepped out onto the sidewalk, "but Mel loved the place, and all the bicycle fish people live in the city, so . . ." She paused. "I did think they'd serve ribs. Rodeo? Barbecue? Shakespeare's Rib and all . . . though they *are* messy to eat."

Pamela and Bettina were quickly swept up by the passing crowd, and it was a minute before Adrienne caught up with them, still talking.

". . . but ice cream bars for dessert! Honestly! And still in their paper wrappers!"

"I liked them." Bettina took Adrienne's arm and pulled her around the corner. The sidewalk that ran past the side of Rodeo was less congested. "You said that man who showed up had a reason to be upset . . ." She let the thought trail off, replacing words with a look—raised brows, insinuating smile—that invited gossip.

Adrienne, not to be outdone, arranged her features to mirror Bettina's expression. "Now I know what put Mel in the state she was in when she took refuge with me in Arborville."

"Oh?"

"One word," Adrienne said. "Or is it two? *Lovesick.* And I can see why—that guy was *hot!*"

"The flowers!" Bettina exclaimed. "They must have been from him!"

"And she was trying to resist, trying to stay true to the Shakespeare's Rib group and the Womanifesto," Pamela added.

"Sounds like." Adrienne nodded. "Of course, she wouldn't confide in *me*—we didn't have that kind of a relationship. But some of the bicycle fish people knew, and one of them—that little blond woman with the unflattering hair—was happy to tell me all about it. Martin Cotswold is his name, by the way."

"Was that Zoe?" Pamela said. "We were talking to her too, but that was before the man arrived."

"Zoe . . . whatever." Adrienne shrugged. "How they can all stand to look at themselves in the mirror is beyond me." She fingered the wavy strands of hair that framed her carefully made up face, then tilted her arm to consult her watch. "I should get going," she said. "I'm in one of those lots where after three hours you pay as much as if you'd been there all day. I can just make it before it goes up if I hurry."

And then she was on her way, disappearing into the bustling crowd. Pamela had been persistent enough to find a free parking spot on the street, and barely a block from Rodeo. Thus she didn't mind lingering a bit longer on the sidewalk, especially because a thought had just occurred to her and she wanted to explore it with Bettina while it was still fresh.

"So now we know more about the flower man," she said, drawing Bettina toward a rustic bench positioned in front of the long wood-framed windows that looked out from the party room.

"It's emptying out now," Bettina noted parenthetically as she peered through one of the windows and then took a seat. And in fact, a small group of women Pamela recognized from the event had just turned the corner.

"I'm positive the flower man was Martin Cotswold," Pamela continued. "Remember, the florist said he was taller than usual, with jet-black hair and dreamy blue eyes."

"And that he was *hot*." Bettina laughed. "Funny— Adrienne had the same impression."

"Do we still think he could be the killer?" Pamela asked. "We had that idea he'd tried and tried to win her love but then just gave up."

"He seemed so distraught." Bettina's own expression took on a sorrowful cast. "If he was the killer, why would he be distraught? Why would he even show up?"

"To avert suspicion?" Pamela suggested. "And his misery could just have been an act."

"We'll never know." Bettina sighed and shook her head, setting her pearl earrings in motion. "On the other hand"—she brightened up—"he *is* very tall, and according to the police the figure in the surveillance footage was either a tall woman or a medium-sized man. And he said he came to the event because he *wanted to see the people who did this to her.*"

Pamela shrugged. "What did he mean?"

Bettina mirrored the shrug. "I don't know, but that's not something her killer would say, is it?"

Pamela smiled. "I know you think he's hot, and that's why you don't want him to be guilty."

"Anyone would think he's hot." Bettina laughed. "He *is* hot."

A man had detached himself from the passing crowd and was lingering near the bench where Pamela and Bettina were sitting, alternating between glancing through one of the windows that looked into the Rodeo party room and studying the people turning the corner from the street the restaurant's entrance faced. He seemed so caught up in these activities as to be unaware that the bench behind him was occupied.

He was attractive in a low-key sort of way—slender, with short-cropped brown hair and dressed in jeans and a dark woolly jacket. Seen in profile as he peered through the window, his features were regular and his expression was open and eager. He shifted his gaze back to the corner and suddenly his body tensed. He strode away from the bench and intercepted a woman who had just come into view.

"Roxanne!" Pamela heard him exclaim.

Pamela recognized the woman. She had seen her at the event in the Rodeo party room, carrying an empty plate back to the buffet table for a refill. The woman had paused to respond when Martin Cotswold said he wanted to see the people who did . . . whatever they did . . . to Mel—but her response had implied that Mel had actually done something to the people present at the event.

Now she was staring at the man who had confronted her. Her pretty lips were parted and her eyes were wide.

"What are you doing here?" she whispered.

"Looking for you, of course." He took her arm and drew her to the side as people continued to flow past. He was facing away from the bench where Pamela and Bettina still sat, and he was tall enough that his torso screened the woman from view.

Pamela could hear him—he was speaking loud enough to be heard above the din from the street—but the woman's responses were muffled.

"Can we take up where we left off now?" he asked. "I miss you so much." There was a pause, and he tipped his head forward as if listening to a response. "But she's gone now. Everything's different." Pause. "I know the group is important to you, and to your career . . ." Pause. "I know about the Womanifesto. You explained the whole thing to me, but can't it be revised now?"

"I have to think! I have to think," the woman moaned. She darted around him and sank down onto the bench right next to Bettina.

The man whirled around and planted himself in front of her. His face was no less pleasant when seen from this new angle than when seen in profile, though at the moment he was obviously in considerable distress.

"You don't need them," he said, "but I won't stand in your way—whatever you want to do, wherever you want to go."

"You all say that," Roxanne moaned, "but once a woman commits herself to a man, the whole traditional thing takes over. She enhances his life but diminishes her own."

"It wouldn't be like that, it wouldn't be like that. I promise!"

For a moment, he seemed on the point of sinking to his knees, but Roxanne half-rose and extended her hands, palms facing out as if to push him away. She tipped her head toward Pamela and Bettina as if to call attention to the fact that he had a larger audience than just one person.

He gaped at Bettina, who was sitting closest to Roxanne, in seeming amazement, straightened up, and cleared his throat.

"We'll talk later," he said, addressing Roxanne. "I'm sorry to have caught you unawares."

He headed down the sidewalk, and Roxanne folded her hands primly on her lap and closed her eyes.

On her occasional trips to the city for work or pleasure, Pamela had witnessed other dramas, both happy and sad, playing out in public. People in Arborville had spacious houses to contain their joys and sorrows, but apartment dwellers seemed to live more of their lives in the open, with a park as likely a spot to knit or read, or maybe argue, as a living room.

Bettina, meanwhile, was stirring. First she nudged Pamela, responding to Pamela's questioning look with a questioning look of her own. Then she shrugged and focused on the other occupant of the bench.

"Sad event, wasn't it," she remarked in an offhand way. Pamela felt herself frown. As a conversational gambit the statement couldn't be faulted, but as to its accuracy . . .

"Um?" Roxanne turned.

Bettina followed up with, "Were you and Mel close friends?" Pamela couldn't see her friend's face, but she could picture the expression that likely accompanied the question: delicately furrowed brows and lips poised to offer sympathy.

"What?" Roxanne scowled.

"I believe I saw you inside," Bettina added, tipping her head toward the long window and the party room beyond.

Roxanne scowled harder. "I hated the woman. Didn't you?" She surveyed Bettina, even examining her shoes, perhaps trying to determine her connection with the group that had attended the Rodeo event.

"I didn't actually know her," Bettina said. "Her sister, Adrienne, is my neighbor."

"You're lucky you didn't know her." Roxanne folded her arms across her chest and contemplated the passing crowd. "It was almost like she was hypnotizing us," she murmured, more to herself than to Bettina, then she turned back to Bettina. "Mel was . . . what's that word . . . very charismatic. People wanted to please her, and the way to do that was to resist the lure of *romance*. She said it was a trap, and that once we gave in, we'd be trading all our work, our careers, everything for . . . a lesser life."

"Your young man seemed pleasant," Bettina observed.

"He's not my young man." Roxanne laughed, but not happily. "Wasn't that clear?"

"Does he have a name?" Pamela felt her eyes widen. Bettina was really incorrigible, she reflected. Given the circumstances, the question could only strike Roxanne, who was all but a complete stranger, as outlandish.

And apparently it did. Roxanne stood up. "Of course," she said. "Everyone has a name, but why on earth should I tell *you* the name of the person who is *not* my *young man*?"

Bettina reached into her handbag, pulled out one of her business cards, and thrust it at Roxanne. "I'm a reporter," she said.

Roxanne took the card, but she hurried away before Bettina could say more. Bettina watched her go, then looked at Pamela and shrugged.

"I know why you asked her that," Pamela said. "It would be interesting to know more about him . . . because, obviously, he thought Mel was the impediment standing between him and the woman he loves."

"Obviously." Bettina sighed and pushed herself up from the bench. "But we don't even know *her* last name. I can't think how we could ever track *him* down."

# CHAPTER 9

Pamela's first task the next morning, after feeding the cats but even before making her own breakfast, had been to send her evaluations of "Victorian Hair," "Dark Arts," and "New Black" off to Celine Bramley at *Fiber Craft*. She was not surprised when a response came almost instantly, a message with three more articles attached and instructions to copyedit them by the following Wednesday. The short titles ranged across the top of the message—"Pocket Change," "Putting on the Dog," and "Needle Spells"—revealed little about their actual content, and Pamela was too eager for her morning infusion of caffeine to open the files in search of more detail.

Downstairs, she set water to boil and headed for the entry, en route to fetching that morning's *Register*. She didn't have to make her usual trip to the end of the front walk, however. She opened the door to find Bettina preparing to climb the porch steps, both hands clutching a plate covered with foil, and a newspaper in the

*Register*'s familiar plastic sleeve tucked under one arm. Bettina was already dressed for the day in a cozy fleece tunic whose flamingo-pink hue echoed that of her leggings.

"No point in hurrying to read it," she said as Pamela intercepted her and slipped the *Register* out from under her arm. "There's nothing new about the case." She nodded toward the foil-covered plate. "Nothing new here either. Adrienne has a very limited baking repertoire."

"She came around already this morning?" Pamela moved aside, and Bettina started up the steps. Pamela followed her across the threshold, but not before pausing to admire the glorious autumn morning—deep blue sky, cloudless, with red and amber foliage fairly vibrating in the clear air.

"Yes, she came around." Affecting a comically insincere smile, Bettina simpered, "*I thought your handsome husband would like something sweet to go with his coffee.*" She thrust the foil-covered plate at Pamela. "Chocolate chip pound cake again."

They were standing in the entry now, and Bettina made a show of sniffing the air. "Is there coffee?"

At that moment, the kettle began to hoot. "There will be very soon," Pamela said. "But maybe I'll add more water to the kettle first. I wasn't expecting you."

"Adrienne was on her way to see Clayborn," Bettina reported as Pamela led the way to the kitchen. "She thought he'd like to hear about the memorial event." In a change of topic, she added, "I think she dresses much too young for her age, don't you? She's Mel's older sister, after all. Much older, I'd say. Didn't the article in the *Register* say Mel was forty-two?"

Pamela limited her responses to nods and murmurs as she moved about the kitchen, setting the foil-covered plate on the table, adding extra water to the kettle, and taking cups, saucers, and little plates from the cupboard where she kept her wedding china.

Some minutes later, the two friends were seated in their usual seats at the table with steaming cups of coffee before them—Bettina's a bit less steaming thanks to the copious amounts of sugar and cream she had added—and little plates holding golden slices of pound cake studded with chocolate chips.

"Blair is very tall," Bettina said suddenly. She went on to explain: "In the images captured by the surveillance camera, the attacker is either a tall woman or a medium-sized man."

Pamela, with a mouth full of chocolate chip pound cake, could only nod. She swallowed, took a sip of coffee, and nodded again. "She could definitely have a motive. Both she and Mel were vying to be president of Shakespeare's Rib—and it sounded like there were some very fundamental contrasts in their visions for the group."

"One especially." Bettina's coffee cup paused partway to her mouth. "Should they let men in or not?"

"It would all have come down to what the membership wanted, wouldn't it?" Pamela said. "The ones who wanted to let men in would have voted for Blair, and the ones who wanted to keep things like they were would have voted for Mel . . . but if Blair was left as the only one running . . . she'd become president by default . . ."

"Killing someone in a squabble over the leadership of Shakespeare's Rib seems pretty extreme." Bettina compressed her lips into a tight knot and wrinkled her nose. "If Blair wants to be in a scholarly group with men, I'm sure there are plenty of others she could join."

Pamela didn't answer right away. She was recalling the conversation she and Bettina had had with Blair at the memorial event. After they identified themselves as neighbors of Mel's sister, Blair had said something to the effect that the house where the murder occurred was on a very pretty block. And then she had frowned and stared at her plate, as if realizing she had just given something away.

She described the recollection to Bettina, adding, "How would Blair know it was a pretty block unless she had been here? And why did she frown?"

Bettina shrugged. "She could have been here some other time, not necessarily on Halloween night, or with murderous intent. Maybe Mel liked to show off her sister's nice neighborhood in the suburbs. Or maybe Mel had just described the neighborhood, or shown pictures . . ."

"But then she frowned and stared at her plate," Pamela said.

"People frown for all kinds of reasons. Maybe she was wondering what was in the enchiladas. Maybe she doesn't like spicy food. Personally"—Bettina raised her fork to emphasize the point she was about to make—"I think that man who accosted Roxanne on the sidewalk is a more likely suspect."

"Thwarted love . . ." Pamela nodded. "Is that more of a motive than thwarted ambition?"

The question went unanswered, however, because at that moment the doorbell chimed and Pamela rose to her feet. From the vantage point of the kitchen doorway, she didn't recognize the figure behind the lace that curtained the oval window in the front door, though it was obviously female. But when she opened the door, she discovered that her visitor was Adrienne. Bettina had by this time joined Pamela in the entry and, after crossing the threshold, Adrienne spoke first to her.

"Your sweet husband told me you were here," she explained. "I thought you'd like to hear about my meeting with Clayborn. He was quite sympathetic—after all, Mel was my sister."

She took several more steps and peeked into the living room, where Precious gave her an appraising look from the top platform of the cat climber. Adrienne had dressed for her meeting with Clayborn as if for a professional appointment, in a feminine skirt suit, rosy pink in color. The luxuriant waves of her blond hair seemed arranged with particular care.

"I love your house, Pamela." She turned back to where Pamela and Bettina stood. "It's full of so many interesting *old* things." She glanced at Bettina and winked.

Next to Pamela, Bettina growled but didn't speak.

"So, do you want to hear what all he said?" Adrienne smiled expectantly.

"Uh—" Pamela glanced at Bettina, whose eyes widened in exasperation but who nodded assent. "We could go into the kitchen. I think there's even a bit of coffee left."

"That chocolate chip pound cake looks familiar!" Adrienne exclaimed as she stepped through the kitchen doorway. "But there's not much left. I guess you both liked it, but I hope Wilfred got his share."

"He got plenty," Bettina said with a scowl. "I don't really care for it that much, and neither does Pamela. You can see there's quite a bit still on our plates."

Pamela, meanwhile, had set an extra cup, saucer, and little plate on the table and lit the burner under the carafe.

"Watch that so it doesn't boil," she instructed Bettina and darted into the dining room to fetch another chair.

Soon Pamela and Bettina were back in their usual seats and Adrienne was stationed at the end of the table with a slice of cake—just a tiny bit, she had said—and a cup of coffee. Bettina pointedly ignored the remains of her own cake while Pamela sipped at her coffee, surprised to discover that it was still quite hot. The process of greeting Adrienne at the door and settling her at the table had actually taken only a few minutes.

Despite Bettina's understandable pique, Pamela was curious to hear what Adrienne had to say, and Adrienne seemed eager to relate the details of her meeting with Detective Clayborn.

"First of all," she said, "he interviewed some of the bicycle fish people and so he knows all about the rivalry between Mel and Blair."

"Is he planning to follow up?" Pamela asked. "Most obviously by checking whether Blair has an alibi for Halloween night?"

Apparently quite happy to have a chance to enjoy her own creation, despite her stated aversion to sweets, Adrienne had just closed her lips around a large forkful of chocolate chip pound cake. She nodded as if to signal that an answer would be forthcoming.

When it came, however, the answer was disappointing. "He's cagey," Adrienne responded. "That was not revealed."

"What about Martin Cotswold?"

"I told him about Martin Cotswold." Adrienne followed up her bite of cake with a swallow of coffee. She'd added no cream or sugar, and Pamela hoped it wasn't too bitter in its reheated state.

"And?"

"He seemed surprised, though trying not to show it. *I* was surprised that he was surprised, because I'd have thought the bicycle fish people . . ."

She broke off. Bettina was staring at her, shaking her head slowly and smiling a pitying smile. "*Duh!*" she said. "Obviously the bicycle fish people wouldn't have revealed to a man the fact that some among their number had been tempted to stray from the group's mission."

"Or perhaps to anyone . . ." Pamela murmured.

"And once I'd told him about Martin, I'd have thought he'd have wanted me to tell him all I knew." Adrienne shrugged. "But he just brushed it off."

"He didn't think of it himself." Bettina spoke up, obviously unwilling to let this interesting conversation proceed without her input. "I mean, asking the bicycle fish people if they knew of any romantic entanglements—though that's usually one of the first questions when there's been a murder."

"Or maybe he *did* ask them," Pamela suggested, "but like you said, they didn't reveal anything, and he was chagrined to hear from you"—she tilted her head toward Adrienne—"that perhaps a man *was* involved."

"Perhaps," Adrienne agreed. "At any rate, I came away feeling a little disappointed."

They all focused on their cake and coffee for a minute or two, but Pamela wasn't willing to abandon the topic of Martin Cotswold quite yet.

"What did it mean," she asked half to herself, "when he said he had come to the event because he wanted to see the people who did this to her? And what was the *this* he was referring to?"

"Made her give him up?" Visible over the rim of her coffee cup, Bettina's eyes signaled puzzlement.

"But"—Pamela punctuated her thought with a sharp tap on the table—"it was Mel who was most adamant about renouncing men."

"Then she met a man she couldn't resist," Adrienne murmured. "The heart wants what it wants."

"Was killing her some kind of retribution for hypocrisy?" Pamela's tone suggested she found the idea no less horrifying for its improbability.

"The killer could have been almost anyone in the group then," Bettina said, and Adrienne cut in right away with an emphatic, "Yes!"

"Yes," she repeated. "It could have been any one of those people who were being spied on and reported on, assuming they knew about Mel's feelings for Martin!" She glanced at Pamela and then at Bettina as if to make sure they understood the significance of this realization.

"They were only identified by initials," Pamela pointed out. "I don't see how we could find them." She paused. "The police could. They could collect all those papers from Mel's apartment and collate them with a membership list from Shakespeare's Rib."

"They won't, though." Bettina sighed. "Clayborn didn't think of it himself, and he doesn't like it when I give him ideas about what he should do."

"ZZ!" Pamela exclaimed suddenly. "ZZ was one of them, and I'm pretty sure we met her. That blond woman with the bowl-cut hair was named Zoe Zander. It's a name that kind of sticks in the mind."

"She was on Blair's side, as I recall," Bettina said, "in favor of admitting men."

"Did she know about Mel's feelings for Martin, though?" Pamela asked. "In order to consider Mel a hypocrite worthy of punishment, members of Shakespeare's Rib would have had to know that she wasn't being faithful to the mission."

"We don't know what she—or any of the group— knew." Bettina looked up from pursuing an errant chocolate chip with her fork.

Pamela raised her cup to her mouth and tipped her head back to drain the final swallow. Then she pulled the plate with the remaining slice of cake closer, picked up the knife, and cut the slice crosswise into four narrow portions.

"There are only three of us," Bettina commented, "unless you're saving one for Wilfred."

"Four motives," Pamela said with a mysterious smile. She nudged the leftmost portion away from the others. "Motive number one: Supplant Mel, become president, and revise the group's mission."

"One suspect?" Bettina peered at Pamela. "Blair?"

Pamela nodded and nudged off a second portion of cake. "Motive number two: Remove Mel so the group's mission can be revised and his girlfriend will come back to him."

"One suspect? That nice man who accosted Roxanne outside Rodeo?"

Pamela nodded again. She nudged off a third portion of cake. "Motive number three: Unrequited love—though not because she didn't actually love him."

"Martin Cotswold." Bettina nodded sadly. "He finally decided if he couldn't have her, he didn't want her to exist." She picked up the knife and poked at the last, skinny, portion of cake. Saying, "Motive number four . . . punishment for hypocrisy . . . lots of suspects," she chopped that portion into little bits.

"Whew!" Adrienne gestured as if wiping her brow. "That's complicated!" She reached for one of the intact cake portions and ate it with her fingers. "What next?"

"I think the man who Roxanne broke up with has the *strongest* motive," Pamela said. "The heart wants what it wants."

"Not Martin?" Adrienne signaled surprise by lifting her precisely shaped brows. "The heart wants what it wants, but if it can't have it . . ."

"We all saw him at the Rodeo event," Pamela said. "He's very tall, and the figure on the surveillance video appeared to be either a tall woman or a medium-sized man. Of course, how a person looking at a video could really judge height unless there were other people to compare with . . ."

Across the table from Pamela, Bettina was consulting her watch, a pretty gold watch in a bracelet style. Adrienne noticed the action and raised her wrist to consult her own watch.

"I guess you both have work to do or places to go or something," she remarked as she scanned their faces. There was no response, but she climbed to her feet.

"Do you want to take your plate?" Bettina asked. The plate was the same yellow one that had held the last batch of chocolate chip pound cake.

"No, no, no. Don't bother." Adrienne fluttered one hand in a shooing gesture. "Your sweet husband can drop it off this afternoon."

They escorted Adrienne to the door, past the spot on the entry carpet where the patch of sunlight in which Catrina took her morning naps still lingered.

"By the way . . ." Adrienne paused on the threshold and addressed Bettina. "Do you by any chance know if Clayborn is single?"

"No," Bettina said. "I don't know."

She managed to contain her laughter until Pamela had closed the front door securely, but once she and Pamela were alone, she exploded in a raucous hoot. "*Is Clayborn single?*" She fairly shrieked the words. "What on earth does the woman have in mind?" She paused, and her voice took on a mincing quality. "And what about, *Your sweet husband can drop it off this afternoon?*"

Bettina headed back toward the kitchen.

"I thought you had to leave," Pamela said. "You were looking at your watch."

"That was only to get rid of Adrienne. My heavens, that woman is annoying!" She shook her head spasmodically, and the scarlet tendrils of her hair vibrated.

By the time Pamela reached the kitchen doorway, Bettina had already seated herself back at the table. "Now," she said, "what are we going to do first?" She picked up one of the cake fingers and took a bite. "I liked the way you sorted things out with the motives and the suspects, but it's okay to eat the suspects now, isn't it?"

Pamela returned the chair that had been Adrienne's to the dining room. She took her customary seat across from Bettina and said, "I'd like to know what the man Roxanne broke up with was doing on Halloween night."

"We don't know his name or anything about him," Bettina pointed out as she reached for another of the cake fingers. "We don't even know Roxanne's last name."

"Shakespeare's Rib might have a website, though. And the website might talk about the doings of the members."

"Like breaking up with their boyfriends?"

"Of course not." Pamela laughed. "Academic accomplishments . . . things like that. Roxanne isn't the most common of names. Maybe we can learn more about Zoe Zander too."

Bettina popped up from her seat with barely an assist from the table. Alarming Ginger, who had just stepped into the kitchen from the entry, she dashed through the doorway, returning seconds later with her phone.

Even before settling back into her seat, Bettina pushed the button that would bring her device to life, and her fingers began to flutter over its screen. She lowered herself into her chair, murmuring, "Yes, yes . . . Shakespeare's Rib . . . yes." More fluttering, then, looking up, she said, "They have a group blog."

Pamela watched from her side of the table as Bettina peered at the little screen, alternately smiling and frowning. Finally, she rose and circled around the table to lean over her friend's shoulder and learn firsthand what the Shakespeare's Rib bloggers had to say.

"'Notes from Underground,'" she read aloud, "by Roxanne Ballard."

"Posted before the Rodeo event," Bettina pointed out, "but after Mel was killed."

"It doesn't seem to have anything to do with Mel, though," Pamela commented, scanning the text rapidly as Bettina scrolled.

"More like the hard life of a would-be professor without a full-time job. It sounds like she's dashing all over the place, teaching courses here and there as an adjunct." Bettina set the phone on the table and sighed. "Poor thing—hoping the Shakespeare's Rib contacts will lead to something permanent and working part-time at the Little Corner Bookshop in the Village to make ends meet."

Pamela had returned to her seat. "We've found our lead!" she exclaimed. "Not only do we know her last name now—Ballard—but we know where to find her . . . except . . ." Pamela felt her lips twist into a disappointed knot. "Her boyfriend—ex-boyfriend—is the person we're really interested in, and she already made it clear that, understandably, there's no reason she should reveal his name to a couple of women she doesn't even know."

But Bettina was on her feet. "I can't go to the city dressed like this," she said, looking down at the flamingo-pink tunic and leggings outfit in which she had started the day. "No time like the present, though. I'll pick you up in an hour."

"What if she's not even there?" Pamela asked. "She only works part-time at the bookshop."

"All the better if she's not there." Bettina smiled mysteriously. "That's what I'm hoping. I have a plan."


The bell that jingled as Pamela pushed the bookshop's door open welcomed them into a world much different from the world its windows now surveyed. Yes, the cobbled streets whose intersection had given the bookshop its name were already old when the building that housed the bookshop—narrow storefront below and walk-up apartments above—was built. But that building itself, with its multipaned windows and ornate wood trim, was now old. And the slender young people, tattooed and jeans-wearing, who constituted the passing scene seemed out of place—though, paradoxically, so very at home in the Village.

"Hello?" A pleasant-looking older woman looked up from behind a wooden counter whose patina linked its age with its surroundings.

"Books Old and New" read a sign, and the shop's aroma, musty with ancient paper and binding glue, bore that claim out. Tall bookcases formed narrow aisles that blurred into shadows before they ended. Flashes of color were rare as it appeared that most of the books were old, with dust jackets either lost or faded to neutral tones.

"Hello!" Bettina responded, stepping up to the counter. She had exchanged the flamingo-pink outfit for navy-blue corduroy pants and a matching turtleneck, topped with a red leather jacket lent extra flair by its fetching peplum. On her feet were red leather bootees with wedge heels. "Is Roxanne Ballard here today?" Bettina peered down the nearest aisle.

"Oh, no." The older woman shook her head. With her gray hair, cardigan sweater, and glasses dangling around her neck like a curious necklace, she seemed of a piece with her environment. "She doesn't come in on Thursdays. It's one of her teaching days, poor girl. So busy."

"What a shame!" Bettina clasped her hands in a gesture that echoed her mournful tone. "I'm visiting the city from . . . um"—she mumbled something unintelligible—"and Roxanne's mother asked me to look in on her. So sad when there's a falling-out between mother and daughter . . ."

"Oh!" The older woman raised a hand to her mouth,

and above her fingers, her eyes looked worried. "Roxanne never said anything about that—but why should she?"

"Anyway, I hope I can report back that she's fine. That will be some comfort to her mother."

"Fine . . . fine, I guess." The words were accompanied by an uncertain nod. "As fine as such a busy person can be."

"And that nice beau? Is he still in the picture?" Bettina's sociable manner made the question seem friendly chitchat rather than a nosy intrusion. "Arnold, was it?"

"Arnold?" The older woman seemed momentarily startled. "Maybe you mean Graham? Graham Tuttle?"

"Graham, of course!" Bettina laughed. "And he *is* still in the picture? We were all hoping this one would stick. Roxanne isn't as young as she used to be."

Pamela cringed. The passage of time and its cruel tendency to limit romantic opportunities was a favorite theme of Bettina's, one she often invoked with reference to Pamela's love life. But it hardly seemed appropriate in this context. The older woman, however, just chuckled and said, "None of us are, are we?"

"Have you met Graham?" Bettina asked. "Is he everything Roxanne's mom might want in a son-in-law?"

"He hasn't been around lately," the older woman said, "and that's odd because he lives right over there"— she glanced toward one of the multipaned windows— "and he seemed to have one of those work-at-home jobs."

Guided by the glance, Pamela and Bettina turned. Visible through the window, a narrow brownstone faced the bookshop across the cobbled street. They looked at each other. Trying to suppress her glee, Pamela maintained her window-facing pose while Bettina offered a few pleasantries in keeping with the visiting-the-city persona she had created.

Out on the street again, with the jingle of the bookshop's bell still echoing as the door closed behind them, Pamela and Bettina contemplated the brownstone.

"They usually have doorbells with names," Bettina said.

"The bookshop woman will think it's odd if she looks out and sees us trying to pay a call on Graham. Chatting with Roxanne's coworker as if on a mission from her mother is one thing, but tracking down a boyfriend who the bookshop woman seems to realize might not still be a boyfriend . . ."

Saying, "I'll take that chance," Bettina set out across the street, treading delicately over the cobblestones in her red leather bootees.

Indeed, the brownstone did have doorbells with names, lined up vertically alongside an impressive pair of wooden doors lacquered deep green. The doors were reached by climbing half a flight of stone steps to a stone stoop.

"It looks like he has a roommate," Bettina said as she studied the collection of doorbells, "Abe Woods. And it looks like their apartment's on the top floor." She sighed. "The stairs in these walk-ups are narrow and steep, but we really need to talk to Graham, so . . ." She aimed a finger tipped with a red-painted nail at the doorbell.

"You can save yourself a walk," said a jaunty voice behind them. "The G-man isn't home."

They had been joined on the stoop by an imposing figure, tall and muscular, with a shaved head that contrasted dramatically with a lush dark beard. He would have seemed menacing but for the cheerful smile that revealed well-tended teeth.

"Woody Woods," he added with a bow. "At your service."

"Do you know when he'll be home?" Bettina responded to the smile with a flirtatious smile of her own.

"Can't say." Woody Woods tightened his lips into a thin line that nearly disappeared into the thicket of his facial hair. "The G-man has been unpredictable lately."

"Unpredictable how?" Bettina asked, and continued with, "We're friends of his mother, visiting from out of town. She's been worried about him."

"Sad, sad, sad—the G-man, I mean, not his mother. Then, starting last Friday, happy, happy, happy. Excited, like. Not contented happy. Then, last night, he comes home and says he can't be here anymore and packs a bag and cuts out."

"That *does* sound unpredictable." Bettina gazed at Woody Woods as if awed by his eloquence. "Tell me," she said after a brief pause, "was he around on Halloween night?"

"Can't say." He tightened his lips again, but despite his effort they curved into a grin. "Can't say," he repeated, "because I wasn't." He bent down to peer into Bettina's face. "*Hello?* Village Halloween parade? How many times a year does a straight guy have a chance to rock a feather boa?"

Bettina was still giggling as she and Pamela made their way back to the parking garage where Bettina's faithful Toyota waited. "I'll bet he looks cute in a feather boa," she commented between giggles. "And why not? Girls shouldn't get to have all the fun."

"But on a more serious note"—Pamela's steps slowed—"Woody's description of . . . the G-man's . . . moods fits with what I'd expect if he's the killer."

"*Sad, sad, sad . . .*" Bettina slowed her pace to match Pamela's. They were passing an antique shop, and she paused to look in the window, where a display included an angular chair, a streamlined table made from blond wood, a free-form pottery bowl, and a black-and-white photo of the Brooklyn Bridge. "Then *happy, happy, happy* starting on Friday, the day after he murders Mel—"

Pamela cut in, "And last night, having failed in convincing Roxanne to come back to him even with Mel out of the way, he decides he's got to get away from the sight of the bookshop where she works—"

"Not to mention"—Bettina took up the thought—"the possibility of seeing her coming and going from the shop."

"What do you think we should do?" Pamela asked. The parking garage had come into view, and exhaust fumes drifted out of the vast open bay that yawned to the street.

"I could drop a hint to Clayborn," Bettina said, "but

I won't. Adrienne thinks so much of him, let her feed him hints."

"He doesn't always pick up on hints," Pamela murmured.

"Another reason for me not to drop a hint."

The serenity of Arborville was a welcome contrast to the bustle of the Village, with its crowded sidewalks, narrow one-way streets that intersected at strange angles, and traffic clogged by stop signs at nearly every corner. Bettina pulled the Toyota into Pamela's driveway but left the engine running.

As Pamela reached for the door handle, Bettina said, "We haven't eaten at Hyler's lately. Why don't we sleep on the discoveries we made today and meet for lunch tomorrow? I've got an event to cover for the *Advocate*, but I'll be finished by noon."

Pamela confirmed the plan, gave Bettina a hug, climbed out of the car, and headed for her own porch.

# CHAPTER 10

The full title of "Pocket Change" turned out to be "Pocket Change: Women's Pockets and the Evolution of Personal Space." Pamela hadn't been the one to evaluate the article when it was submitted to *Fiber Craft* and so its content, as she worked at her copyediting task, was all the more fascinating for being unfamiliar.

She was to meet Bettina at Hyler's for lunch, but Friday morning was to be devoted to *Fiber Craft*. The cats had been fed and she had breakfasted, and now she sat at her desk blinking in the bright glow of her computer monitor's screen as she scrolled through the article, pausing to add a comma here, remove a comma there, and—gritting her teeth—change commas to semicolons.

She knew that for most of their history, the pockets that served women as repositories of items necessary and not so necessary had been detachable rather than integral to a garment. She had seen such pockets in museums. Sewn from sturdy cloth and often decorated with fanciful embroidery, though they lurked unseen beneath skirts, they were teardrop-shaped and generally occurred in pairs joined by a narrow sash that allowed them to be tied around the waist. Slits in the side seams of the wearer's skirt allowed the pockets to be accessed in the same way that a modern woman would reach into a pocket inset in the seam of a skirt or pants.

Pamela worked contentedly for a few hours, taking a break from copyediting now and then to pore over the illustrations that accompanied the article. The author had traveled through the British Isles in doing her research, finding examples of pockets in venues as large as the Victoria and Albert Museum and as small as the collections assembled by small-town historical societies in Wales.

At eleven thirty, she pushed back her chair from her desk, closed her eyes—though the imprint of the screen remained behind her eyelids—and raised her arms over her head in a luxurious stretch. Humans, she often reflected, could learn a great deal from cats, whose languorous stretches gave them such obvious pleasure.

Downstairs, she stepped onto the porch to check the weather. She'd found the landscape softened by an autumn mist when she ventured out earlier in quest of the *Register* and, because it was Friday, the *Advocate*. But now the mist had given way to a clear and bright day. Soon she was headed up Orchard Street, enjoying the rosy golden tint lent to the air by the trees' vivid foliage. In her hand she carried a few canvas totes, planning to combine the lunch date with an errand at the Co-Op.

\* \* \*

Bettina was already seated when Pamela reached Hyler's, visible through the luncheonette's front window even before Pamela pulled open the heavy glass door and entered. She half-rose and waved, and in a moment Pamela had joined her.

"It was a wonderful event," Bettina announced without preamble. "Career Day at the high school. I was so happy to see all the young women showing up for the sessions on careers in scientific and technical fields. And I'll have plenty of time to get my article in next week's *Advocate*." She paused. "By the way, did you get your *Advocate* this morning?"

"Yes, yes," Pamela assured her friend. Bettina often lamented the unreliability of the carriers charged with delivering Arborville's weekly paper.

Bettina had dressed for her visit to the Career Day event at the high school as if to demonstrate her professional approach to her own job, despite the lack of respect in some circles for Arborville's weekly newspaper. (Bettina refused to countenance the term *throwaway*.) She was wearing a chic skirt suit in a navy-blue pinstripe wool, wide white pinstripes, their color echoed by a white silk blouse with a floppy bow at the neck. On her feet were navy suede pumps, and elegant gold and pearl earrings added the final touch.

She handed Pamela one of Hyler's distinctive oversize menus, said, "I told the server that you were on your way," opened her menu, and bent forward to study its many offerings.

Pamela did likewise, but she paused to scan the printed card headed "The chef recommends." The chef's recommendation for Friday was "Denver Sandwich on Toasted Sourdough," a new offering, Pamela believed.

She looked across the table and addressed Bettina, or rather the menu that obscured all but a scarlet pouf of Bettina's hair. "The chef's recommendation sounds interesting," she said. "Denver sandwich?"

"Egg and ham," Bettina responded, lowering her menu, "other things too. It's like a Denver omelet between slices of bread"—she consulted her menu—"or toast, I see, in this case."

A few minutes later, the server was on her way to the kitchen with orders noted in her pad for two Denver sandwiches and two strawberry milkshakes.

"We decided we were going to sleep on the discoveries we made yesterday," Bettina said once the server was out of earshot. "One big discovery, mainly—that Graham Tuttle's moods, as described by his roommate, mesh exactly with what one might expect if he killed Mel to remove her influence over his girlfriend, but then discovered that she still resisted his overtures."

"And that he could well have been in Arborville on Halloween night," Pamela added, "or at least that Woody couldn't give him an alibi."

"Do you think Woody knew about Mel's murder?" Bettina asked. "It might have been in the New York papers because she was a New Yorker—but an awful lot of dramatic things happen in New York all the time."

"If it *was* in the New York papers, it wouldn't necessarily strike him as noteworthy—unless he knew who Mel was. And why would he?"

"Maybe Graham confided in him . . . ?" Bettina suggested, but her voice trailed off and she looked past

Pamela to smile at the server, who was arriving with two tall frosted glasses in hand.

"Denver sandwiches coming right up," she said as she lowered the milkshakes onto the paper place mats.

The milkshakes were a creamy shade of pink, and each was topped with a foamy crest from which a straw emerged at a jaunty angle. Bettina pulled her milkshake close for a sample. Apparently satisfied that it met her expectations, she returned to the thought that had been interrupted by the arrival of the server, rephrasing it as a question.

"Do you think Woody knew about Graham's romantic difficulties?" Bettina studied Pamela's face as if confident that Pamela would have an answer.

"Men—most men—don't really talk about personal things the way women do," Pamela said, "and with rental prices so high in the city, having a roommate can be more about economics than friendship."

Bettina nodded. "If they were friends, and Woody knew the whole story—really the *whole* story—he'd have been more likely to give his friend an alibi than not."

Pamela shrugged. "If he was willing to lie and if he'd been talking to the police, which we're not sure about."

At that moment, the server reappeared with the sandwiches. The puffy edges of the omelets were visible between oval slices of toasted sourdough, and that oval shape was echoed by the large oval platters on which the sandwiches were centered. The sandwiches had been cut in half crosswise, and each half speared with a toothpick sporting a cellophane frill. Tucked alongside the sandwiches were small portions of slaw in pleated paper cups.

Pamela lifted a sandwich half from her platter. The cross section revealed by the cut surface gave a clearer sense of the omelet's composition, with bits of onion and green pepper and larger bits of ham speckling the buttery yellow of the egg. She took a bite, enjoying the interplay among the salty ham, the slightly sweet onion, and the piquant green pepper against the delicate egg and the sourdough, whose yeasty texture had been enhanced by toasting.

Across the table, Bettina was nodding with delight after sampling her own sandwich. She replaced the sandwich half with one bite missing on its platter and murmured, "Very good choice. I hope the chef continues to recommend Denver sandwiches at least once a week."

She followed up the bite of sandwich with a long sip of milkshake, leaning forward to reach the straw protruding from its foamy pink crest. "The strawberry milkshake is good, don't you think? I don't know why we always order vanilla."

The strawberry milkshake *was* good, Pamela agreed. Hyler's vanilla milkshakes were mild and sweet, but not too sweet, allowing the rich dairy taste of the milk and ice cream to prevail. To that, the strawberry shake added the slight acidic tang of strawberries frozen at the peak of freshness.

No words were exchanged for the next few minutes, with the pleasures of the meal, including the slaw, demanding full attention. The slight bitterness of the finely shredded cabbage contrasted appealingly with the sandwich's nod to comfort food.

Partway through her second sandwich half, and after a few forkfuls of the slaw, Bettina broke the silence to comment, "I hope Penny's still coming to Arborville this weekend."

"Definitely!" Pamela nodded. "I had an email from her this morning and she's taking the bus, aiming for early afternoon tomorrow. I'm going to stop at the Co-Op on my way home to stock up for her visit."

"Don't cook tomorrow night," Bettina said. "Come to us. Wilfred loves the chance to do a fancy meal."

After a few more bites of sandwich and a few more sips of milkshake, Bettina spoke again. "It's great that she and Sibyl Larkin are sharing a place in the city."

"Roommates." Pamela smiled. "And good friends. Sibyl's a little older and very sensible, which makes it easier for me thinking of Penny over there across the Hudson."

"She's all grown-up now and out on her own."

Reflections like this on Bettina's part often segued into themes touching on Pamela's romantic prospects. She tried to keep her expression neutral, not sure of what was to come. But what actually came was unexpected.

Bettina turned toward the window with its view of Arborville Avenue and frowned, murmuring, "What on earth does she want?"

Pamela turned too. Someone was peering at them from the sidewalk, bending close to the glass and mouthing something unintelligible while gesturing with a pointing finger.

"It's Gayle Witherspoon," Bettina said.

Indeed it was Gayle, gray hair loose today, straying onto the shoulders of her nondescript fleece jacket. As they watched, she edged toward Hyler's door, pulled it open, and greeted them with a wave once she had stepped over the threshold.

"I was trying to tell you I was on my way inside," she explained as she neared their table. She perched on one of the vacant chairs and added, "Such a coincidence, running into you both like this, because I was planning to get in touch today.

"Go ahead, go ahead—eat!" She gestured toward their plates, on which partly eaten sandwich halves remained. "I don't mind if you eat in front of me." She looked up to wave away the server, who was approaching with a menu, and said, "No, no. I'm not staying."

When the server had gone on her way, Gayle leaned forward. "I had an idea about the murder," she whispered. Like her sturdy body and her wardrobe, Gayle's unremarkable features might best be described as serviceable, Pamela reflected.

At the moment, her expression was wary. "And because Nell isn't here . . ." She looked around as if to make sure, then interrupted herself to add, "I know she didn't like it at your meeting when someone brought up the murder."

Bending low to glance under the table for good measure, she went on, still whispering. "Because Nell isn't here, I can tell you . . ." She paused dramatically. "I'm almost sure the real target was Adrienne, not her sister."

Bettina had been picking at the last bits of slaw with her fork, but she dropped it with a clatter. "Why on earth?" she whispered back, aware that the clatter had attracted stares from a neighboring table.

"Easy and obvious!" Gayle sat up straight and gave the table an authoritative tap. "It was Adrienne's house. The power was out for a while, and it would have been easy for the killer to stab the wrong person on the assumption that a woman answering the door at Adrienne's house would be Adrienne."

"But why would someone want to kill Adrienne?" Pamela asked, though she acknowledged to herself that Gayle had a point about the possibility of mistaken identity in the dark.

Gayle leaned forward again, this time explicitly addressing Pamela. "There's a resentful wife out there . . ." She nodded knowingly, a swaying motion that involved her whole body from the waist up, then she opened her eyes so wide that the white around her irises was visible. "Maybe more than one resentful wife."

Bettina had been paying close attention, remnants of her meal—even the milkshake—forgotten for the present. "Resentful because . . . ?" she inquired.

"Why do you think?" Gayle laughed. "Everybody knows what kinds of things Adrienne gets up to."

"*I* don't—" A crease appeared between Bettina's brows, and she shifted her gaze to Pamela. "I mean, she *is* flirtatious, but my Wilfred would never . . ."

"Not every man is a Wilfred." Pamela laid a hand on Bettina's arm.

"All that chocolate chip pound cake," Bettina murmured. "So *that's* what she was up to. I thought Adrienne was just an annoying flirt . . ." She shook her head. "And the pound cake wasn't even that good."

Alone again once Gayle had gone on her way, Pamela and Bettina stared at each other. Pamela picked up the bit of sandwich left on her plate but then put it down again.

"Gayle could have a point," she observed. "It was dark when we got home from the Halloween festivities, and the murder could easily have happened while the power was out."

"A resentful wife could definitely have a motive," Bettina said. "What if the very same thought has occurred to Adrienne, and that's why she's been pushing for the idea that the answer lies across the Hudson?"

"Doesn't seem logical," Pamela commented. "Adrienne could be in danger if the killer was really after her and is determined to do it right the next time. Wouldn't she want the police investigation to focus on residents of Arborville, assuming her dalliances have been local?"

Bettina had been nibbling at the remaining bit of her sandwich and didn't speak for a moment. When she did speak, it was to say, "She might not have thought that far ahead. And if she *had* thought that far ahead, what would she have done? Gone to Clayborn and pointed out a likely suspect or suspects by identifying local wives whose husbands were unfaithful?"

"That doesn't seem like something she would do." Pamela picked up the remains of her own sandwich and took a large bite.

"Would anyone?" Bettina asked with a giggle.

"It could be a tricky conversation." She felt her own giggle welling up. "Can you picture Detective Clayborn on the receiving end of a confession like that?"

She accompanied the amusing thought with a long slurping sip that left her glass empty but for a film of milky pink.

"I think we should talk to Adrienne, though," Pamela said after the amusement had passed. "She could really be in danger."

"Do we care?"

"Bettina!" Pamela spoke louder than she intended, and a few heads turned in her direction. "You can't really mean that," she added in a lower voice.

"I don't! No, no, I don't!" Bettina's head sagged forward until her face was nearly hidden by her scarlet curls. "It was an awful thing to say, even if she is annoying and a flirt. Of course we should talk to her."

"What if we stop by her house tomorrow morning?" Pamela suggested. "Our excuse can be that we wanted to deliver a goody as a thank-you for the goodies she's delivered to your house."

"We'll need a goody." Bettina's cheer seemed restored.

"Something from the Co-Op bakery counter, I'm thinking," Pamela said. "As I said, I'm going there anyway."

"I've got my car." Bettina signaled to the server for their bill and reached for her handbag. "I'll come too, and you can stock up on heavy things like cat food because you won't be walking home."

\* \* \*

Sometime later, Pamela and Bettina stood before the Co-Op bakery counter. Pamela had guided her shopping cart over the Co-Op's worn wooden floors and through its maze of narrow aisles, collecting provisions for the coming week. This was the final stop, and they were studying the array of tempting treats displayed on shelves protected by sloping panes of glass.

There was the familiar crumb cake with its buttery, rumpled topping, and next to it loaves of marble cake and pound cake. A tray of Danish occupied an upper shelf, yeasty rounds encircling splotches of soft pale cheese or syrupy fruit. Near them, doughnuts and crullers glistened with sugary glaze. Pies and cakes and tarts had their own display case, along with cupcakes and cookies and so much more.

"How about cheese Danish?" Bettina inquired.

"The last time we had Co-Op Danish we decided the cherry was the best kind." Pamela leaned closer to the glass to study the crullers, which, with their oblong shape and twisted effect, always brought to mind sugar-glazed skeins of yarn.

"Cherry then," Bettina said. "I'm fine with cherry."

"Half a dozen?" Pamela half-turned toward Bettina, who nodded. "Three for our visit to Adrienne, one for Wilfred, and two for Sunday morning when Penny's home. They'll still be fresh then, don't you think?"

The bakery counter attendant approached, and Pamela made her request. She and Bettina watched as a hand shielded by a leaf of waxed paper scooped six of the cherry Danish, with their gooey red centers and sticky glaze, into a white bakery box. Two hands then encircled the box with string and, with a flourish, tied the string in a bow.

Bettina had parked along Arborville Avenue when she arrived for her lunch date with Pamela. It was only half a block's walk from the Co-Op to the spot where her faithful Toyota waited at the curb. The canvas tote bags, now bulging with groceries, that Pamela had brought from home for her Co-Op errand were swiftly stowed in the Toyota's trunk, and she settled into the passenger seat, holding the bakery box on her lap.

"Tomorrow night then?" Bettina said as she pulled into Pamela's driveway. "Wilfred and I are so anxious to catch up with Penny." She turned the key and the engine growled into silence.

"I'll bring dessert." Pamela reached for her door handle.

"Wilfred has something in mind, and you know how he loves to bake." Bettina stepped out onto the asphalt. "I'll help you carry your groceries inside. We can set two cherry Danish aside for you and Penny, and I'll store the rest at home till tomorrow morning."

As they made their way across the grass with its faded autumn tint, Bettina spoke again. "Pete's welcome to join us tomorrow night too. I hope you didn't cancel plans with him—though, of course, with Penny visiting . . ." Her voice trailed off, then she added, "Maybe you're doing something with him tonight?"

They had reached the porch steps. Pamela turned to see Bettina gazing at her, eyes bright with expectation.

"Not that I know of." Pamela started up the steps.

"Sunday? After Penny goes back to the city?"

"No comment." The phrase popped out, surprising Pamela herself. Perhaps she'd absorbed it from watching British mysteries, she reflected, where it was a favorite response of uncooperative suspects.

"I won't say anything else," Bettina murmured. "I know how you get. But you'd tell me, wouldn't you, if . . ."

If what? Pamela wondered. If it was over? He'd canceled their last date and that was the last she had heard from him. Did that mean it *was* over? He hadn't seemed the kind of person to disappear with no explanation.

In her kitchen, after Bettina had gone, Pamela put her groceries away—cat food in the cupboard, butter and Vermont cheddar in the refrigerator, whole-grain bread in the bread drawer, and clusters of glowing red and green grapes in the wooden bowl on the counter.

The ground beef would become a meat loaf that very evening, accompanied by a baked potato. The cucumbers and the cherry tomatoes, preferable in chilly months to the larger tomatoes flown in from who-knew-where and tasting like nothing, would become salads.

With grocery shopping done, one chore remained: Penny would be spending the night, and her bedroom needed to be prepared. Upstairs, Pamela opened the door to her daughter's room, located at the front of the house right next to her own. The afternoon sun was still bright behind the white eyelet curtains that Pamela had sewn so long ago. Michael Paterson had still been alive then, and decorating their lovingly restored fixer-upper house had been undertaken on a frugal budget. A bargain bolt of white eyelet fabric had provided curtains for all the upstairs rooms.

The wallpaper—tight pink rosebuds against a pale blue background—had been a rare splurge, though she and Michael had papered the room themselves, a challenging exercise in teamwork that she still chuckled to remember. Penny had never asked to have the room's décor changed—the dresser, desk, and chair painted white to match the woodwork were classic. But she had added her own touches, most notably a gallery of art produced over the years by her own hand: art-class still lifes of flowers and fruit rendered in oil, pencil sketches of Arborville scenes, portraits of family and friends in various mediums.

As she gazed at the room, Pamela felt a furry presence at her ankles and looked down to see Ginger. The door to this room was never open unless Penny was in residence or expected, and Ginger clearly sensed that an interesting development along those lines was in the offing.

Pamela had stripped the bed after Penny's last visit. The patchwork quilt Pamela's grandmother had made for her long ago and which had been handed down to Penny covered a bare mattress and pillow. She peeled it off and folded it loosely. Fresh sheets, scented with a sachet containing her own homegrown lavender buds, would be fetched from the linen closet and Penny's down comforter from the attic, but first there was cleaning to be done.

Pamela gathered up the rag rugs, which would go outside for a good shaking, and retreated down the stairs. When she returned it was with the rag rugs, now shaken, along with a dustcloth and a dust mop.

Once the room was done, Ginger seemed to want to stay, as if expecting Penny at any moment. Pamela propped the door open with the brass cat doorstop she had found long ago at a rummage sale. A quick check of email across the hall brought a message from Penny saying to look for her at about ten the next morning. The day's final chore was dinner preparation, a meat loaf that would provide dinner as well as many meat loaf sandwiches in days to come.

# CHAPTER 11

Pamela stepped out to fetch the *Register* the next morning to see Bettina en route across the street carrying the white bakery box from the previous day.

"I thought you'd be dressed by now," she called as Pamela bent toward the newspaper.

Bettina herself was already dressed, dressed to impress another fashionista perhaps, given the nature of the errand she and Pamela had planned for that morning. She was wearing burgundy wool pants in a chic wide-legged style, paired with a boxy jacket the same color but made from a quilted velvet fabric. Under the jacket a black turtleneck was visible, and a striking pair of garnet earrings echoed the burgundy of the outfit.

Pamela straightened up with the paper in its plastic sleeve dangling from her hand. "I didn't know we were going first thing," she said.

"The point"—Bettina paused to catch her breath after her sprint across Orchard—"is to deliver the Danish in time for breakfast, breakfast with Adrienne. That will give us a chance to chat, and after we chat for a bit about . . . whatever . . . we bring up the idea that maybe she was the intended victim."

"You'll do the bringing up," Pamela said. "I'm not good at asking people whether they are having affairs with married men."

Bettina laughed. "I won't exactly put it like that. I'll find a way." She made a shooing motion with the hand that wasn't holding the bakery box. "Get back inside and put some clothes on. I'll sit on your porch—we won't have too many more of these warm fall days."

Less than ten minutes later, Pamela rejoined Bettina. Her toilette, as Bettina often pointed out, was quite unimaginative, but once summer was past she enjoyed pairing her usual jeans with one of her handknitted sweaters. Today's sweater was the one she had made from the wool imported from the Shetland Islands. The design involved wide cables like multistrand braids decorating the front and sleeves.

They proceeded across the street with Bettina still carrying the bakery box. Stepping onto Adrienne's porch brought back memories of Halloween night, and Pamela felt herself shudder, though the chair that Mel's body had occupied was long gone. In its place was a tiered plant stand holding several potted chrysanthemums in colors ranging from amber to deep maroon.

Bettina rang the bell, which echoed inside, and they waited for the sound of footsteps within as prelude to the door swinging open.

There were no footsteps, however, and the door didn't swing open.

"She's got to be here," Bettina commented. "She's not like you with the walks, and her car is here." Indeed, Adrienne's BMW was parked in her driveway. Bettina pushed the doorbell's button again, this time more forcefully, and she left her finger in place as the bell chimed again and again.

Now they did hear footsteps, and the door swung back so swiftly that the outer storm door rattled.

"You two!" Adrienne addressed them from behind the storm door, her voice slightly muffled. She was wearing a silky negligee trimmed with much lace.

Bettina pulled the storm door toward her and stepped around it. "Good morning!" she said brightly. "We've brought some cherry Danish. Not homemade like your delicious chocolate chip pound cake, but we thought it would be good with coffee and—"

Adrienne reached out and seized the bakery box. "I'm terribly busy," she said, "but thanks." She retreated and started to close the door.

"Wait, wait, wait!" Bettina leaned forward and pushed the door open. For a moment, there was a struggle as Adrienne pushed back. Her expression as she peeked through the narrowing crack between door and doorframe mixed irritation and surprise.

"You could be in danger!" Bettina added. "Big danger! Don't you want to hear why?"

Adrienne stepped away from the door and Bettina, who was still pushing, nearly lost her balance, rescuing herself by grabbing onto the doorframe.

"Big danger?" Adrienne put her hands on her hips,

still looking both irritated and surprised, though her forehead remained smooth. The bakery box had apparently been parked somewhere. "What on earth do you mean?"

"The killer is still out there," Bettina said, relinquishing her grip on the doorframe. "Has it ever occurred to you that your sister might not have been the intended victim? After all, it was very dark, and the killer could have been expecting to find you at home."

"But who would want to kill me?" Adrienne sounded genuinely mystified.

"A resentful wife, jealous because her husband and you . . ."

Bettina's voice trailed off as Adrienne's eyes expanded and she inhaled, squaring her shoulders as if preparing to do battle. Words rather than actions were forthcoming, however.

"I would never . . . never . . . get involved with a married man," she said, her voice low and grating. "The fact that you even *think* this makes me wonder about your own morals. Here you are with that sweet husband, but I always suspected that you had a wandering eye. I've seen the way you look at Richard Larkin and that sexy handyman who comes around."

Bettina stiffened, and a guttural screech escaped from her lips. Pamela rested a hand on her shoulder and she retreated, growling, as the storm door slammed shut. After taking a moment to compose herself, Bettina spoke.

"We tried to help you," she said, raising her voice to be heard through the storm door. "Just remember that . . . when it's too late."

Adrienne's response came back, muffled by the storm door's glass. "I'm not worried about my safety at all, and I'm sure Lucas will get to the bottom of things very soon." She lifted her chin and smiled a serene smile.

"Lucas?" Bettina whispered.

"Clayborn," Pamela reminded her.

"Whatever." Bettina addressed the comment to Adrienne, who was still smiling serenely behind the glass.

They turned to leave, but they had barely stepped off the porch when the storm door opened. "By the way," Adrienne's voice sang out, "Lucas very kindly got back in touch with me about Blair. She has an alibi—in fact, the whole feminist group does. They were all at their annual Halloween event, the Witches' Sabbath."

Neither Pamela nor Bettina spoke again until they reached the street. But as they crossed Orchard, Bettina murmured in a small voice, "I was looking forward to eating one of those cherry Danish." A glance at her profile revealed a mournful cast to eyes and mouth.

Pamela reached an arm around Bettina's shoulders and squeezed. "Not everyone understands what's expected when a neighbor comes calling first thing in the morning with a bakery box from the Co-Op. Adrienne will never know that pleasure."

"Her coffee probably wouldn't have been that good anyway." Bettina's tone suggested the statement was her final word on the subject.

"I happen to know where there are two more cherry Danish," Pamela said as they neared her front walk. "Why don't *I* make some coffee and we can sit at my kitchen table and eat them?"

"But we bought those other two for you and Penny to eat tomorrow morning."

"I can always go back to the Co-Op." Pamela laughed. "Come on . . . you know you want to."

Five minutes later, the ritual of grinding beans and boiling water had commenced. Soon Pamela and Bettina were inhaling the aroma of brewing coffee as the steaming water dripped through the fresh grounds in the filter cone and into the carafe beneath. On either side of the little table, a wedding-china cup and saucer waited, as well as a wedding-china plate bearing a cherry Danish with a fork and napkin tucked alongside.

Bettina filled the cut-glass cream pitcher from the carton in the refrigerator and settled it on the table next to the matching sugar bowl. Pamela stood near the carafe, peeking into the filter cone as the water saturated the grounds and disappeared beneath.

"It's ready," she announced at length. "Take your seat."

She removed the filter cone, set it in the sink, and slipped on an oven mitt to grasp the carafe. At the table, she tipped the carafe over the cups one at a time, and the dark brew swirled against the pale porcelain of their interiors. She returned the carafe to the counter and sat down across from Bettina.

Another ritual was underway on Bettina's part alone. First she added two spoonfuls of sugar to her coffee, then she dribbled in cream, stirring all the while. The contents of her cup changed from dark and clear to pale and opaque, the mocha color that resulted only hinting at the nature of the liquid that had been transformed.

"Perfect," she announced after an exploratory sip. "I'm glad Adrienne didn't invite us in."

Pamela, meanwhile, had postponed tasting her own coffee in favor of sampling her cherry Danish. They seemed sticky to pick up, thus the forks. She carved off a bite from the glazed and pillowy pastry edge and lifted her fork to her mouth. The pastry had the satisfying chewy texture of yeast dough, and it was barely sweet in itself, that lack being made up by the sugary glaze. She took another bite and followed it with a sip of coffee, savoring its bitterness.

Bettina had moved on to her cherry Danish as well, making inroads that had reached all the way to its deep red center, where a small puddle of syrup submerged a few cherry pieces.

"I still like the cheese Danish too," she said, "but it's good to try other things. Maybe the pineapple next time?"

Attention was focused on pastries and coffee then, until only crumbs remained on the plates, along with streaks of red syrup. Pamela rose and crossed to the counter where she transferred the carafe to the stove and lit a low flame beneath it. She and Bettina had things to discuss, and freshly heated coffee would stimulate the mental processes.

Even before small bubbles began to form in the warming coffee, however, Bettina spoke.

"I don't see any point in going on with this Mel question," she announced. "After those insulting things

Adrienne said to me, why should I want to help her untangle the mystery? The only reason we got involved in the first place was that she practically *begged* me to come to the city and browse around for clues in Mel's apartment—because she didn't think the Arborville police knew what to look for."

She dismissed the idea with an explosive exhalation, and her voice took on a simpering quality. "Now it's all *Lucas this* and *Lucas that* . . ."

"You don't think he'll figure it out?" Pamela said, trying to sound serious but feeling her lips curve into a teasing smile. She was still standing at the stove and turned away to hide the smile from Bettina.

"Do *you*?" Bettina raised her voice, put her elbows on the table, and leaned forward.

The coffee seemed warm enough now, and Pamela refilled both cups before responding.

"Adrienne seems awfully sure, and she's even on a first-name basis with him now."

Bettina straightened up, doing her best to tame her natural cheer and muster a serious expression. "*I* prefer to keep my relationship with Detective Clayborn professional."

"Okay," Pamela said. "It's probably for the best. When the case is all solved, you can interview him and get the story for the *Advocate* . . ."

Bettina frowned and addressed herself to sugaring and creaming her coffee. She completed the task and took several meditative sips. A minute or two passed. She took another sip, then returned her cup to its saucer with a clunk.

"It seems that none of the bicycle fish people, including Roxanne, could have been in Arborville on Halloween night because they were at the Witches' Sabbath," she murmured, as if speaking to her coffee cup. "So if Graham and Martin have alibis too, Adrienne could really have been the intended victim and the killer could really have been a resentful wife."

She looked up. "Wouldn't it be something if that turned out to be the case? I can see the headlines in the *Register*—" She paused for dramatic effect and then went on. "MISTAKEN IDENTITY IN ARBORVILLE HALLOWEEN MURDER. Then, below, KILLER'S INTENDED TARGET WAS WANDERING HUSBAND'S GAL PAL."

She paused again. "Of course, the *Advocate* would never use such a headline because, unlike the *Register*, the *Advocate* doesn't pander to its readers."

"Of course not," Pamela replied, secretly delighted at the vision of *Register* subscribers unfolding their morning paper to discover such a headline. "So does that mean you want to look into what Graham and Martin were doing on Halloween night?"

"Yes!" Bettina nodded vigorously, and her garnet earrings swayed. "As a journalist I feel bound to seek the truth."

"I suggest we start with Graham," Pamela said, "for a couple of reasons. First, Martin is tall, likely taller than the figure in the surveillance video." She took a sip of coffee as her mind shaped the other reason into words. "Second, people *do* kill the people they love sometimes. But killing the impediment that you think stands between you and the person you love seems a more likely motive to me. And besides, we know where

Graham lives. The roommate wasn't helpful, but there must be other neighbors in that building."

Catrina had been making her lazy way across the kitchen floor en route from the dining room. Suddenly, she stopped, froze, and stared toward the doorway that led to the entry. Her mobile ears rotated until they faced that direction too.

A sound like a key turning in a lock was heard. Bettina looked startled, then puzzled, but Pamela lifted a soothing hand and said, "It's Penny."

With a blur of little paws, Catrina scurried through the doorway.

"Hello!" Penny's voice called from the entry as Pamela and Bettina rose and followed Catrina. Ginger arrived to make up part of the welcoming committee, and they all converged on a small figure with dark curls wearing a violet jacket.

"Welcome back to Arborville!" Bettina exclaimed, standing aside to give Pamela the first chance at a hug.

Pamela pulled her daughter close, her chin grazing the top of Penny's curly head. Penny still carried a canvas duffel bag in one hand, but she snaked the other arm around Pamela's waist and gave a squeeze. Then it was Bettina's turn for a hug as the two cats prowled around Penny's feet, quite aware that a familiar person had returned after an absence. Precious surveyed the scene from a perch on the arm of the sofa.

"And how was your trip, Miss Penny?" Bettina inquired as she loosened her hold and stepped back.

"Not very arduous." Penny laughed. "It's a twenty-five-minute bus ride."

She deposited the duffel bag on the floor and unbuttoned her jacket. Pamela recognized the jacket, which was one of Penny's thrift-shop finds, and she recognized the sweater that was revealed once the jacket had been shed. It was deep gold in color, almost glowing, and knit from yarn of remarkable silkiness.

"You still have that!" She smiled. "It's so old."

"Not that old." Penny smiled back. "I love it and I wear it all the time—and I remember that at first I didn't want you to make it because I didn't think the cool people wore sweaters that their mothers had made."

"I remember that too," Pamela said, "and then you met Laine and Sybil next door and discovered they thought hand-knit sweaters were cool . . ."

Penny bowed her head in mock-shame.

Bettina spoke up then. "And now Sibyl Larkin is your roommate in the city and I want to hear all about everything—tonight, though, when you come for dinner. You and your mom have catching up to do."

Penny stooped for the duffel bag. "I'll take this upstairs, and I'll see you tonight, Bettina, and"—she turned to Pamela—"I'll be right back down and we'll catch up."

She headed for the stairs with Ginger at her heels.

"So . . ." Bettina stepped closer to Pamela and whispered, "Back to Graham's on Monday for sure. I'll pick you up at eleven. We might not have time to talk about . . . our plans . . . with Penny here." She stepped back and raised her voice. "Okay, Miss Pamela. Wilfred and I will expect you and Penny at about six, and now I'm off."

The front door closed behind her just as Penny's feet sounded on the stairs.

Pamela greeted her with the words, "Grilled cheese sandwiches?" and Penny nodded.

As Pamela worked at the counter, Penny talked about her work in the mail room at her father's old architecture firm. One of her tasks consisted in delivering materials to clients or picking up materials from clients. She laughed as she described her adventures traveling around the city, sometimes by cab, sometimes by subway, sometimes by bike, and sometimes just on foot—and often at her destination being directed to the service entrance and the special service elevator.

Pamela, meanwhile, was busy with a chunk of Vermont cheddar, four pieces of whole-grain bread, and her griddle. She carved off several slices of cheddar, buttered two pieces of the bread, and lit the flame under the griddle. As it began to heat up, she placed the bread buttered side down on the griddle's surface and arranged several slices of the cheese on each piece. Then she buttered the other two pieces of bread and placed them on top of the cheese buttered side up.

The sandwiches were ready to eat, after careful monitoring, a few minutes later, served on wedding-china plates with knives and forks at hand. The bread was toasty and golden with a buttery sheen, and molten dribbles of the paler golden cheese were visible in the joint between the top slice and the bottom.

Seated across from Penny at the little kitchen table, Pamela took her first bite. Grilled cheese sandwiches made with Vermont cheddar were a lunchtime staple, but she never tired of the contrast between the supple texture of the melted cheese and slight crustiness of the toasted bread.

"It's really good, Mom," Penny said after her first few bites. "Sibyl and I make grilled cheese sometimes too, but yours always tastes better."

That comment led to a pleasant chat about Penny's and Sibyl's sharing of domestic chores, and soon the plates were empty.

"So . . . what do you want to do this afternoon?" Pamela inquired. "Are any of your old Arborville friends still in town?"

"Everybody grew up and moved away," Penny said.

Penny too—though studying her daughter across the table, Pamela felt she might as well be looking at the Penny of ten years ago, or even more. Penny's dark curls framed a smooth forehead and softly rounded cheeks, her complexion was clear and rosy, and her blue eyes were bright and eager.

This pondering was apparently reflected in Pamela's expression because Penny reached for her hand and added, "But anyway, I came out here to visit you— and the Frasers, of course." She paused for a moment and then said, "Let's walk down to the nature preserve. Living in the city is great, but it can be intense."

Instantly, she was on her feet and heading for the doorway with no explanation. But the sound of feet on the stairs to the second floor indicated that her intention hadn't been to put the nature preserve idea into effect by dashing out the front door that minute. Pamela transferred the plates and silverware to the counter and fetched her jacket from the closet.

She was sitting on the chair that was the entry's main piece of furniture, holding Penny's violet jacket in her lap, when Penny reappeared carrying one of her old sketch pads.

"It was still in my closet," she said. "I used to love to go down to the nature preserve and sketch."

Pamela handed Penny her jacket and they were on their way, out into mild golden afternoon, with the sun coming at an autumnal slant and the air pungent with the aroma of composting leaves.

# CHAPTER 12

On the stroke of six that evening, Bettina opened the Frasers' front door and welcomed Pamela and Penny into her comfy living room. She had exchanged the stylish ensemble of that morning for an equally stylish but more casual look: a jumpsuit fashioned from a silky fabric in shades that echoed the yellows, ambers, and rusts of the fall foliage.

"Come on into the kitchen," she said after taking their jackets. "Wilfred has made a special treat for us to nibble on while he puts the finishing touches on the main course."

The entire Fraser household was on hand in the kitchen. Wilfred, with an apron tied over his bib overalls, emerged from behind the high counter that separated the cooking area of the kitchen from the part where a scrubbed pine table served for breakfast and casual meals. Punkin the cat was curled up on the seat of one of the chairs that surrounded the table, and Woofus was sprawled along the wall by the door that communicated with the dining room.

A long platter of interesting tidbits occupied a prime spot on top of the high counter, with four champagne flutes stationed nearby. The aroma of the tidbits, though nearly overshadowed by another deeper aroma, gave a hint as to their composition.

"Shrimp toast," Wilfred explained, obviously pleased with the admiring looks aimed at the platter. "Help yourselves—it's finger food." He pushed a small pile of cocktail napkins closer to his guests. "And meanwhile, I have some champagne cooling in honor of Penny's visit."

He edged around the end of the counter and opened the refrigerator. Bending toward its bright interior, he seized a shapely green bottle whose neck was swathed in gold foil.

Pamela, Penny, and Bettina responded to his invitation, and each picked up a shrimp toast. On a base consisting of a baguette slice, lightly toasted, Wilfred had piled a mixture of chopped shrimp, onion, and celery, sautéed and then blended into a rich cheese sauce with salt and pepper and a hint of cayenne. The final step had been to bake the assembled toasts long enough to meld the flavors together.

"Delicious!" was the verdict, delivered in chorus after the first taste. The toasts were a perfect pre-dinner nibble, with the bread crusty but light and the shrimp sweet and mild. The cayenne-flavored cheese sauce added piquancy but didn't overpower.

Attention was diverted from the shrimp toasts as

Wilfred, now standing behind the high counter, began the ritual of serving the champagne. He peeled away the gold foil to reveal a bulbous cork held in place with a cage of delicate wire and twisted the wire cage from the cork. Then he turned, aimed the neck of the bottle away from his audience, and nudged at the cork until it began to loosen. One final nudge freed it with a pop and a wisp of vapor.

He turned back toward the counter and tilted the bottle over the closest champagne flute, tipping the slender glass to receive the liquid. It caught the light like liquid gold imbued with tiny silver bubbles.

When all the glasses had been filled, Wilfred raised his in an invitation to a toast. The other three followed suit, and the glasses collided gently in the air with a melodious clink.

"To the future," Wilfred proclaimed, "Penny's future specifically!"

"Penny's future," Pamela and Bettina echoed as Penny blushed.

"And what have you heard from your graduate school applications?" Bettina inquired after her first sip of champagne.

"Nothing yet," Penny responded. "It's too soon."

"What are you hoping for?" Bettina accompanied the words with a sociable smile, as if to indicate that her question's benign intent was merely to make conversation.

Pamela had been wondering the same thing but hadn't wanted to pry. She knew that the assortment of architecture schools Penny had applied to ranged from close to home—Columbia—to the opposite coast—UC Berkeley—and points in between. She had been sipping her champagne while nibbling a second shrimp toast, enjoying the play of the champagne's chilly sparkle against the slight tongue tingle of the shrimp toast's peppery cheese sauce. But now she paused to wait for Penny's answer.

Penny laughed. "I'm hoping to get in . . . somewhere."

"Fingers crossed for that, then!" Bettina raised her glass again, and the conversation turned to the doings of the Frasers' Arborville granddaughter. Penny had a lively interest in the topic, knowing how eager Bettina had been to welcome a little girl upon whom she could lavish girly gifts.

"Not like Morgan, up in Boston," she reminded an audience already well aware of the contrast from Bettina's frequent laments, "though I love her dearly. Why Warren and Greta are so bent on raising a *person*, who isn't allowed to have dolls or wear pink, is completely beyond me. Morgan is a little girl."

Wilfred had left the three women to their chatting and was busy at the stove. He lifted the lid of the stout Dutch oven on a back burner, and the aroma already permeating the room—that of rich beef sauce accented with thyme and bay leaf—intensified. Pamela had noticed two other pots when they arrived, on the stovetop but with burners not alight.

Now Wilfred removed the lid from one, peeked inside, and lit the flame beneath it. He did the same with the other but replaced the lid after peeking.

"Twenty minutes," he announced, his ruddy face aglow with anticipation.

\* \* \*

Indeed, twenty minutes later they were seated around the table in the dining room. Orange place mats and napkins set off the sage green of Bettina's favorite pottery, and an arrangement of multicolored chrysanthemums in a low bowl carried out the autumnal color scheme. On either side of the flower arrangement, a tall white taper rose from a pewter candleholder of Scandinavian design. Stainless steel tableware and tall Swedish crystal glasses echoed that sleek style.

The glasses had been filled with beer, which Wilfred declared was more suited to the menu he had prepared, and the dishes that composed that menu were arrayed before them on the table. The Dutch oven, which was a deep enamel green in color, occupied a thick straw trivet in front of Wilfred. The cover had been left behind in the kitchen, revealing the contents: oxtails bathed in a thick sauce with a rosy hint of tomato. An oval bowl from the sage-green set held a mound of steaming white rice, and a similar oval bowl held a tangle of cooked greens gleaming with butter.

"Who wants some oxtail stew?" Wilfred inquired as he picked up a big serving spoon. He held out a hand for Penny's plate, to his right. Bettina passed her plate to Penny and Pamela passed hers to Bettina, and the plates, now bearing generous portions of oxtail stew, made a circuit around the table and ended up back where they started, with Wilfred serving himself last.

The rice and greens, which were collard greens, were closer to where Bettina was sitting, and their containers more manageable for self-service. The oval bowls were handed here and there, and after a genial bustle Wilfred surveyed the table with a contented sigh.

"Bon appétit!" he exclaimed, raising his fork.

The aroma alone was enticing, not to mention the tempting sight presented by the food arrayed on each sage-green plate. The oxtails—meaty rounds with their central cross sections of bone—were bathed in sauce that glistened with fat rendered by slow braising. The white rice, each grain distinct, offered a contrast in both color and texture, as did the collard greens, which Wilfred had sliced into thick ribbons before boiling.

The meat yielded easily to a fork, coming away from the bone at the oxtail's center as a tender sauce-covered gobbet. Savoring such a dish required concentration, and no one spoke until several oxtails had been consumed.

"This is delicious!" Penny said as her fork paused before tackling another oxtail. "I'm glad I came home."

Pamela had been alternating bites of meat, rice, and greens. The meat was meltingly tender and the sauce that enveloped each morsel was beefy and intense, with hints of tomato and aromatic herbs. The rice was the perfect neutral backdrop and the slight bitterness of the collards offset the sauce's richness. And Wilfred was right—the cold beer was the ideal complement to the dish.

Penny's praise was taken up by Bettina, and Pamela joined in, adding that she had often noticed oxtails among the offerings available at the Co-Op's meat counter but had never been sure how to cook them.

"Lots of recipes," Wilfred said, "French, of course,

and they're popular among the West Indians. Braising is the key though, long and slow—not that much different from pot roast."

"Speaking of coming home . . ." Bettina turned to Penny, who was sitting to her left. "You'll be in Arborville for Thanksgiving, I hope."

Penny's mouth was full so she nodded enthusiastically.

"We'll be hosting the whole family," Bettina went on, smiling as if already picturing the happy scene. "The Boston children are coming down and the Arborville children are already in Arborville, and you and Pamela are right across the street and you're family too."

Penny meanwhile had swallowed. "It's funny to think about Thanksgiving already," she said in a meditative voice. "The year has gone so fast. Wasn't it just Thanksgiving, like, hardly any time at all ago?"

Pamela set down her fork and stared at her daughter. If she'd had any doubt that Penny was indeed grown up, that doubt had just been dispelled. The sense that time was passing faster than one could keep track of was definitely a hallmark of adulthood.

A hallmark of adulthood, indeed, to the point that Penny's reminder of time's swiftness had an effect she likely did not intend. Conversation faltered. Pamela glanced at Bettina, whose expression had become uncharacteristically bleak. Facing his wife across the table, Wilfred too appeared downcast.

"You have so much to look forward to," Bettina ventured at last, focusing on Penny.

"We *all* do," Pamela said. "Thanksgiving, Christmas, watching grandchildren grow up . . . so many things."

As if a spell had been broken, Bettina smiled, her cheer restored. At his end of the table, Wilfred too seemed himself again. He leaned on the table and half-rose from his chair to survey his fellow diners' plates.

"There's plenty more food," he said, "and beer too."

Because the plates were far from empty, the statement seemed aimed more at enhancing the restored cheer with the assurance of bounty than suggesting an immediate need for second helpings.

Forks were picked up again, accompanied by a small chorus of "Not quite yet," and eating and chatting proceeded at a comfortable pace.

Sometime later, after additional oxtails had joined fresh mounds of rice and tangles of collards on the sage-green plates, and had in turn been reduced to small puddles of sauce, stray grains of rice, and the odd collard strand, Wilfred leaned back in his chair with a happy sigh. At her end of the table, Bettina echoed the sigh, her expression so resembling that of a cat content with its dinner that Pamela expected the sigh to modulate into a purr.

They all stared at one another in the dazed silence of the slightly overfed, until Penny climbed to her feet and said, "Let me clear away, please."

"No, no . . . I'm the host . . ." Wilfred stirred and began to rise, but Pamela scooped up her own plate and utensils, nodded at Penny, and reached for Wilfred's plate and utensils.

She and Penny made quick work of clearing the table, and in the kitchen they stored the leftovers in plastic containers, rinsed dishes and utensils in the sink, and arranged all neatly in the racks of the dishwasher. As they were finishing, Wilfred joined them.

"It wouldn't be a company dinner without dessert." He edged past Pamela to access a long baking dish covered with foil, adding, "By the time I make coffee, I expect we'll all be ready for some cake."

He hefted the foil-covered dish and backtracked to the high counter that marked off the cooking area of the kitchen, where he set down the dish. Then he stepped to the stove, seized the kettle, and filled it with water at the sink. Sensing that they were now superfluous, Pamela and Penny circled the high counter and watched as Wilfred began making coffee.

Bettina joined them as they watched, and indeed, once the dark and spicy scent of coffee began to rise from the filter cone over the carafe, the prospect of cake and coffee came to seem very enticing. Wilfred, meanwhile, had opened a cupboard and transferred a small stack of sage-green dessert plates to the counter where the cake waited. He added four coffee mugs from the same set, as well as the matching cream pitcher, freshly filled with heavy cream, the sugar bowl, and four dessert forks.

Foil still covered the long baking dish, but the foil didn't entirely contain the tempting aroma of what was beneath: sweet and intense with a dark complexity. Then Wilfred peeled the foil away to reveal a sweep of pale icing, not thick and not smooth but like a sugary glaze hinting at chopped nuts and other interesting components lurking beneath the surface it skimmed.

"Carrot cake," he announced. "Shall we eat dessert in the living room? I have a fire laid and it might be welcome. It sounds like a cold front is blowing in."

The view through the sliding glass doors that opened onto the Frasers' backyard was of a dark sky and darker shrubbery. But the wind could be heard rushing across the patio, and the upper branches of the maple tree, where some leaves still clung, were swaying fitfully.

Wilfred fetched a knife and spatula from a kitchen drawer and returned to the counter to study his cake. With a decisive nod, he sliced it in half crosswise, cut that half in half, and divided each of those halves into thirds. Then he traded the knife for the spatula to delicately nudge one piece at a time free and transfer it to a plate. One half cake plus two slices remained in the baking dish.

"Dear wife," he said when that operation was complete, "I will get the fire going if you will serve the coffee, and we can rendezvous in the living room."

Five minutes later, they were all gathered around the coffee table, enjoying the fire's warmth and the play of the flickering flames. The old-fashioned comfort of the carrot cake added to the coziness.

"Grated carrots," Wilfred explained. "Lots of them, but plenty of sugar and spices too."

The carrots were evident in each forkful, delicate orange shreds embedded, along with chopped walnuts, in the moist dense-textured cake. The flavor was complex, a hint of carrot perhaps, but also a hint of pineapple and certainly hints of cinnamon and nutmeg. The icing, which Wilfred explained was largely composed of butter, cream cheese, and confectioner's sugar, added a note of less complex sweetness.

"It's perfect for this time of year," Pamela said, and Bettina and Penny nodded in agreement.

They were joined then by Woofus, who sprawled on the carpet along the edge of the hearth and immediately lost himself to sleep. Pamela, however, was reflecting on the last time she and the Frasers had sat like this with a fire in the fireplace and wind moaning outside. It had been Halloween night, and over a week later the mystery of the murder next door had yet to be solved.

By Sunday morning, the cold front had brought a sharp chill and the wind had done its work. The air was calm as Pamela dashed to the end of the front walk to collect the *Register*, but the trees were noticeably barer than they had been and heaps of bright, variously colored leaves lay heaped in sheltered spots where the wind had pushed them.

Quick as the trip to fetch the newspaper had been, the kettle was already hooting by the time she stepped back into the kitchen. She turned off the flame, slipped a paper filter into the plastic filter cone atop her carafe, and spooned coffee beans into her grinder.

Catrina was still finishing her breakfast. She gave a momentary start as Pamela pressed on the lid of the grinder and the beans clattered in syncopated counterpoint to the grinder's whir. Once the ground beans had been tipped into the filter and the steaming water had begun its brewing task, Pamela slipped the *Register* from its flimsy plastic sleeve and unfolded it on the kitchen table. Unsurprisingly, no urgent headlines announced progress in the Halloween mystery.

Penny arrived as the aroma of toasting whole-grain bread was competing with the aroma of freshly brewed coffee. She stepped through the doorway leading from the entry wearing her fleecy robe and slippers and with hair tousled from sleep. In her arms she bore Ginger, the cat's butterscotch color vivid against the sky blue of Penny's robe.

"She'll be disappointed that you're leaving again so soon," Pamela commented.

"I'll miss her," Penny responded as she seated herself in one of the kitchen chairs and lowered Ginger into her lap. "I wonder if she'd like to live with me in the city."

"She's so used to her life here." Pamela smiled at the cat.

"You're right," Penny said. "It wouldn't be fair to uproot her—but maybe I could adopt another cat."

"Of course you could." The toast had popped up, just one piece, because Pamela hadn't known how soon Penny would be down. She extracted it from the toaster and slipped in another piece of whole-grain bread. "There are certainly enough cats in need of homes."

Pamela added a jar of boysenberry jam and the cream pitcher and sugar bowl to the china, silverware, and napkins she had already arranged on the table. A few minutes later, the rose-garlanded cups had been filled with steaming coffee, golden-brown slices of toast occupied the rose-garlanded plates, and Pamela had taken her seat across from her daughter.

She had moved the *Register* to the counter when she began preparing the table for the meal, but once the toast had been eaten and the coffee cups refilled, Penny fetched it back. She glanced at the front page and browsed a bit through the other sections, which were more numerous given that she was looking at the Sunday edition. Pamela cleared away everything but the coffee cups, which were still in use, and rummaged through the pile of newsprint for LIFESTYLE, which often had features dealing with home décor on Sunday.

As she read an article about a local house that had been built in the 1930s by a ship captain who incorporated ship-building techniques, Penny suddenly spoke up.

"I guess they already solved that Arborville murder," she said. "There's nothing at all about an investigation in the *Register*."

Pamela remained staring at the sentence she had been in the middle of reading. Aware after a moment that she had not only not been reading but also not breathing, she inhaled deeply.

"What murder is that?" she inquired, raising her eyes to meet Penny's.

"*Mo-om!*" Penny lifted a skeptical brow. "I think you know."

"Maybe," Pamela murmured, lowering her eyes again. "But how do you know?"

"Sibyl reads the *Register* online sometimes, so I know all about it. And I suspect, now, that you and Bettina were up to something more than *strolling* when I came upon the two of you, *plus* the sister of the murdered woman in the Village last weekend."

"She had an errand at her sister's apartment," Pamela said, "and she didn't want to go alone. She's Bettina's next-door neighbor . . ."

"And the murder happened right across the street, and I don't know why you and Bettina are always somehow *around* . . ."

The doorbell's sudden chime intruded then. Grateful for the interruption, Pamela jumped to her feet, startling Ginger, who had remained in the kitchen though not on Penny's lap.

"It's probably Bettina," she said as she hurried toward the doorway. "I can't think who else it would be."

But the figure visible through the lace that curtained the oval window in the front door lacked Bettina's distinctive scarlet coif and appeared to be quite slender. Pamela opened the door to greet a pleasant-looking middle-aged woman with dishwater-blond hair. The woman was carrying a shopping bag from one of the mall stores. After staring for a moment, Pamela recognized her caller as the woman who seemed to have taken up residence next door.

"Hello," the woman said with a friendly smile. "I'm Maureen . . . and I think you're Pamela?"

"Yes?" Pamela wasn't sure why she echoed Maureen's tentative intonation.

"I'm sorry to bother you," she said, extending the shopping bag, "but my daughter Sibyl left her favorite jeans behind the last time she was in Arborville and she just got in touch to say Penny was next door and could Penny please bring them back to the city?"

"Oh . . . yes . . . certainly." Pamela reached for the bag, scarcely aware of what she was doing. It was as if her mind had become devoid of all but a kind of buzzing thought—that if this woman was Sibyl's mother, that meant she was also Richard Larkin's ex-wife. "Yes, yes, certainly," she repeated. "And . . . uh . . . very nice to meet you."

"I hope we'll have a chance to get acquainted," Maureen said, smiling again. "But I know you're busy now with your daughter here." She took a few steps backward and added, "So, thank you."

Pamela stood in her doorway unmoving as Maureen headed down the steps and across the grass in a short-cut back to Richard Larkin's house. She was aware of something in her hand, and looked down to see the shopping bag from the mall store dangling by its handles from her fingers.

"Who was it?" came Penny's voice at her back.

Pamela turned and held up the bag. "Sibyl's favorite jeans," she said, "from her mother."

"Oh." Penny's voice was matter-of-fact. "I knew she was missing them."

"I'll get dressed," Pamela said. The front door was still open and she still stood on the threshold.

"Mom?" Penny approached, tilting her head to study Pamela's face as a small rumple marred her normally smooth forehead. "Are you okay?"

"Yes, certainly." Pamela blinked, as if to awaken her brain from its curious lassitude. "I'll get dressed," she repeated, handing Penny the shopping bag and proceeding toward the stairs as Penny closed the front door.

Upstairs, she sat on her unmade bed as the buzzing in her mind gradually cleared. Richard Larkin had a perfect right to get back together with his ex-wife, of course. She, Pamela, had no claim on him at all. She'd lost her chance when she spurned his advances, as Bettina never tired of reminding her.

Penny hadn't seemed surprised at the fact that Sibyl's mother was in residence next door, so she must have known what was afoot. Bettina probably even knew. Why hadn't they told her? Or maybe Penny assumed she already knew—otherwise she would have reacted differently when Pamela handed over the jeans. And Bettina, of course, was wary of bringing up anything to do with Richard Larkin anymore.

Pamela sighed. Then she stood up and started to make her bed.


Dressed and back downstairs sometime later, she discovered that Penny had cleaned up the breakfast dishes but was nowhere to be seen. She checked the front porch and the yard on the chance that the bright though chilly day had lured Penny outside to enjoy a bit more of nature in its suburban form before returning to the city. There was no sign of Penny outside either, and Pamela retreated to the entry.

She heard feet on the stairs then and turned to see her daughter descending with a skein of yarn in one hand and a pair of knitting needles in the other.

"I found these in my closet," she said. "I remembered I had yarn and knitting needles somewhere from that time you taught me to knit, and I was just thinking the other day that it would be fun to have a knitting project again."

She veered toward the sofa, took a seat at the far end, and clicked on the lamp.

"What will you make?" Pamela asked.

"I don't know." Penny shrugged. "What's one skein enough for? That's all I could find."

"Nothing to wear—at least for an adult . . ." Pamela stepped through the arch that divided the entry from the living room and picked up her knitting bag, which was on the carpet at the near end of the sofa, where she usually sat. "I have an idea, though . . ."

She described her current project, intended as a gift for Penny—the patchwork sweater made with odds and ends left from a lifetime of knitting. Penny listened with an expression that reminded Pamela of a much younger Penny reacting when her mother offered a magical solution to a quandary.

"So," Pamela said, "you can get busy making squares, lots of squares—and I'll give you some of my leftover yarn to take back with you so you have a nice variety of colors—and the next time we get together, we can experiment with how to shape all our squares into a sweater. And the sweater will be for you."

She settled into her customary spot at the other end

of the sofa and took out her own yarn and her own needles bearing her own in-progress square. Joined by Catrina and Ginger, mother and daughter spent a companionable few hours knitting and chatting. And thankfully, in Pamela's mind, the topic that had been interrupted by Maureen's visit—the Halloween murder and Pamela and Bettina's interest in it—did not resurface.

After a lunch of sandwiches made with leftover meatloaf, Pamela walked Penny to the corner of Orchard Street and Arborville Avenue to catch the bus back to the city.

Two more articles remained to be copyedited from the three that were due back on Wednesday. That morning had been given over to knitting and enjoying the company of Penny, and Monday would be busy, with the errand into the city to see what could be discovered about Graham's whereabouts on Halloween night. A session of work at the computer seemed an appropriate use for a Sunday afternoon, so Pamela climbed the stairs to her office, settled into her desk chair, and pushed the buttons that would bring her computer and monitor to life.

The choice was between "Putting on the Dog" and "Needle Spells"—both titles that piqued interest. Pamela knew that people collected hair shed by or combed from dogs, often beloved pets, and spun it into yarn, sometimes adding other fibers to make the dog hair more manageable. But "Putting on the Dog," whose full title was "Putting on the Dog: The Canine Origin of Coast Salish Blanket Fiber," dealt with a method of harvesting weavable fiber both more conventional—in that it involved shearing—and less conventional—in that the sheared creatures were dogs.

The author was an anthropologist who studied the material culture of indigenous people in the Pacific Northwest. While analyzing blankets made by the Coast Salish people and dating from the mid-nineteenth century, he had come to the conclusion that the fiber used was dog hair—a *lot* of dog hair. How the weavers could have access to so much dog hair was initially puzzling because, as he explained, the author himself had experimented with collecting dog hair for craft projects by combing his own dog, and he had found that it accumulated very slowly. In fact, the article was accompanied by a photo of a year's worth of dog hair collected from his own dog: a paltry amount. The article was also accompanied by some photos of Coast Salish blankets, which were striking in their design.

His breakthrough came when he turned to written materials documenting interactions between the nineteenth-century Coast Salish people and the trading posts they did business with. Journals kept by a European stationed at a trading post described seeing dogs resembling lambs shorn of wool in the canoes of the native people, and the author drew the conclusion that these dogs had actually been bred for the weavable quality of their coats.

Pamela had not been the one to evaluate the article when it was first submitted, so its contents were a total surprise to her—and the author made the description of his quest to discover how dog hair could be collected in such abundance as fascinating as any BBC mystery. When she reached the final paragraph, she realized she had made no corrections at all for the last several pages.

After another pass through "Putting on the Dog," she descended to the kitchen, made and ate a cheese omelet, and settled on the sofa with her knitting to watch one of her favorite BBC mysteries unfold.

# CHAPTER 13

In a plot twist that would have suited a Shakespearean comedy, Graham Tuttle, the unrequited lover, turned out to be himself an object of unrequited love—or so it seemed to Pamela and Bettina after they had been ushered into his apartment by his extremely solicitous neighbor.

"I'm Joyce," she explained, "from next door. I just dropped by to see how Graham was feeling and bring him some food—he's been so down lately, poor thing."

The object of her concern was lying on his sofa, a serviceable but low-budget piece of furniture that reflected the same aesthetic as the mismatched armchairs and the footlocker repurposed as a coffee table. Its surface was occupied at the moment by a tray that held a bowl of soup, a few crackers, and a glass of tomato juice.

"I'm Bettina Fraser," Bettina said, adjusting her expression to mirror the concern on Joyce's face. "And this is Pamela Paterson. We're friends . . . uh, friends of . . ."—Bettina's voice trailed off, then brightened—"and we were nearby . . . and thought we'd check in."

The figure on the sofa stirred and opened his eyes, which had been closed. Pamela was not sure she would have recognized him but for the fact that she was standing in the apartment known to be his and his neighbor had referred to him as Graham. The eager expression that had made his low-key looks appealing had vanished, leaving his eyes weary and his mouth slack.

"You were sitting outside Rodeo," he said in a toneless voice, "witnessing my misery. Why are you here now?"

Bettina was seldom at a loss for words, and Pamela had watched her extract information from people under the most challenging circumstances imaginable. She had imagined, *they* had imagined—Pamela supposed—that Graham, if they found him, would be inclined to chat. And that Bettina, with her wiles, could work the conversation around to Halloween night and trick-or-treaters and the Village parade and whatever—and easily figure out whether Graham had been in the city while Mel was being murdered. Or else, if they hadn't found Graham, they could find a neighbor who could vouch or not vouch for Graham's presence on the night in question.

Things weren't working out the way they had imagined. Joyce, however, came to their rescue. She had rushed to the sofa, knelt, and begun stroking Graham's forehead as he spoke. Now she rose and stepped toward one of the room's long windows, beckoning them to follow her.

She reminded Pamela of a young *Fiber Craft* employee she dealt with on the occasions when her job took her into the magazine's offices, a bookish young woman with a serious mien, looking out at the world through glasses that made her eyes seem larger than normal.

"He's not up to entertaining visitors," she whispered. "He recognized you from the . . . event . . . at Rodeo? I guess that means you know him through Roxanne and her cohort?"

"Yes!" Bettina exclaimed, sounding relieved to have been offered a plausible explanation for her presence. Joyce made a shushing noise, and Bettina's voice dropped to a whisper. "Roxanne asked us to stop by and see how he's doing—"

Joyce didn't utter a word, but her eyes grew so large behind her glasses that her stare served as admonition enough. When she did speak, it was to say, "Roxanne is a cruel woman who has broken his heart, and any concern she's showing now is just to make herself feel better. You could have saved yourselves a trip. And don't you dare tell him that and get his hopes up."

A fierce crease had appeared between Joyce's brows, but when her glance strayed toward the recumbent figure on the sofa her expression softened.

"It sounds like he confides in you," Bettina commented, still whispering. "You and he must be very close."

"Yes," Joyce said. "Yes, you could say that we're very close . . . even closer lately."

"In a romantic way?"

Joyce peered at Bettina, the glasses making her gaze all the more probing. Was she deliberating how much to confide in this sympathetic stranger? Pamela wondered.

"I'm right next door," she said after a bit, "so I'm around a lot, around Graham a lot. And eventually, when you're around someone a lot, they're bound to fall in love with you." Her voice faltered. "Aren't they?"

"It's been known to happen." Bettina's tone was encouraging. "Were you around Graham on Halloween night?"

Joyce took a step back. "Why on earth would you ask me that, of all things? Don't tell me Roxanne thinks Graham had something to do with what happened to that awful creature Mel."

"Oh, no, no, no." Bettina waved a carefully manicured hand as if to bat away a pesky insect. "Just making conversation. We get so many trick-or-treaters in the suburbs where we live. Are there even any children in the Village? Or do people just have dogs?"

"Of course people have children in the Village." Joyce wrinkled her nose and made a sound like a cross between a cough and a laugh. "I'll . . . we'll . . . have children someday. There are children right in this building, and on Halloween Graham and I were handing out candy together just like an old married couple."

Bettina cast a stealthy glance at Pamela and her lips twitched in a half smile. The conversation with Joyce was interrupted then as Graham stirred once more. The three women watched him shift his feet from the sofa to the floor and push himself into a sitting position.

"Feeling better?" Joyce cooed. She skipped across the floor and perched at his side. "Maybe try a little soup now? It's that recipe you especially like—and if it's gotten too cold, I can heat it up."

Graham shook his head and waved Joyce away but not unkindly. "Maybe in a bit," he murmured. Then he looked over at Bettina. "Did Martin Cotswold send you to bring comfort to a fellow sufferer?" Pamela realized that Joyce had obviously been successful in shielding him from the claim that Roxanne had sent them.

"Where's Martin been keeping himself?" Bettina inquired as if the question made perfect sense—and maybe it did, in the context. Apparently Graham assumed Bettina knew Martin.

Graham shrugged, as if accepting that his question wasn't going to be answered. "Gone," he said. "Gone back where he came from. Somewhere out West. He's on sabbatical from Fulham—just came back for the Rodeo event."

"Poor things," Bettina commented as they walked back to the parking garage where the Toyota waited. "She's obviously smitten, and he'd rather have somebody around than nobody—especially if that somebody is fussing over him and feeding him—but he's still pining for Roxanne."

Pamela murmured agreement. The visit to Graham *seemed* to have answered the question that had brought them to his apartment—whether he had an alibi for the night Mel was murdered—but the visit deserved discussion nonetheless.

They had reached the parking garage, however, and

were descending the concrete ramp to the exhaust-smelling lower level where the cars were stored. Bettina plucked the claim ticket from her handbag, a burgundy shoulder bag that lent a pop of color to her stylish camel coat. She handed the ticket to the garage attendant as Pamela produced some bills from her wallet. Soon they were on their way—though their exit involved braking at the top of the concrete ramp until pedestrian traffic was clear in both directions and then a perilous lurch into the street.

Neither of them spoke as Bettina negotiated the narrow one-way streets with stop signs at every corner that led to Fourteenth Street. But once they had turned onto the West Side Highway and were speeding along surrounded by trucks, vans, and all manner of other vehicles including motorcycles, Pamela turned to Bettina and asked, "What do you think—besides that Joyce is obviously smitten?"

"I don't think she just made up the story about them handing out Halloween candy to give Graham an alibi."

"So that occurred to you too?" Pamela said.

"People have done worse things for love—" Bettina yelped and hit the brakes as a van that had cut in front of her screeched to a stop at a red light. Pamela took a deep breath, grateful that the pause for the light gave them both a chance to collect themselves.

"But I believed her," Bettina said after the light changed and they were once again underway.

"Even the part about handing out Halloween candy like an old married couple?"

"That part was wishful thinking." Bettina chuckled.

"She had no reason to assume we were wondering whether Graham had an alibi," Pamela observed. "We're not the police. So that's in her favor. A person doesn't make up an alibi if they don't think an alibi is needed."

The Hudson River was coming into view on the left and New Jersey beyond, with clusters of high-rise apartment buildings jutting up along the shore.

But an idea had taken shape in Pamela's mind and now she spoke again. "Joyce wouldn't have wanted Mel to be dead because with Mel alive, Shakespeare's Rib would maintain its no-consorting-with-men rule and Joyce would have a chance with Graham."

Traffic was flowing smoothly now that they were past Midtown and the Upper West Side, and Bettina took her eyes off the road to glance at Pamela. "So does that mean she would want the person who killed Mel to be punished, even if it was Graham?"

"She wouldn't give Graham an alibi then. But she's smitten with Graham, so she *would* give him an alibi, even if he hadn't been handing out Halloween candy with her." Pamela laughed. "Things are getting convoluted. Let's just say we don't think he did it and we have one suspect left, Martin Cotswold."

"Who's gone back to wherever he's spending his sabbatical, and where he might well have been on Halloween too."

They drove in silence for a while, spiraling around the ramp curving up to the bridge and sailing across with the grand sweep of the Hudson stretching far below on either side.

"It was odd," Bettina observed as the Toyota coasted

down the hill that led from the bridge to Arborville Avenue, "odd that Graham thought Martin might have sent us and odd that he even knows Martin in the first place. He referred to himself as Martin's *fellow sufferer.*"

"There was that faction—the Blair faction—that wanted to admit men to Shakespeare's Rib," Pamela said. "I suppose they could have come in contact with each other through some connection with Blair."

"Knit and Nibble tomorrow night," Bettina commented. "At Holly's. I wonder what goody she has in mind for us."

Pamela spent Tuesday morning cleaning her house and doing laundry, but her mind was busy too. It seemed quite likely they had been barking up the wrong tree in pursuing the New York City angle, and if that was true, perhaps Adrienne really had been the intended victim.

Satisfied that all was in order once again—at least in regard to the house—she smiled as the cats, who had been driven into hiding by all the noise and bustle, reemerged. In the kitchen, she rewarded them with a handful of cat treats and rewarded herself with a meat loaf sandwich. As she sat at the kitchen table eating and browsing through the LIFESTYLE section of the *Register*, to which she had given only a quick glance over morning coffee, the phone rang.

Bettina was on the other end and her message was brief: "I'm not walking up that hill to Holly's so I'll pick you up at a quarter to seven."

Lunch finished, Pamela climbed the stairs to her office, where she pushed the buttons that brightened her monitor's screen and brought her computer to beeping and whirring life. One article remained to be copyedited. The abbreviated title that identified the document was intriguing, and the full title "Needle Spells: Power and Meaning in Traditional Ainu Embroidery," even more so.

She knew the Ainu people had something to do with Japan, but she learned as she read the article before beginning the copyediting task that they were an indigenous group quite distant genetically from the modern-day Japanese people. They were particularly associated with Hokkaido Island in the north, though they once had occupied more territory, including land in Russia.

The needle spells in the article's title referred to the distinctive embroidery patterns passed on from mother to daughter through generations. Illustrations accompanying the article showed tuniclike garments with patches of embroidery at neck, sleeve openings, and hem, the embroidered designs incorporating swirls and spirals that made them seem to dance against the background fabric.

Most interesting was the notion that the designs were not purely decorative. Rather, they were intended to protect the wearer of the garment from evil spirits. The swirls and spirals so prevalent in the designs evoked thorns or barbs that one might see in a hedge or fence set up to repel a corporeal invader. Similar designs, the author pointed out, appeared in traditional tattoos, tattooing being another distinctive art form cultivated by the Ainu. Though the author didn't explicitly make the connection, it occurred to Pamela that the *needle* in "Needle Spells" could refer not only to the embroiderer's tool but also to the needle used by the tattoo artist.

Once she had absorbed the article's content—again, this particular article was one she hadn't been asked to evaluate for publication—she shifted her mindset from reader to editor. The author appeared not to be an academic or professional writer but rather part of a group attempting to revive the art form she wrote about, and English seemed not to be her native language, so for the next several hours Pamela was oblivious to all but text slowly scrolling in front of her.

Holly's house smelled like cookies, warm and sugary. She greeted Pamela and Bettina with a sly smile and, as if she had intuited their unspoken question, said, "You'll see what kind they are when the time comes, but they have something to do with Halloween." Holly's jewelry had been chosen in acknowledgment of the recent holiday as well. Her earrings were dangly skeletons wrought from silver, long enough to nearly touch her shoulders and quite visible with her abundant hair drawn up into a high ponytail.

She beckoned them into her living room, where Karen had already taken a seat on the long ochre sofa, and Nell occupied the comfortable love seat, with its orange and chartreuse print, that was usually reserved for her.

Holly's décor was striking, befitting her artistic flair and her love of the vintage and the unusual. Other seat-ing was supplied by twin chairs with angular chrome frames and dark green leather seats and backs. A 1950s sunburst clock was a bright accent against a graphite-colored wall, and the coffee table consisted of a free-form slab of granite supported by spindly legs.

Holly's own handiwork was in evidence too. An amusing knitted throw pillow the shape and color of an eggplant decorated the sofa, as well as an afghan for which she had pieced together knitted squares and rectangles in vivid shades of orange, green, and turquoise.

The ochre sofa was very roomy, and Pamela and Bettina joined Karen there as the doorbell chimed and Holly backtracked to answer it.

"Not late, I don't think." Roland stepped over the threshold and set down his briefcase to consult his impressive watch. "No," he murmured. "No, it's just seven." He picked up the briefcase again and glanced around the room.

"Take one of the green chairs," Holly said. The gesture that accompanied the words displayed a manicure featuring nearly the same deep green color. "If Gayle comes again tonight, she can have the other and I'll sit on the sofa."

Nell and Karen were already hard at work, Nell on another Christmas stocking for the children at the women's shelter in Haversack. Nell's frugal impulse to use up odds and ends of yarn left from other projects meant that the stockings she produced could be any color at all. The current one was a festive, if not specifically Christmas-themed, hot pink.

Karen, on Pamela's left, was midway through a band of ribbing, powder blue, likely the start of a sleeve for the pullover that was to be a Christmas gift for her husband. On Pamela's right, Bettina hadn't yet taken her project from her knitting bag but rather was chatting with Karen about a library program aimed at children in Lily's age group.

Holly had remained on her feet, surveying the room as if to check that everyone was comfortable. Seemingly content that they were, she settled into the chair next to Roland and reached under the coffee table where her knitting bag was waiting. Soon a feeling of calm descended on the room as breathing slowed and hands relaxed into the pleasant rhythms of crisscrossing needles and looping yarn.

Minutes passed. The purple square currently underway on Pamela's needles grew by three rows as Bettina labored away on the sleeve of the maroon pullover destined for Wilfred Jr. and Roland bent toward his four-needle sock project as intently as if he was studying a complex legal document. Holly, in contrast, smiled to herself, perhaps contemplating the fashion statement that her chartreuse cable-knit leggings would make when complete.

The doorbell, however, intruded on this scene of placid industry. Holly set her work on the coffee table, rose, and made her way to the door.

"Gayle, I suppose," Bettina murmured. "I guess she wants to become a knitter after all."

"Showing up on time would be a good start," Roland commented from across the coffee table as his fingers continued their steady motion.

The caller was, in fact, Gayle, stepping over the

threshold in response to Holly's cheerful welcome. The contrast between guest and hostess could scarcely have been more striking. Everything about Gayle was nondescript: the loose-fitting jeans and fleece jacket, the graying ponytail, and the already plain face fading into middle age. Holly's outfit tonight was a pair of black leggings and a black turtleneck that suited her shapely figure, and her raven hair set off her radiant complexion and dark eyes. Wine-colored lipstick added the final dramatic touch—along with the dangling skeleton earrings.

Gayle glanced around the room looking uncertain, brightening slightly as she recognized Roland. Holly guided her toward the other green leather chair where the in-progress legging project awaited close at hand on the granite table.

But Gayle noticed Holly reaching for her project and said, "No, no. You were sitting there. I'll just"— she edged toward the sofa—"I'll just perch here."

The sofa was plenty long enough for four, and Karen moved over a bit to make extra room at her end. The placid industry resumed, with Holly back in her seat and Gayle's needles in motion. Pamela was curious whether Gayle had made progress beyond the careful rows Roland had coached her through, but Karen was between her and Gayle and it would have been hard to see what Gayle was actually doing without seeming nosy.

A quiet conversation sprang up between Bettina and Nell, and Pamela asked Karen about her progress on the powder-blue pullover. The front and back were yet to be made and only one sleeve was complete, Karen said, but both she and Pamela agreed that Christmas was still a long way off.

"It seems to come faster every year," Nell remarked from the love seat, "and Thanksgiving will be here in no time at all."

At that point the conversation became general, with everyone except Roland joining in, praising the decorations that had begun appearing along the commercial stretch of Arborville Avenue. Tall bundles of cornstalks with dried ears of corn still dangling from them had been lashed around the light poles, with wide orange ribbons adding an extra flair.

"Messy to clean up," Roland grumbled suddenly, "after the birds and squirrels have been at the corn. Arborville isn't a farming community, so why the town fathers feel these harvest displays are appropriate is beyond me."

"Some of the town fathers are town mothers," Bettina pointed out.

Roland looked up from his work, but his fingers kept moving. "What do you mean?" he inquired.

"There are more women than men in the town government," Bettina said, "as of the last election and for the first time in Arborville's history. I did an article on it for the *Advocate*."

"They should all know better." Roland frowned and seemed to address himself to his busy needles. "Fathers and mothers. The corn makes a horrible mess and the sanitation people have enough work as it is."

Suddenly Holly was on her feet, bending down to

rest the leggings project on the seat of her chair and then swiveling to face Roland, who stared up in alarm.

"Do not look at your watch!" she commanded, then she whirled around and darted toward the arch between the living room and dining room, en route to the kitchen. "Making coffee," she called over her shoulder, "and tea."

Pamela stole a peek at her own watch. It was just eight. She turned to glance toward the dining room and Holly's sleek Scandinavian-inspired table. In preparation for the evening, Holly had set out cups, saucers, and little plates from the collection of pastel Melmac she had sourced from eBay. A supply of fancy paper napkins, also in pastel shades, sat nearby. Sounds could be heard from the kitchen, of cupboards and drawers opening and closing.

Roland was still contentedly knitting, apparently confident that preparations for refreshments had been launched, albeit belatedly. Bettina, however, had set her work aside, and Karen had left her spot on the sofa and headed for the kitchen. With Karen gone, Pamela was able to take a discreet look at Gayle's project, which did not seem to have grown very much since the end of the last meeting. The black yarn Gayle had chosen made it hard to see without close examination whether the individual stitches were tidy and regular, with no gaps from dropped stitches, so Pamela couldn't tell whether Gayle had taken to heart Roland's admonition that anything worth doing was worth doing well.

The seductive aroma of brewing coffee began to waft from the direction of the kitchen. Pamela turned again when she heard soft footsteps in the dining room and saw that Karen had arranged Holly's chrome cream and sugar set, as well as several spoons, next to the Melmac. Then Karen retraced her steps to the kitchen and returned with Holly's elegant chrome coffeepot.

"Holly's coming with the teapot," she announced in her meek voice, "but coffee drinkers, please come and take a cup."

She tipped the coffeepot over the nearest cup, and a stream of dark liquid poured into its pale blue interior. Holly joined her then, holding her squat brown teapot aloft.

"Nell," she called, "stay where you are and I'll bring your tea."

"One spoonful of sugar and no cream," Nell responded.

Bettina was among those who had gathered in the dining room to claim their coffee. "I believe there were to be cookies," she commented as she waited for Karen to fill a pink Melmac cup for her.

"There are," Holly said, "and they're finger food, so we'll have them in the living room."

She stirred sugar into Nell's tea and stepped through the arch to deliver the steaming cup to the small table next to the love seat, then she darted back through the dining room and returned to the kitchen. Karen, meanwhile, had completed her coffee-pouring task. Now she picked up the stack of Melmac plates and the napkins and carried them to the coffee table.

Holly appeared in the kitchen doorway carrying a chrome platter. On it, large cookies had been layered atop lacy paper doilies.

"Cookies on the way," she sang out. "Please get comfortable in the living room."

After a few moments of bustle, during which Bettina, Pamela, Karen, and Gayle lined themselves back up on the sofa and Roland returned to his chair, Holly set down the platter on the coffee table and stood back to gaze at it with satisfaction.

"To use one of your favorite words," Bettina said, "these look *awesome*!"

The cookies were indeed impressive. They were golden brown with streaks of chocolate and a moist nubbly texture hinting at interesting things within.

Karen passed around the plates and napkins, and many hands reached simultaneously for cookies. Nell wasn't close enough to the coffee table to help herself to her own cookies, so Karen slipped a few onto a plate and bobbed up to deliver it to the small table at Nell's elbow.

Pamela lifted a cookie delicately because of its size and soft texture. It was still slightly warm, which enhanced its sugary seductive aroma. The first bite offered the expected discovery of chocolate embedded in the cookie's tender interior, but there was another taste as well—a taste that seemed a most appropriate complement to the chocolate.

Holly was surveying the group lined up on the sofa from the vantage point of the chrome and green leather chair, her lips twitching as she suppressed a tiny smile. Pamela turned to her left and right to see expressions of delighted bewilderment that she imagined mirrored her own.

"Peanut butter cups!" Holly crowed. "The mini ones

that people give out for Halloween. Peanut butter cups are my favorite, favorite candy, so we always get them for the trick-or-treaters and I eat the leftovers. But this year we had a huge bag left and I didn't want to eat them all myself."

"I would have." Bettina laughed. "That's why you're thin and I'm not, but I'm glad you made them into cookies instead."

"You cut them up, I guess?" Roland was holding a cookie from which he'd taken a few bites, and now he turned it over to examine the bottom.

"Chopped them up," Holly said, nodding, "though I thought about wrapping cookie dough around whole peanut butter cups. But I decided to model them on chocolate chip cookies. I used my vintage recipe for chocolate chip cookies and just stirred in the peanut butter cup pieces instead of chocolate chips."

Holly took a bite of her own cookie and followed it with a swallow of coffee. No one else seemed inclined to talk, unless hums of satisfaction and groans of pleasure counted.

"I guess you all like them," Holly said after a bit with a bright smile that brought her dimple into play. "At first I wasn't sure . . . if I should remind people of Halloween in any way, given what happened."

"It would be nice if the police could figure out who did it." Bettina had finished her first cookie and reached for another. "It's a shame that a holiday everyone in Arborville enjoys so much had to be spoiled."

Heads nodded in agreement, Holly's in particular, causing her luxuriant ponytail to bounce this way and that.

"Odd, though," she said when she stopped nodding. "Someone at the salon today was talking about a Halloween tragedy that happened exactly twenty-five years ago in Arborville. Four girls were roaming around in a lightning storm on Halloween night, and one was struck by lightning and killed."

"I'll take another cookie now," came a voice from the direction of the love seat.

Holly swiveled to face Nell, who was holding out her plate. "You will?" she exclaimed. "You don't think they're too sweet?"

"Of course they're sweet!" Nell's eyes looked out merrily from their nests of wrinkles.

As Holly took the plate and bent toward the doily-covered tray to select a cookie, it occurred to Pamela that Nell's request had been a good-natured ploy to change the subject to one less fraught, instead of the usual scowl or growl she employed. It seemed that the same idea had occurred to Bettina.

"Somebody contacted the *Advocate* this morning to suggest I do an article on the dog park controversy," she said. "That was the first I'd heard of a dog park controversy."

"Oh!" Holly laughed, punctuating her laugh with a handclap. "They've been talking about that at the salon all week. It seems this amazing town wants to make things even more amazing for Arborville's dogs by expanding the dog park."

"Who could object to that?" It was Karen who spoke up. Pamela had been going to ask the same question, but her mouth was full of cookie.

"It would expand at the expense of the children's

play area," Holly explained. "Just that one play area by the existing dog park, though. Arborville has several parks with play areas for children, but only one park with a section for dogs."

Roland's gaze was focused on the cookie platter. All that was left of his first cookie was a dusting of crumbs on the yellow surface of his Melmac plate. His hand had begun to move toward a particularly tempting cookie at the platter's edge, but it halted in midair and he looked up.

"Why can't children—and dogs for that matter—play in their own yards?" he inquired.

Bettina sighed. "Roland . . ." she began. She sighed again, and her mouth settled into a grim line, very unlike her usual expression. "We all know—well, most of us anyway, but maybe not Gayle because she's not a longtime Knit and Nibbler—what you're going to say next."

Roland grabbed the cookie he had been aiming for, deposited it with unnecessary care in the middle of his plate, and kept his eyes downcast as Bettina continued.

"Why should your tax dollars subsidize playgrounds for other people's children and dogs?" She paused, and Pamela noticed she had become quite pink. "The playgrounds for children and dogs have existed in Arborville for decades, if not longer, and many young families move here for that very reason. We all owe it to the next generation to create communities that foster families, and . . . and . . ."

Pamela glanced at Nell, across the room on the love seat. Nell's suddenly tense posture and the fact that her eyes had grown large suggested that she was about to elaborate on Bettina's views, with perhaps even more vehemence.

Roland stole a look at his watch and took two bites in a row from his cookie. The minute hand on the sunburst clock was nearing the quarter past mark.

"Oh, my goodness! Look at the time!" Holly exclaimed with perhaps more animation than necessary. "I know we all want to get back to our projects, so I'll just clear away . . ."

She hopped to her feet as Roland finished off his cookie in two more large bites and relinquished his plate, seeming relieved that the discussion of playgrounds and taxes had come to an abrupt conclusion.

# CHAPTER 14

Holly had baked several dozen peanut butter cup cookies. That fact had become clear to Pamela in the process of helping with cleanup duties. Not only did cookies remain on the doily-covered platter, but cookie sheets still covered with cookies crowded the stovetop and counter in Holly's kitchen.

Now, as the hands of the sunburst clock approached nine p.m. and people began to tuck away their projects after the post-break session of knitting, Holly rose to announce that cookies were available for the taking. She gestured toward her dining room, where a row of ziplock bags bulging with cookies waited on the pale wood surface of her sleek table.

"I certainly won't say no," Gayle said as she pushed herself up from the sofa.

Soon six people were gathered around the table claiming bags of cookies. Holly stood by and watched, smiling delightedly.

"Tell me again how you made them." Gayle edged out of the crowd to join Holly near the kitchen doorway.

"Just like chocolate chip cookies," Holly replied. "Recipes are everywhere, even on the chocolate chip package."

Pamela was distracted then, as Karen pretended good-natured amazement at the fact that Nell had succumbed to the temptation of cookies to take home.

"They're all for Harold," Nell said with a wink.

Soon the table was bare and people began migrating back to the living room. Gayle, still chatting with Holly, headed for the door, leaning to pick up her knitting bag from the sofa on her way past. As Holly lingered in the open doorway after seeing her on her way, Roland bid the remaining knitters a courtly good night, added a slight bow, and followed Gayle into the chilly air.

Nell was still chatting with Karen, on a new topic, though—Nell's insistence that because she had walked to the meeting she was perfectly capable of walking home.

"It's dark and cold," Karen protested in her meek voice.

"It was dark and cold at seven p.m. too," Nell pointed out. "And I got myself here in one piece."

"But it's uphill going back," Karen said. "It was downhill coming. I'll go and get my car . . ." Karen was Holly's neighbor and lived just a few houses away.

"No, no!" Holly shook her head, setting her ponytail

and earrings in motion. "Desmond will be home from the salon any minute. He can take Nell home."

"No need." Bettina stepped forward and laid a hand on Nell's arm. "Pamela and I are just leaving and we'll take you home. It's hardly out of the way at all and . . ." The sentence trailed off, and she gazed toward the stairway leading to Holly's second floor.

As she spoke, Nell was speaking too, inquiring with great concern whether Holly had saved cookies for Desmond.

"Yes, of course." Holly smiled her dimply smile.

"Kitty, kitty, kitty," came Bettina's voice. She moved toward the stairway, half-crouching and with one hand extended.

"Oh!" Holly laughed and swiveled around. "Here's my little sweetie. She's usually too shy to venture out when there's company."

At the foot of the stairs was a ginger cat, poised on her haunches with her tail wrapped like a narrow, furry stole to cover her front paws. She was nearly identical to Pamela's Ginger and Bettina's Punkin, and with good reason. She too was one of Catrina's daughters.

A tapping at the door distracted them then. Holly opened it to admit Harold Bascomb, bundled in a rugged plaid wool jacket. He was a rangy man in his eighties with a thick crop of white hair that flopped over his forehead.

"Harold!" Nell regarded her husband with a look that tempered exasperation with affection. "I'm perfectly capable of walking home and you know that."

"All too well, my dear. All too well." Harold added a jovial grin. "So I'll just turn around and drive back home if you're sure you don't want a ride . . ."

In the event, Nell did accept a ride, and Karen too, leaving Pamela and Bettina the last to leave.

Returning to the sofa to collect her knitting bag, Bettina exclaimed, "Oh, my goodness!" She held up a knitting needle from which hung an inch or so of work knit from black yarn. "Gayle left her project behind. Excited about the cookies, I guess." She peered at it more intently. "She certainly didn't make much progress tonight—it doesn't look much different from what she ended up with after Roland helped her last week."

Pamela was standing nearby, collecting her own knitting bag. She bent closer. Gayle seemed not to have mastered the difference between knit and purl—or maybe she just didn't care—not to mention the puckers that marred the surface of the small swatch where stitches had been dropped but then extra loops had made their way onto the needles in other spots.

"I don't know why she even bothers." Bettina shook her head slowly and made a clicking sound with her tongue.

Holly delivered Pamela's jacket and Bettina's pumpkin-colored down coat. They slipped jacket and coat on, and the group moved toward the door as their voices overlapped with thank-yous and goodbyes. Holly pulled the door open but then stiffened in surprise. Peeking around her, Pamela could see Gayle standing on the porch, her unremarkable features illuminated by the porch light.

"I didn't mean to startle you," she said. "I was just about to ring the bell." She made a tentative gesture toward the doorbell, a brass plaque with a button in the center.

"Your knitting. You took your knitting bag but not your knitting." Holly pulled the door open all the way and backed up toward the sofa, where Gayle's unimpressive project still reposed.

"Why did you pick black yarn?" Bettina asked as they waited for Holly to return with the project, "considering you're just getting back into knitting? It's really hard to see what you're doing with black. Everything blends together."

Gayle's lips twitched in the facial equivalent of a shrug. "It seemed appropriate," she murmured.

"To the season?" Pamela inquired. "Do you mean Halloween?"

"Yes, I guess." Gayle's lips twitched again. "Halloween."

After another chorus of thank-yous and goodbyes, augmented by Gayle's voice this time, Pamela, Bettina, and Gayle made their way down Holly's front walk to where Bettina's Toyota waited at the curb.

"I'm parked just behind you." Gayle pointed to a nondescript car rendered more nondescript by the darkness that made Holly's porch seem a bright oasis.

But instead of stepping away she lingered, and Bettina, with keys in hand and about to circle around to the driver's side, remained on the sidewalk.

"I was wondering," Gayle said, "did you follow up on the idea that a jealous wife was actually after Adrienne and Mel wasn't the target at all?"

"I wish I hadn't." Bettina laughed. "Adrienne can be kind of fierce."

"Ask her about Brock Pomfret." Gayle's voice came out of the gloom. "That's all I'll say."

The next day, even before feeding the cats or collecting the newspaper, Pamela had returned the three copyedited articles to her boss at *Fiber Craft*. Now, breakfasted and dressed and with morning chores out of the way, she sat down once again at her computer and watched a message from Celine Bramley with attachments appear in her inbox.

The message itself read, "Please evaluate these and get them back to me first thing Monday. The third one is too late for Halloween this year, but it looks like a fun topic. If you agree that it's publishable, we'll accept it and use it next October." The short titles accompanied by the Word logo were lined up across the top: "Woven Song," "Cat Mummies," and "Fashioning Witchcraft."

When Pamela dashed outside for the *Register*, the morning had seemed to augur such a perfect autumn day that she had been almost unwilling to return to the house, robe and slippers notwithstanding. The articles had only to be evaluated, not copyedited, and the task would not take long, but such a day as this was rare with winter fast approaching. She deleted a few pieces of junk mail, responded to a note from her mother, and then descended the stairs, where she took her jacket from the closet and stepped out into the golden sunlight.

* * *

An hour later, she was en route up Orchard Street after a ramble through the nature preserve when she caught sight of a familiar figure heading toward her porch. She reached her house just as that familiar figure had begun to retrace her steps and was halfway to the curb.

"There you are!" called Bettina, for that's who the familiar figure was.

Bettina was dressed for the day, albeit a casual day at home, in a harvest-gold fleece tunic and matching leggings. An appliqué design on the tunic's front featured autumn leaves in shades of amber, rust, and brown.

"I was having a walk," Pamela said.

"I suspected as much because your car is here." Bettina continued to advance. When she got closer, she added, "I came over to invite you to lunch. Wilfred is making bean soup with the ham bone he's been saving in the freezer since Easter."

"Sounds great." Pamela smiled. "When do we eat?"

"Not for a while, but in the meantime . . ." Bettina's gaze strayed toward Pamela's house. "I don't suppose there's any coffee left . . ."

"I can make more." Pamela beckoned and started toward the porch.

Once they entered the kitchen, Bettina headed for the cupboard where Pamela stored her wedding china as Pamela set water to boil in the kettle. While Bettina transferred cups and saucers to the little table, Pamela arranged a paper filter in her carafe's filter cone and measured coffee beans into the grinder. The beans clattered briefly as the grinder reduced them to aromatic grounds. Meanwhile, Bettina had moved the cut-glass cream and sugar set from the counter to the table and was filling the pitcher with heavy cream.

Soon the sound of rhythmic dripping and the seductive aroma filling the room signaled that fresh-brewed coffee would soon be at hand. Bettina took her accustomed seat at the little table and turned toward where Pamela waited near the carafe.

"I'd have brought some of Holly's cookies," she said, "but I know you have them too and probably haven't even touched them."

"As it happens"—Pamela raised her brows, smiled a mysterious smile, and reached up to open a cupboard—"I have them right here. I don't suppose you could be persuaded to have a few."

"You know I could!" Bettina hopped to her feet with an assist from the table, detoured past the cupboard that housed the wedding china to pick up two small plates, and held out a hand for the ziplock bag of cookies.

By the time Pamela approached with the carafe, Bettina had added the plates, napkins, and a few spoons to the table setting and had placed a cookie in the middle of each rose-garlanded plate.

"Just as good as last night," was the verdict once the cookies had been tasted, which in Bettina's case occurred even before she tipped the first spoonful of sugar over her steaming cup.

As Bettina stirred in sugar and dribbled in cream,

Pamela followed her first bite of cookie with a hot and bitter sip of her own coffee. The peanut butter cups added not only a peanut dimension to the classic chocolate chip cookie idea but also a hint of saltiness, unexpected in a cookie but somehow enhancing the sweetness with its contrast.

The ramble through the nature center on this breezy day had swept Pamela's mind as clean of day-to-day concerns as it had swept fallen leaves from yards and pathways. But now, stimulated by the combination of sugar and caffeine, thoughts that had occupied her earlier returned.

"Have you thought any more about what Gayle told us last night?" she asked.

On the drive home from Holly's, Pamela and Bettina had discussed Gayle's suggestion that they ask Adrienne about Brock Pomfret, and Bettina had been noncommittal.

"I know you're reluctant to approach Adrienne again with the idea that a jealous wife might have been targeting her rather than Mel, because obviously that implies she's been getting up to things with other people's husbands."

Bettina gazed at Pamela with a facial expression that wordlessly communicated *duh*. Then she elaborated. "Why should I try to save her if . . . whoever it is . . . tries again, after the horrible things she's said to me, and the way she acts with Wilfred?"

"You could scoop Marcy Brewer . . ." Pamela added a teasing smile. "Remember, KILLER'S INTENDED TARGET WAS ADULTEROUS HUSBAND'S GAL PAL."

Bettina's response was a haughty, "The *Advocate* doesn't pander."

She reached into the ziplock bag for another cookie and addressed herself so earnestly to its consumption as to make clear the subject was closed.

"The cookies are just as good as last night," Pamela commented after a bit, aware that that point had already been made but eager to launch a new subject. "It's funny that Holly hears more about Arborville doings than we do and the salon isn't even in Arborville."

Bettina nodded, busy with her cookie and coffee.

"Are you going to follow up on the dog park controversy?"

Bettina swallowed. "People complaining at a hair salon in Meadowside about something that might happen in Arborville isn't a story. The *Advocate* would have been informed if the council had made the plan official."

"True." Pamela nodded. "Arborville has hair salons of its own, but I guess a lot of Arborvillians like Holly and Desmond's salon better."

"That other Arborville tidbit Holly mentioned was interesting," Bettina said. "The twenty-five-year-old Halloween tragedy with the girls in the lightning storm?"

"Nell obviously didn't want her to elaborate, so we'll never know more."

"It was probably in the *Register* when it happened, even the *Advocate*, though that was before my time."

"The *Advocate* doesn't pander," Pamela reminded her with another teasing smile.

"It doesn't have to." Bettina assumed a dignified pose, with raised chin and brows. "People read the

*Advocate* for other things besides gruesome news. I'm covering the battle of the bands at the high school on Sunday afternoon. Somebody named Nadine Dennis called me, and I promised to do a story."

The conversation meandered from there to other town events and then to the doings of children and grandchildren. Half an hour passed in this pleasant way until, with coffee cups refilled and emptied once again and the supply of cookies seriously depleted, Bettina rose from her chair.

"Come over in about an hour," she said. "I've got to write up some material about the library's display of Thanksgiving-related books in time to get it in this week's issue. By noon I'll be done and the bean soup will be ready."

Catrina still lingered in the sunny spot on the entry carpet as Bettina stepped out onto the porch, waved on her way by Pamela.

Wilfred had busied himself not only with ham bone and bean soup but also with corn bread. As soon as he opened the front door, jovial in the expansive apron that reached from his chest nearly to his ankles, Pamela was greeted by the mingled aromas of the soup, with its smoky hint of ham, and the corn bread, smelling of sweet earthy grains. Bettina was sitting on the sofa as Pamela entered, holding her phone.

She stood up and followed Pamela and Wilfred across the living room floor and through the dining room. In the kitchen, Pamela remained standing, chatting with Wilfred as he circled around the high counter to station himself in front of the stove. Bettina lowered herself into one of the chairs that surrounded the scrubbed pine table, which was already set in preparation for lunch.

Bettina fingered the phone's screen as Wilfred, on the opposite side of the room, donned an oven mitt, extracted a square metal baking dish from the oven, and set the baking dish on the stovetop with a clunk.

"Corn bread," he announced with a flourish.

Though behind her, Pamela could hear Bettina murmuring, "Melissa Wilson . . . Trish Unger . . . Nadine Barnes . . . and Heather Cotton," Wilfred's activity was more immediately engaging. Removing the oven mitt from his hand, he patted the gentle swell of golden-brown crust that was the corn bread's surface. The tantalizing aroma, which evoked the bounty of sun-drenched fields, had intensified now that the bread was out of the oven.

Wilfred turned his attention to his soup, which was simmering in a large Dutch oven on a back burner of the stove. He removed the lid from the pot, releasing a cloud of fragrant steam, and picked up the wooden spoon lying nearby. After a few moments of stirring, he exchanged the wooden spoon for a set of tongs with which he probed the soup's bubbling surface and then lifted out what remained of the ham bone.

As Wilfred addressed himself to carving from the bone the few bits of ham still clinging to its soupy surface, Pamela turned her attention to Bettina. Noticing Pamela looking at her, Bettina rose holding her phone and seeming embarrassed.

"I'll put this away," she said. "I shouldn't have been

ignoring my guest, but I was curious about that thing Holly mentioned." She darted through the dining room doorway and returned in an instant.

"Who's ready for soup?" came Wilfred's voice from behind the high counter.

The question seemed formulaic because both Pamela and Bettina were approaching the counter carrying bowls from the place settings laid out in advance on the scrubbed pine table. The bowls were sturdy and deep, part of Bettina's sage-green pottery set, and the tawny raffia place mats and plaid linen napkins in tones that evoked fallen leaves had been chosen to complement them.

A few minutes later, they had all taken their places at the table with steaming bowls of soup before them. In the center of the table, a large sage-green plate held squares of golden corn bread, the cut sides revealing the delicate spongelike texture of the interior. Next to the large plate, a smaller one held a stick of butter, already missing several pats. Those pats were slowly melting into the surfaces of corn bread squares, halved crosswise and waiting on bread plates to be consumed.

The soup seemed to contain every kind of bean one could imagine, from huge pale ones that resembled limas through medium-sized kidneys and pintos to tiny black beans. Instead of broth, they were suspended in a medium that itself was like soup, like a thick split-pea soup, which Wilfred explained was exactly what it is.

"I throw the beans and peas in the pot together," he said, "along with diced onion, carrot, and celery and my ham bone, and let it all cook and cook. The split peas eventually disintegrate and the bigger beans remain beans."

The soup was declared a success as Pamela and Bettina sampled the result of Wilfred's alchemy. It was hearty and flavorful, with the bits of ham and essence of ham bone adding a savory dimension to the legumes. The moist and tender corn bread was the perfect accompaniment. The small glasses of beer Wilfred had delivered to the table were welcome and refreshing.

The conversation had progressed from its focus on the meal to Bettina's summary of her article about the library's plans to commemorate Thanksgiving, which had proved to involve more than just a book display, when the doorbell's ring interrupted. Woofus had been sprawled out along the wall near the sliding glass doors, watching the squirrels rearrange the dirt in the patio planters, but he swung his shaggy head around in alarm. A short bark emerged from his throat like a ragged cough. The doorbell's ring was followed by pounding, as if the caller wasn't sure the bell was working.

Murmuring, "What on earth?" Wilfred rose to his feet with an assist from the table. With the back edges of his apron flapping behind him, he hurried toward the doorway that led to the dining room and the living room beyond. The pounding continued.

Bettina reached out and clutched Pamela's arm. So uncommon was it to see her in anything but a state of contented cheer that she was almost unrecognizable, pale and staring.

"Why would someone pound like that unless . . ." she left off, but her mouth remained open.

Wilfred's voice, carrying from two rooms away, however, provided a hint of comfort. Sounding notably unperturbed, he was saying, "No problem, no problem. We were just finishing lunch."

"We weren't!" Bettina whispered urgently. "I wanted more soup."

Footsteps approached and then a woman with a cap of bouncy auburn curls appeared in the doorway. Her face was a shade of pink that implied recent agitation, and Wilfred was visible over her shoulder.

"June Pomfret has come to call," Wilfred said as he followed the woman into the kitchen. He addressed June then. "Please have a seat, and can I offer you a bowl of soup?"

"I don't want soup," she muttered, but she did slip into the one vacant chair as Wilfred reoccupied his own. "I want to get to the bottom of what's going on."

"June feels that someone has been spreading rumors about her," Wilfred explained.

"More than rumors!" June pounded the table, and the butter knife balanced on the butter plate jangled. "Someone has been saying that I'm the Halloween killer and I really meant to kill Adrienne."

"Who's the *someone*?" Pamela inquired.

"I traced it to Gayle Witherspoon, but I just came from her house and she told me that *you* told her that"—June aimed a quivering finger at Bettina, who shied away—"and you said I'm jealous of Adrienne because my husband is having an affair with her."

"I never said anything like that at all." The seat that June occupied was directly across from Bettina, who now leaned toward her, gripping the edge of the table. A deep crease had appeared between Bettina's carefully shaped brows. "Gayle told *me* that, and I've kept it totally to myself, except that Pamela knows because she was there too when Gayle said it."

"Well!" June uttered the word as if it was a prolonged sigh, and the outpouring of breath seemed to leave her a bit deflated. "Gayle should mind her own business and not go spreading gossip that isn't even true. I'm certainly not a killer, my husband is the most devoted of men, and I'm certainly going to let Gayle know that."

"You should." Bettina was once more her sympathetic self, her hazel eyes fairly glowing with concern. "What Gayle did was shameful. Are you sure you won't have some soup?"

"No thank you." June waved the idea away, but with a small smile. Bettina's powers to comfort and soothe were indeed remarkable.

"A piece of corn bread? It's very good."

"No, no, really. You're very kind." She continued waving and smiling. After a moment, she said, "There's a reason a rumor like that might circulate about Adrienne, you know."

Was she about to produce a tidbit of information in appreciation of the offer to share their meal? Pamela wondered.

"Oh?" Bettina's posture changed subtly and her eyes seemed to enlarge. Pamela stifled a laugh as she recognized the emergence of her friend's reporter persona, not to mention that Adrienne was far from Bettina's favorite person.

"My husband is blameless, but I don't think Paulette Hodges can say the same about her husband, Kurt."

June Pomfret went on her way then, escorted to the door by Wilfred. Bettina finished a second bowl of soup, but the diners lingered at the table.

"Everything is such a confusing jumble," Bettina said after a prolonged silence. "Gayle told us June Pomfret's husband was having an affair with Adrienne, but then June told us that Gayle told her that that was my idea and that some whole other husband is having an affair with Adrienne."

"Does Gayle have a husband?" Wilfred asked. "Maybe he's having an affair with Adrienne and Gayle killed Mel by mistake thinking she was Adrienne, and now she's trying to deflect that crime and that motive onto someone else."

Bettina scooted her chair back and darted through the doorway. In a moment she was back with her phone, and in a few more moments she looked up from the screen to say, "She's the only owner listed for her address in Arborville, but there's an eighteen-year-old Witherspoon and a twenty-year-old Witherspoon living there too. So likely there was a husband Witherspoon at some point."

"But not now," Pamela said, "so Gayle isn't a jealous wife with a reason to go after Adrienne."

"She's up to something, though." Bettina's lips formed a thin line and her head twitched in a puzzled shake. "I just can't figure out what."

"I don't suppose you want to ask Adrienne if she knows Kurt Hodges . . ." Pamela let the sentence trail off with a questioning lilt. "Straight from the horse's mouth, one might say." She nodded at Wilfred to acknowledge his fondness for old sayings.

"You suppose correctly." Bettina tapped on the table for emphasis. "And besides, horses are nice and Adrienne isn't."

# CHAPTER 15

Back at home sometime later, Pamela discovered a phone message from Pete Paterson. "I'd like to see you today," he said, his voice rendered tinny by the answering machine. "Maybe this evening? I'll call again later to check."

*Odd*, she thought. *I wouldn't have minded calling him back—but maybe he's crawling around on someone's roof or something*. She climbed the stairs to her office, sat down at her desk, and let her mouse meander on its mouse pad until her monitor woke from its nap.

First on the agenda for *Fiber Craft* was "Woven Song: Work Chants as Codes to Enable Complex Weaving Patterns." Pamela opened the Word file and read the first paragraph to discover that, interesting as the topic seemed, English did not appear to be the author's native language. She could recommend that it be published, though, if the material warranted publication, but point out that it would need a copyeditor's serious attention—and because she was *Fiber Craft*'s chief and only copyeditor, that would be her.

The phone message from Pete was nagging at her. He hadn't meant to tease her with suspense, she was sure, but she was finding it hard to concentrate, so she closed the file and closed Word. She would return to the article later, when she could give it her full attention. Meanwhile . . . her cursor hovered in the center of the screen, seemingly at loose ends. Then it wandered upward and landed on "Favorites." A moment later, Pamela was looking at the current batch of messages on the AccessArborville page.

"I personally am insulted," read the title of one post. The writer had evidently looked up the Womanifesto when it was mentioned in the news reports on Mel's death and was now citing the line, "You weave the web that is your prison."

"I am sorry that this woman was killed," the writer went on to say, "and I hope the police figure out *soon*—I'm looking at you, Lucas Clayborn—who did this dreadful thing, but Mel 'Wordwoman'—as she called herself—did not make any friends in the fiber arts community with that ignorant statement. We women don't need traitors in our mist"—*I think you mean midst*, Pamela whispered to herself—"and maybe that's what her killer was trying to say."

The post had not attracted any responses, but the message directly below it seemed to have struck a nerve, as indicated by the circled number 15—indicating responses—that accompanied its title, "Dogs or Children: Which Side Are You On?"

Pamela clicked on the title and scrolled down to

read the message and the responses it had occasioned. Many people—dog owners most likely—were in favor of expanding the existing dog park. They pointed out that a number of public areas in Arborville were devoted to children—from the kiddie playground behind the library to large expanses of lawn suitable for team sports—whereas dogs had only one small, fenced yard in one park where they could run free and socialize with other dogs.

But those opposed had made their views known as well. "Another case where our elected officials have conspired to foist decisions made in secret upon the taxpayers," one person wrote. "It just does not seem right. Arborville is going to the dogs in more ways than one."

"I beg your pardon," was the response. "Your statement is demeaning to dogs and *going to the dogs* should be purged from the lexicon. Moreover, the date, place, and time of the meeting to discuss the expansion was announced on this very listserv, and I and one other person were the only Arborvillians who took the trouble to show up. Your conspiracy talk gets very old."

A flurry of messages following that one argued that it was a free country and people could say whatever they wanted about dogs, and that people who chose dogs over children were responsible for the declining birth rate and were selfish besides.

"And why would that be a bad thing?" someone interjected, while Trish on Catalpa Street asked, quite logically, why a family couldn't have both dogs and children, and someone else pointed out that having dogs taught children to be responsible.

"I live across from the existing dog park," wrote a woman who signed her post Ellin Taylor Mordaunt, "and the barking is already unbearable. In my view the dog park should be removed, not expanded. What happened to the enforcement of our noise ordinance? Or have our elected officials done away with that in secret too? Never forget that the ancient Egyptians worshipped dogs and look what happened to them."

Pamela frowned. It seemed to her that the ancient Egyptians had endured extremely long and successfully as a culture. What could Ellin Taylor Mordaunt be thinking? She clicked on the back arrow to return to the main message page.

Another new post had just popped up, relating to the dog park issue but calling for action rather than discussion. Titled "Children or Dogs?" it read, "North End Arborville Avenue Park, tomorrow at two p.m., be there to protest the dog park expansion if you care about our children."

The controversy was edging into newsworthy territory, it seemed. Pamela brought up her email page and sent a quick note to Bettina, referring her to the listserv and pointing out that a protest might be worth covering for the *Advocate*, even though it would be too late to get anything into that Friday's issue.

Pamela was about to return to "Woven Song" when she heard the doorbell's chime. Ginger had been lounging on the floor near the radiator, but she jumped up and scurried ahead of her mistress as Pamela headed down the stairs.

It wasn't dusk yet, though dusk came early this time of year, and from the landing a figure was visible on the porch—though obscured by the lace that curtained the oval window in the front door. More readily recognizable than the figure, however, was the vehicle parked at the curb, a sleek silver pickup truck gleaming in the late-afternoon sun.

Pamela hurried down the remaining stairs and opened the door to admit Pete Paterson.

"I know I said I'd call again." He fastened his gaze on her face as if preparing to react to some expected change in her expression. The hint of melancholy always present in his eyes now seemed to fit his subdued manner.

"Come in." Pamela beckoned him to advance beyond the doorway. "Do you want to sit? Has something happened?"

"I don't know what to say." Pete glanced toward the living room.

"*Do* you want to sit?" Pamela took a few steps in that direction.

He shook his head, then suddenly reached out to grasp both of her hands. "My wife . . . my ex-wife . . . came back."

Now it was Pamela's turn to study *his* face. Whether Pete's wife coming back was a good thing or a bad thing wasn't clear. But the question she heard herself ask was, "Where was she?"

The question surprised her with its irrelevance. Clearly the key point was the return. From where was immaterial.

But Pete answered, "Renting a condo in Timberley."

"Not so far, then."

He was still holding her hands and he squeezed them. "Pamela," he said, his voice deepened by emotion, "she came back *to me*."

Pamela sensed her expression must be as blank as her mind was at that moment. Her silence seemed to alarm Pete. He leaned closer to peer at her.

"You're getting back together," she said then, and blinked—surprised again by her words, by the fact that her unconscious had drawn the conclusion that eluded her conscious mind.

"She likes the new version of me and she wants us to be married again." He let go of Pamela's hands. "And I want to be married. I never stopped loving her, even when I thought she had stopped loving me." He paused and laughed tentatively. "She didn't love the Wall Street guy, though."

The mood had lightened. Perhaps Pete was surprised that Pamela wasn't weeping or obviously angry. He had shown up clearly expecting a difficult encounter. Decent of him, though, she reflected, to come and explain in person rather than on the phone, or just disappearing.

"I really like you, Pamela," he said, with that probing gaze she'd noticed when he first stepped inside, like he was searching for some reaction beyond blankness. "The divorce was final when I met you—otherwise I'd never have . . . led you to . . ."

She shook her head but looked at the floor rather than him as she spoke. "It's okay," she said, "really. I didn't think we'd ever . . ." She paused. "I like you too." She raised her eyes to meet his and felt a tiny smile begin. "We had some nice meals, like at that French restaurant you took me to on our first date."

He returned the smile. "And lots of the nice meals were meals that you cooked."

After she saw Pete on his way with a chaste kiss, Pamela sat on the sofa, not exactly sure how she felt and staring at nothing in particular. Would she wake up tomorrow grieving this loss once the implications sank in? She hadn't been in love with Pete, but he had brought her out of her romantic solitude, and it had been pleasant to have a handsome, interesting man in her life.

Catrina wandered in and posed on her haunches, gazing up with her amber eyes unblinking, as if she realized that it was unusual for her mistress to sit on the sofa with no knitting in her hands—all the more so at this time of day. Distracted from her musings, Pamela focused on the cat. Was she concerned that a change in the routine could portend other changes? Pamela wondered. Or was she merely eager for dinner and curious about whether the bowl that descended from on high would contain seafood medley or liver with gravy?

The telephone's ring summoned Pamela to the kitchen then, and Catrina scampered along.

The voice on the other end of the line was Bettina's. "I saw Pete's truck," she announced without preamble. "Is he okay?"

Pamela lowered herself into the chair on the side of the table nearest the phone, but she didn't respond and the silence lasted until Bettina spoke again.

"I didn't call about that, really," she said. "I just happened to notice he was there."

Pamela took a deep breath and willed her voice to sound pleasantly curious rather than exasperated. "What *did* you call about?"

"Your email. The dog park protest. It *is* newsworthy and I definitely plan to go." She paused and then went on, talking quickly. "Why don't you come along? It's way up at the north end of Arborville Avene and it's too far to walk, but we'll be outdoors once we get there, and that's sort of like a walk."

Pamela agreed to go and hung up the phone wondering why she hadn't just told Bettina that Pete was now, as Bettina would put it, out of the picture. Along with, apparently—and permanently this time—Richard Larkin, but she hadn't discussed that development with Bettina yet either.

The protest was at two that afternoon. Bettina wanted to get there early to do some interviews but wouldn't be picking Pamela up until one. *Fiber Craft* work was waiting, so after breakfast, newspaper, and morning chores, Pamela sat down at her desk. The computer came alive with beeps and chirps, the monitor brightened, and the mouse snuggled into Pamela's hand as if eager for another productive day. Pamela opened the "Woven Song" file again and began to read.

Yes, the author's native language was most definitely not English. His name sounded Scandinavian, he was affiliated with a British university, the research had been done in India, and the article proved to be fascinating—well worth recommending for publication despite the work that would then be needed to tidy up the syntax.

The author began by citing, with photos, complex woven patterns found in ancient textiles from various cultures preserved in museum collections. He then reminded the reader that such textiles often date from preliterate eras, and even if the cultures that produced them were literate, universal literacy extending to the people who spent their days weaving could not be assumed.

Therefore, he asked, how was the information required to produce and reproduce the patterns stored and transmitted? His fieldwork in India had provided an answer. He had observed and recorded traditional weavers accompanying their work with memorized rhythmic chants and concluded that the chants actually encoded the information needed to create the desired patterns.

Pamela wrote up a recommendation that the article be published and added that the extra time needed for thorough copyediting would be well spent.


Pamela and Bettina arrived at the protest site before two, but things were already well underway—and the atmosphere was more carnival than protest. The park's leaf-strewn lawn was crowded with people, cheerful people with seemingly not much more on their minds than enjoying the excuse to gather outdoors on a bright fall day. It was hard to tell from their demeanor which protestors were on the anti-dog side and which on the pro-dog side, though the signs that many carried gave a hint.

"LIE DOWN WITH DOGS, GET UP WITH FLEAS," read one sign, carried by a man pacing within view of cars slowing for the traffic signal on Arborville Avenue. "SUPPORT OUR FURRY FRIENDS," read another, its bearer pausing to rest on a bench. Someone in a dog costume was loping here and there, and a man in cowboy boots was strumming on a guitar and singing "Hound Dog." His voice was barely audible over the hubbub, which included the sounds of many dogs barking. And there were dogs everywhere, large and small, both within the chain-link fence that enclosed the current dog park and roaming freely.

As Pamela and Bettina proceeded across the lawn, Bettina in her bright red sneakers, navy corduroy slacks, and red leather jacket accented with a saucy peplum, they were accosted by a young woman. With a smile that reminded Pamela of the people who rang the doorbell on Sunday morning to offer salvation, she said, "I can tell just by looking at you that you're both dog lovers." She reached into a tote bag and pulled out a leather thong tied in a necklace-sized loop and with a bone-shaped dog biscuit dangling from it. "Wear it to show your support." She handed it to Bettina, then pulled out another and handed it to Pamela.

"I . . . thank you . . ." Bettina tucked the necklace into her pocket. "I am a dog lover, but I'm here as a journalist and I need to be impartial."

"What on earth is that?" Pamela said after they'd progressed farther into the park. A milling crowd had shifted position enough to allow a glimpse of a small wooden structure. It was situated beneath a tree that still retained a few colorful leaves, though most of its leaves lay in rust and golden heaps on the faded grass.

As Pamela and Bettina got closer, the structure was revealed to be a doghouse—with something emerging from the rounded opening that was its doorway.

"It's the mayor!" Bettina exclaimed. Her voice was tinged with delight. She quickly frowned, however, as if to negate the earlier response. "Very disrespectful, I must say."

It was not, actually, the mayor in the flesh. It was a papier-mâché replica of the mayor, or his head at least. A woman standing nearby was brandishing a sign that read "Olson and His Council Cronies Once Again Put One Over on Arborville's Taxpayers." She noticed Bettina observing the scene and said, "I'm Ellin Taylor Mordaunt and we've put him in the doghouse where he belongs."

Pamela felt someone tugging on her elbow. When she turned, a young man thrust a card into her hand. "Ten dollars off your first visit," he whispered. Pamela glanced at the card, which read "Pamper Your Pet at the Newly Opened Pet Pamper Spa." "Here"—he offered more cards—"pass them around to your pet-owning friends."

He wandered off, and Pamela turned back to hear the woman with the sign say, in an affectedly precise voice, "No thank you. I do not wish to be interviewed for the *Advocate*, which I consider an objectionable piece of litter that invades my driveway every Friday."

"Thank you anyway," Bettina responded, though

Pamela could tell, even just observing her friend in profile, that the comment had stung. Bettina looked suddenly older, absent the time-defying effect of her customary cheer.

"Lots of people, *most* people, like the *Advocate*," Pamela murmured as they edged away.

"Maybe somebody from the pro-dog group will be friendlier," Bettina said, "though I should interview both sides to be fair."

A dog lunged past, a dachshund in pursuit of a lively collie twice its size.

"We should have brought Woofus," Pamela suggested. "Being accompanied by a dog would give you an in with the pro-dog faction."

Bettina shook her head. "He's terrified of other dogs. He's—" She'd been watching the dachshund and the collie as they veered toward the fenced enclosure that normally confined the dogs visiting the park. A small crowd of people standing near the enclosure had suddenly become restive.

"I'll tell you who has fleas!" came an angry voice floating across the grass.

A few people in the crowd with signs began waving them in time to a chant that began softly and then swelled. "*Lie* down *with* dogs/*Get* up *with* fleas/*Lie* down *with* dogs/*Get* up *with* fleas," and on and on.

"What's going on?" Bettina picked up her pace, heading straight for the hubbub and pulling Pamela along after her.

A pair of men detached themselves from the crowd, and the dachshund, who seemed to recognize his master, left off chasing the collie and joined them.

"I'll tell you who has fleas!" the angry voice, which belonged to the younger of the men, repeated. "That mangy mutt of yours."

"Schnitzel is not a mutt and he is not mangy!" The older man put his hands on his hips.

"Okay, Grandpa. Some of us have children instead of dogs, and we don't want our children stepping in who knows what when they play in the park." The younger man hopped back as Schnitzel dove for his ankle.

Meanwhile, the bearers of the signs had found another use for them. They were still being wielded rhythmically, but now they were landing rhythmically on the heads and shoulders of anyone within reach who appeared to be pro-dog. Several barking dogs arrived then, as well as the person in the dog costume.

Bettina had taken out her phone when she approached Ellin Taylor Mordaunt about an interview. Now she extended it before her, aiming this way and that to capture photos of the scene, which was rapidly becoming more frantic. The crowd had grown larger as people, pro-dog and anti-dog, bounded across the lawn to offer reinforcements to their faction. More signs were being deployed as weapons, and as the cardboard bearing the messages ripped and shredded, the poles to which the cardboard had been affixed proved useful for both defense and offense.

Grunts, groans, and curses emerged from the flailing mass of angry people, and dogs capered around its perimeter, barking incessantly. Some people who weren't fighting stood by, cheering on the fighters. Other people were fleeing the rampage, dashing along the sidewalk toward the border with Timberley or retreating beyond the fenced dog park where a sheltering stand of trees interrupted the expanse of lawn.

Cars had begun to back up on Arborville Avenue as drivers slowed to take in the spectacle. The traffic signal turned red and then green and then red again with no movement forward. From the south, too far back for those drivers to realize what was causing the sluggish traffic, came a chorus of honks, and very soon the yelp of a siren cut through the cacophony.

"I think you have enough photos," Pamela said, laying a hand on Bettina's arm. "Do you see any reason that we should stay around?"

"This is *news*!" Bettina whirled around. Her cheeks were pink with excitement and her eyes glowed.

"At least back up a little." Pamela tugged her closer to the sidewalk where a small cluster of onlookers who had been cautious enough to retreat but too curious to flee lingered at a prudent distance.

The siren had ceased its yelping, but the police car was nowhere in sight. Then Pamela noticed two uniformed officers loping over the grass from the south. Apparently they had given up trying to thread their way through the backed-up traffic in the police car and had turned onto a side street to park.

Another siren called her attention to the intersection with the light. As she watched, a police car pulled to the curb on the cross street and two officers she recognized as Officer Anders and Officer Sanchez climbed out. A few moments later, they had stationed themselves in the middle of the intersection and were waving cars through regardless of whether the light was red or green.

The officers who had been loping across the grass got closer, and Pamela recognized one of them as burly Officer Keenan. The other, younger and equally burly, didn't look familiar. They continued on their way toward the fracas, and Pamela followed their progress. The fracas, however, appeared to be slacking off of its own accord.

Most of the poles had been tossed to the ground, where they joined the scraps of torn cardboard bearing random words or parts of words, like "FLEAS" or "RRY FR." A few people were lying or sitting on the ground as well, and weary dogs had flopped here and there. Other people, whose stained and rumpled clothes or bloodstained handkerchiefs clutched to nose or cheek indicated they had been among the combatants, were standing, watching, as a last few angry insults were exchanged by a last determined few.

As the officers drew close, even the insults ceased, and belligerence gave way to a sheepish resignation. One man even stepped forward holding out his hands as if inviting handcuffs. Voices drifted across the lawn, low and authoritative on the part of the officers, cooperative and even meek on the part of those who had been engaged in the disturbance.

Bettina took a few last photos, featuring the officers and the chastened protestors, and turned to Pamela. A head tilt and partial shrug served in place of words to ask if Pamela was ready to leave. Pamela nodded, and they made their way to where the Toyota waited at the curb. Traffic had eased with the assistance of Officer Anders and Officer Sanchez, and Bettina was able to pull into the stream of cars now flowing smoothly toward the intersection and make the two right turns that would point the Toyota toward Orchard Street.

# CHAPTER 16

At first neither seemed inclined to talk about what they had just witnessed. Several blocks passed in silence until Bettina said, "At least Marcy Brewer wasn't there." Pamela nodded.

They were driving on a street that paralleled Arborville Avenue a few blocks to the east and, like Arborville Avenue, intersected with Orchard Street. When they reached the corner of Orchard Street, Bettina casually asked, "What are you doing tonight?" as she made her turn.

When Pamela didn't answer, Bettina glanced toward the passenger seat but continued driving. "We still have bean soup," she commented, "unless you have another commitment."

Pamela sighed, more audibly than she intended.

"I think there's even some corn bread," Bettina added, glancing toward the passenger seat once again.

"You might as well just pull over," Pamela said, "if

you're going to keep looking at me instead of the road."

"Okay." Bettina swerved toward the curb in front of a pleasant house whose front steps boasted a profusion of marigolds in decorative pots.

"I guess that means you're going to keep looking at me."

Indeed, Bettina was scrutinizing Pamela quite closely, tipping her head this way and that as if seeking the most illuminating vantage point.

"I don't have another commitment, if that's what you're wondering." Pamela spoke while gazing at the view visible through the Toyota's windshield, which was the cars in the Arborville Avenue intersection up ahead. "Pete Paterson has gone back to his ex-wife."

"No!" It was fortunate that Bettina had pulled over and stopped the car because her reaction to this news involved burying her face in her hands, leaving only scarlet-tipped fingers and scarlet waves visible. When she removed her hands from her face, it was to seize Pamela's hands and squeeze them while muttering, "I never trusted him."

"Bettina . . ." Pamela's throat tightened as a laugh threatened to become a sob. "You thought he was wonderful." She swallowed. "It's really better this way. I was never serious about him, and I think he missed his wife."

She leaned back against the seat and closed her eyes. Her face felt hot, and her eyelids had begun to sting. She put a hand to her cheek to soothe it and discovered that her fingertips were wet.

Even though her eyes were closed she could sense that Bettina was hovering. "Why are you crying," Bettina whispered, "if you were never serious about him?"

Pamela opened her eyes and reached out in an invitation for a hug. Bettina obliged, and Pamela gave in to the urge to weep. Soon gulping sobs blotted out everything but a dark roaring in her brain.

Bettina held on as tightly as if Pamela was in danger of being swept from her grasp by some powerful force. As the sobs abated, she drew back, and Pamela glimpsed a pair of hazel eyes darkened by concern, peering into her own. She disentangled herself from Bettina's embrace and raised a hand to her face, which was feverish beneath the salty slick of tears.

A tissue appeared, and then another, and she accepted them gratefully.

"Richard Larkin's former wife has moved in with him," she said in response to the unspoken question posed by Bettina's rippled forehead and the puzzled tilt of her brows.

"That's what you're really crying about, isn't it?"

Pamela nodded miserably and said, "Did you already know?"

"I knew someone was there . . ." Bettina nodded, also miserably, and added, "But I didn't know who. I didn't *want* to know." She offered another tissue. "You'll come home with me for dinner. That's settled."

After a brief detour to feed the cats and wash her face, Pamela crossed the street to join the Frasers for dinner. Wilfred answered the door and ushered her inside, his genial manner tinged with a curious . . . *deference*, it occurred to her—the deference one affords to the bereaved at a funeral. Bettina was sitting on the sofa, and the imprint of Wilfred's bulky form seemed to linger on the sofa cushion next to her, as if he'd just gotten up from a briefing on the recent and sad developments.

Even the cats seemed deferential. The next morning, instead of dashing down the stairs ahead of Pamela, Catrina and Ginger watched as she pulled on her fleecy robe and slid her feet into her fuzzy slippers. Then they led the way, but slowly, tipping their faces up from time to time as if monitoring her condition.

Precious fell in step with the procession once they reached the bottom of the stairs, and all three cats stationed themselves near the angle formed by the cupboards on adjoining walls, which they knew to be the spot were food appeared. Pamela set a large bowl and a small bowl on the counter and stooped to select two cans of cat food from the cupboard, Pick of the Wharf for Precious and Turkey Trot for Catrina and Ginger. As she peeled the lids back, releasing the aromas of fish and fowl, the cats stiffened, preparing themselves to pounce as soon as their meals were delivered.

Once the bowls had been lowered to the floor, the shared large one for Catrina and Ginger, and the small one for Precious, Pamela filled the kettle and set water to boil for coffee. As the cats hovered over their breakfast, nibbling delicately but with bodies tense, she hurried through the entry, across the porch, and down the steps in quest of the *Register*. The *Register*, in its customary plastic sleeve, lay nearly at the curb, and several feet to the east lay a smaller bundle that she recognized as the *Advocate*.

She headed first for the *Register*, scooped it up, and stepped toward the *Advocate*. As she stooped again, she heard a cheerful female voice greet her with, "Good morning, Pamela!"

A figure in a plaid flannel robe and fuzzy slippers was waving from Richard Larkin's front walk. Her untended hair, dishwater blond, suggested she had only recently climbed out of bed, and the fact that she was holding a partly unfolded newspaper in one hand and a limp plastic sleeve in the other indicated that her aim in venturing outdoors had been the same as Pamela's. Pamela realized that she was being greeted by the woman who had introduced herself as Maureen, Richard Larkin's ex but now apparently reconciled wife.

"Lovely day, isn't it?" Maureen called. She glanced at the unfolded newspaper in her hand and added, "Maybe not so lovely." She looked up. "There's been another of those murders! How shocking, and so soon after the one on Halloween."

"Another . . . what?" It took Pamela a moment to absorb what Maureen had said, then she slipped her own *Register* from its plastic sleeve and unfolded it.

A bold headline stretched across two columns at the top of the front page: BODY FOUND IN ARBORVILLE PARK AFTER PROTEST FRACAS. A smaller headline beneath it read, POLICE SUSPECT LINK TO DOG PARK CONTROVERSY.

Maureen had remained where she was, perhaps expecting a response.

"Shocking, yes," Pamela said after a moment, "and

disturbing, and—" The vision of a kettle hooting frantically while a blast of steam erupted from its spout rose before her eyes. "I've got water boiling on the stove," she called as she whirled around and sprinted for the porch.

The kettle *was* hooting, and the cats had vanished, leaving empty bowls, however. Pamela tossed the newspaper onto the table and lunged for the stove to silence the din. The *Register*'s boldface headline was jarring enough without a nerve-jangling soundtrack. She finished unfolding the newspaper and spread it out on the little table.

The byline was Marcy Brewer's, of course. Pamela skimmed the first few paragraphs and learned that the body was that of Arborville resident Trish Barfield, and it had been discovered in a stand of trees near a fenced area set aside for dogs. The victim had been stabbed. The discovery was made around six p.m. by a maintenance crew charged with cleaning up, after a protest against the town's proposal to enlarge the existing dog park devolved into a fight between those opposed and those in favor. It was not yet known whether the victim was passionate one way or another about the dog park proposal—though Pamela seemed to recall a Trish weighing in on the listserv.

Sustenance would be required to read more, Pamela decided. She accordingly fitted a paper filter into her carafe's plastic filter cone, spooned whole coffee beans into her coffee grinder, and pressed on the lid until their clattering smoothed out into a whisper. She tipped the grinder's aromatic contents into the filter cone and added the still steaming water from the kettle. As the water, transformed into coffee, dripped into the carafe, she toasted a slice of whole-grain bread and soon was seated at the table nibbling on toast and sipping coffee as she read the rest of Marcy Brewer's article.

The body had been discovered in the early evening, so the police had searched the victim's house in time for Marcy Brewer to report on details of that search. Most striking to Pamela was the information that a note had been found in the victim's house, a note reading, "When shall we three meet again?"

Pamela finished her last bite of toast and drained the last few sips from her coffee cup. Bettina had been known to dash across Orchard Street in her robe and slippers when there was dramatic news to discuss, but Pamela's simple toilette required only exchanging robe, pajamas, and slippers for jeans, a sweater, and loafers. Five minutes later, she had locked her front door behind her and was en route to the Frasers' house.

Wilfred, still wearing his robe and slippers, ushered her into a kitchen fragrant with coffee. The feeling of domestic comfort was enhanced by the presence of Woofus sprawled along the wall and Punkin snuggled into a compact loaf shape nearby. A lone coffee mug occupied the scrubbed pine table, whose surface was otherwise covered with scattered sections of the *Register*. Part 1 lay uppermost, open to the page where the continuation of the article about the latest murder appeared.

"Bettina went dashing out first thing," Wilfred said, "as soon as she got a look at that headline." He reached out and flipped the pages over so that the front page was visible. "Clayborn must have granted her an audience because she's been gone for a while."

Yes, the Toyota had been absent from the driveway, but Pamela had been so intent on her errand that its absence had registered only subliminally.

"There's plenty of coffee, toast too." Wilfred pulled a chair out for Pamela and tidied the newspapers. "She'll be wanting to talk to you, and I'm sure she'll be back soon. Clayborn can be stingy with his time."

"Just coffee is fine." Pamela lowered herself into the chair.

Wilfred picked up his own mug and headed for the stove. In a few moments, he was back with a steaming mug for Pamela and a refill of his own. No sooner had they enjoyed a few companionable sips of coffee than Woofus stirred, raising his shaggy head and hoisting himself to his feet as the sound of a key turning in a lock reached them. Seemingly aware that the visitor was not to be feared, he ambled through the doorway leading to the dining room.

Footsteps made their way across the patches of floor not covered by the living room and dining room rugs, and then Bettina stepped into the kitchen with Woofus at her side. She was carrying a white cardboard bakery box fastened securely with white string.

"Dear wife!" Wilfred rose to his feet, as delighted in his welcome as if they'd been apart for considerably longer than the time required for her errand. "Did you have a successful meeting with Arborville's redoubtable Lucas Clayborn?" He edged around the table and held out both hands for the bakery box.

Despite the fact that, according to Wilfred, Bettina had dashed out first thing, she had taken the time to choose an outfit that reflected her view of herself as a serious professional journalist, never mind that few readers of the *Advocate* took it seriously at all. She slipped off her pumpkin-colored down coat to reveal a silky maroon shirt with a floppy bow at the neckline. The shirt was tucked into well-fitted maroon wool pants that matched the maroon leather booties peeking out beneath.

"Well," she sighed as she draped her coat over a vacant chair and set her handbag, also maroon, on the chair's seat, "both these murders have been very ill-timed in terms of the *Advocate*'s publication schedule, not to mention the dog park protest and its aftermath yesterday."

She sat down and accepted a mug of coffee from Wilfred, adding, "For some reason Adrienne was coming into the police department just as I was leaving. I didn't say anything to her, though."

"Least said, soonest mended," Wilfred commented as he set three small sage-green plates, three forks, and three napkins on the table near the bakery box, which remained unopened. Then he folded the newspaper into a compact bundle and edged aside to set it on the high counter.

Bettina leaned forward and untied the bow that had anchored the string around the bakery box, and the string fell away. She folded back the lid, still talking.

"At least Marcy didn't scoop me on the dog park story. Of course, she had to mention it because the maintenance crew found the body while they were cleaning up after the rumpus, but I was there and she wasn't, and I even have photos, and when next week's *Advocate* comes out, everyone in Arborville will be able to read my eyewitness account."

"And they'll be very grateful, dear wife." Wilfred had taken his seat again and he leaned forward to peer inside the bakery box.

"Help yourself! Pamela too!" Bettina distributed plates, forks, and napkins to Pamela, Wilfred, and herself, and Wilfred nudged the box toward Pamela.

She reached in and pulled out a puffy golden round iced with a glossy layer of dark brown chocolate.

"Boston cream doughnuts," Bettina explained. "Obviously they're not actually doughnuts because there's no hole, but there's a surprise inside. Custard!"

Wilfred and Bettina helped themselves to doughnuts too, and the sweet treats, with the complement of coffee—whether bracingly bitter or as Bettina favored it—demanded total concentration then, and silence except for *yum*. The doughnut itself was toothsome and yeasty, the smooth custard filling hinted at vanilla, and the chocolate icing was all sweetness but for the dark undertone of cacao.

"Did you talk to Detective Clayborn?" Pamela asked, after picturing a disappointed Bettina being turned away on grounds of the detective's being too busy and then detouring to the Co-Op for a consolation prize.

But—"Oh, yes, yes, I did." Bettina nodded. "And as usual he's barking up the wrong tree."

"The dog park?" Pamela smiled.

"Why, yes"—Bettina smiled too—"speaking of barking. The body was found near the dog park and after the protest, which ended with the pro-dog people and the pro-children people attacking each other . . . so he thinks Trish Barfield's murder has something to do with the dog park controversy. Apparently she did post on the listserv."

Pamela nearly choked on the sip of coffee she had just taken. She set down her mug. "He has to be the one who told Marcy Brewer about the note his own police department found in Trish Barfield's house, 'When shall we three meet again?' The wording is exactly the same as the note Adrienne found after Mel's murder."

Bettina's lips tightened into a disgusted twist, its import clear despite the dab of chocolate on her chin.

"If I were Detective Clayborn," Pamela said, "I'd be asking myself what Mel Wordwoman and Trish Barfield had in common. In fact *I'm* asking myself that right now."

"He's not, though." Bettina shook her head so vigorously that the tendrils of her hair quivered. "Remember when Adrienne told us about the note she found, and how she gave the original to Clayborn?"

Pamela did remember, and she said, "Adrienne complained that he didn't listen . . . to *anything* she tried to tell him. I imagine that meant he didn't take the note seriously either."

"So . . . he ignored that note then and he's ignoring this one now to save face?"

"Looks like."

Wilfred had been listening intently while finishing his doughnut and sipping his coffee. Now he spoke. "The witches say, 'When shall we three meet again' in *Macbeth*. We were talking about that when Adrienne found the first note. The next line is 'In thunder, lightning, or in rain,' and Mel's murder happened during that Halloween night storm."

"As I recall"—Pamela squinted and felt her forehead crease—"the line after 'In thunder, lightning, or in rain' has something to do with a 'hurly-burly.'"

Wilfred nodded. "When it's done, I think. 'When the hurly-burly's done.'"

These ponderings were interrupted then by a ferocious bark from Woofus. He leaped to his feet and stationed himself at the doorway leading to the dining room. Punkin, startled by Woofus's sudden motion, rushed to take shelter under the table. The cause of all this activity became clear the next moment as the doorbell sounded.

# CHAPTER 17

Wilfred rose from his chair, tugged at his belt to make sure his robe was decently anchored, and crossed to the doorway, where he eased past Woofus.

"A delivery, perhaps?" Bettina shrugged. "Sometimes they ring just to let you know they've left something on the porch."

But soon it became evident that Wilfred had opened the door to find a person rather than a package. "No, no," they heard him say, "you're not interrupting anything. We're just having a midmorning coffee break."

When he returned to the kitchen, he was escorting Adrienne, who seemed exceptionally subdued, with no trace of her usual coquettish manner. Bettina had mentioned that she saw Adrienne entering the building that housed the police department just as she herself was leaving, and Adrienne had apparently dressed for whatever errand she contemplated there. Beneath her creamy leather jacket she was wearing the buttery-yellow sweater and slacks ensemble that nearly matched the color of her hair, but that hair hung in limp strands around a face from which her bleak eyes stared.

Ever the gentleman, Wilfred removed Bettina's coat and handbag from the table's fourth chair and managed them with one hand while pulling out the chair for Adrienne with the other. Bettina was busy watching the interaction as a skeptical pucker appeared between her brows, but Pamela jumped up, relieved Wilfred of his burden, and deposited coat and handbag in the dining room.

"There's still some coffee"—Wilfred gestured toward the stove—"and I think we have"—he lifted the lid of the bakery box and peeked inside—"another Boston cream doughnut."

The pucker between Bettina's brows intensified.

Once seated, Adrienne had seemed to collapse, her head drooping forward and her shoulders bowing. Now she raised her eyes to Wilfred and uttered a meek, "Yes, please."

He hurried off toward where the carafe waited, lit the burner under it, and returned with a plate, fork, napkin, and spoon. Then he was off again, waiting by the stove and watching for the little bubbles that would indicate the coffee was hot again and ready to pour.

Silence settled over the table like a physical presence, with Adrienne's head drooping and eyes downcast, Bettina scowling, and Pamela unsure whether the moment required small talk or something else.

The silence endured as Wilfred delivered a steaming mug of coffee, invited Adrienne to help herself to the remaining Boston cream doughnut, and resumed his seat. Waving away the offered sugar and cream, she sipped the coffee with what seemed like gratitude, and after a few bites of Boston cream doughnut, she murmured, "You're very kind." Her glance as she spoke took in all three people sitting around the table.

Bettina's expression of disbelief was almost comical as she continued scowling but shaped her lips into an amused zigzag.

"I have a confession to make," Adrienne said, addressing the remains of the Boston cream doughnut on her plate. "I lied to you. I *was* involved with a married man."

She looked up as if to assess the reaction to her statement. Pamela herself was merely curious to hear more and imagined that her face reflected only pleasant interest. Bettina's expression hadn't changed, and Wilfred's benevolent gaze hinted at forgiveness to come.

Adrienne continued talking. "Brock Pomfret said he was single, and he liked my cooking. I was shocked when I learned that he was married. I would never have taken up with him if I'd known the truth." She shook her head and repeated, "Never."

Bettina's expression had gradually softened—or maybe sharpened. Reporter Bettina was taking over, Pamela reflected, stifling a laugh.

"What about Kurt Hodges?" Bettina inquired, now clearly in interview mode.

Adrienne's head shake turned into a nod and the word "Yes" squeaked out. "The same thing," she went on. "He said he was single, but he wasn't."

"And now—let me guess"—Bettina allowed herself a satisfied smile—"you're worried either June Pomfret or Paulette Hodges is the killer and you're going to be the next victim, and you showed up at the police station this morning to confess to Detective Clayborn."

Adrienne's eyes grew wide and her lips stretched into a wondering smile. The expression would have suited an actress in an advertisement for some new and amazing product.

"Ohhh," she breathed. "You are truly brilliant, Bettina."

Bettina, who often feigned admiration as she sought the cooperation of an interviewee—much to Pamela's amusement—appeared not to suspect an ulterior motive behind Adrienne's compliment. The satisfied smile took on a tinge of sympathy.

"I *am* afraid of that." Adrienne's expression changed too, and the bleak stare returned. Her voice faltered. "Very afraid. In fact, I don't know what to do, but you always know what to do."

"I suspect Clayborn pooh-poohed the idea that jealousy could be the motive and said the second murder had nothing to do with the first."

"That's exactly what he said, but maybe the second victim had an affair with Brock Pomfret or Kurt Hodges too, and now . . ." The sentence dissolved into a strangled moan, and Adrienne lowered her face into her hands. After a bit, she slid her fingers down far enough to reveal her eyes, smudged with tears and smeared makeup. "June Pomfret or Paulette Hodges is going to come after me, and I don't have anyone"—she glanced at Wilfred—"to protect me."

"Clayborn is ignoring the notes," Bettina said. "According to the *Register*, police found one of those 'When shall we three meet again' notes at Trish Barfield's house too."

"I know that!" Unexpectedly, Adrienne pounded the table, causing Woofus to stir. "And I pointed that out, and it's so clear. The *we three* refers to a lovers' triangle—me, the husband who I didn't know was a husband, and the jealous wife."

"Well!" Bettina straightened her spine and lifted her chin. "We'll just have to figure out what June Pomfret and Paulette Hodges were doing leading up to the time the maintenance crew found the body last evening."

"Great!" Adrienne jumped to her feet and leaned over to hug Bettina. "When do we leave?" She raised a hand to her cheek, which was still damp with tears. "I should wash my face, though . . . freshen up. I must look a fright." The hand strayed to her hair.

"Pamela and I will strategize," Bettina announced. "You go home and wash your face."

Wilfred rose and escorted Adrienne from the kitchen. After they had disappeared, Pamela turned to Bettina, scarcely able to contain her laughter.

"You've certainly changed your attitude toward Adrienne," she said.

"Martin Cotswold is definitely out of the picture," Bettina responded, "after this dog park thing."

"We'd pretty much already agreed that he wasn't a suspect because he's too tall and he might have been out West on Halloween. Remember?"

Bettina's expression and tone implied injured dignity. "You think I was taken in by Adrienne's flattery, don't you?"

"She was being pretty obvious about it."

"Never mind that." Bettina tossed her head as if to shake off the idea. "What I'm thinking is that I need to do a follow-up article on the dog park story. What's the position of the typical Arborvillian? I'll start by interviewing June and Paulette."

"But"—Pamela felt a puzzled grimace supplant her amused smile—"we decided the dog park controversy wasn't the motive for the new murder because the new murder is linked to the old murder."

"*Duh*." Bettina laughed. "I know that, but if June and/or Paulette were at the park, that gives us a hint, and if they weren't at the park, that gives us another hint. If they were far, far away from the park, maybe we can be sure they couldn't possibly have killed a person there before six p.m. when the maintenance crew found the body."

Wilfred spoke up then. "I'm thinking there was a detail in Marcy Brewer's article that could make the time of the murder more specific." He pushed himself to his feet and circled around the table to fetch the *Register* from the high counter.

Back in his chair, he smoothed out Part 1 and flipped to the inner page where the story of the murder continued. He bent over the page, brow furrowed and reading quietly to himself. Then he planted a finger on the page and looked up with a triumphant grin.

"'Based on the fact that the body was cold and rigor mortis had begun to take effect, police estimated that the murder had occurred one or two hours before the body was found.'"

"A little bit after we left," Pamela commented, "or maybe even while we were still there. But it happened back in that stand of trees, and the fight after the protest was just simmering down so people were focused on that."

"How clever you are to remember that, sweetheart!" Bettina beamed at her husband. "So let's say three or four o'clock. What were June and Paulette doing at three or four o'clock yesterday?" She stood up and addressed Pamela. "Let's start with Paulette."

Pamela remained sitting. "What about Adrienne? She's the one who recruited you to do this."

"She'll just get in the way." Bettina waved her hands in a hurry-up gesture. "Come on! Let's get going!"

Paulette and Kurt Hodges lived in the neighborhood called the Palisades, not far from where the Bascombs lived. The house was quite grand, a classic center hall Colonial built of brick and featuring a porch flanked by white columns. A tasteful arrangement of autumn flowers and ornamental cabbage decorated the porch, along with pumpkins of various sizes.

"Wendelstaff College," Bettina commented as they proceeded up the sloping front walk to the house, which looked down from a slight hill. She pointed toward the car parked in the driveway, an Audi with a Wendelstaff College decal on the back window.

"Somebody's home," Pamela responded. "If Paulette's a professor—or a late-in-life student—she could easily have been in Arborville yesterday afternoon. Professors and students have pretty flexible schedules."

But when they met Kurt Hodges, it appeared more likely that it was he who had the Wendelstaff connection. Bettina proffered her business card and introduced herself as a reporter for the *Advocate*, adding that she was surveying townspeople about the dog park controversy for a projected article. Kurt Hodges blinked a few times like a person startled by an unexpected interruption. He was tall and slender with abundant hair starting to gray around the temples, and he was dressed in corduroy pants and a well-worn cardigan sweater. He carried a book in one hand and a pair of glasses in the other.

"Dog park controversy?" he inquired, blinking again. His eyes were a shade of blue that gave him a defenseless air. "I'm not sure I know what that is."

"Perhaps your wife has been following the issue?" Bettina offered a hopeful smile.

"Not here." He shook his head. "I mean *she's* not here. Hardly ever here. Works too hard."

"Maybe not too interested in day-to-day life in Arborville?" Bettina suggested.

"She's not even in Arborville. Hasn't been for a month. Out on the West Coast, working."

Bettina gave Pamela a triumphant glance and Pamela nodded. Kurt Hodges was watching, but he didn't seem surprised by or even interested in Bettina's reaction—though a reporter seeming pleased that a trip in quest of an interview had been wasted might have puzzled another person.

"Is that all then?" Kurt Hodges asked in a pleasant voice. "I was spending the afternoon with Voltaire." He lifted the book, revealing a finger marking a page.

"Of course," Bettina said. "Of course. We'll let you get back to your reading. I'm sorry for the interruption."

"I always pick up my copy of the *Advocate*," he added as they turned away. "I'm not one of those people who lets it litter their driveway."

Bettina was silent until they neared the curb. "I guess Paulette is the main breadwinner," she commented then. "These Palisades houses don't come cheap, and professors don't make a lot of money."

"I can see why he might have strayed, though Adrienne hardly seems his type," Pamela said. "But life with a spouse who's never home could be lonely even for a bookworm."

"We can cross Paulette off our list of suspects." Bettina took her keys from her handbag.

"The idea that the killer was really after Adrienne makes a lot of sense," Bettina said, "especially now that we know for sure—because Adrienne confessed what she'd been up to—that there were two jealous wives in Arborville."

"Motive." Pamela nodded. "And as far as means

goes, everybody has knives, and what better *opportunity* than Halloween night, with people roaming around in costumes in the dark or a brawl providing a distraction from a murder going on elsewhere in the park."

They had reached Bettina's car. Pamela paused as Bettina unlocked the doors, they settled into their seats, and Bettina twisted her key in the ignition. With a sound like the engine clearing its throat, the Toyota came to life. Soon they were cruising along the street that sloped downhill to Arborville Avenue, past yards whose lawns were buried in fallen leaves like patchworks of red, gold, amber, and yellow.

"June is the only one left," Pamela said. "Unless she very definitely was somewhere else while Trish Barfield was being murdered, I'd say that Adrienne has reason to be worried."

"Maybe there's a different way to do it than talking to June herself." Bettina braked as they reached the stop sign at Arborville Avenue.

"Neighbors," Pamela said.

"She lives way down at the other end of town near Roland's house, and we never ate lunch." Bettina edged forward and then made her turn.

Bettina had a point. They'd been drinking coffee and eating Boston cream doughnuts when Adrienne arrived, and they'd gone dashing out with only that to sustain them. Pamela's own stomach was telling her that it was time for something more nourishing.

As they neared the corner of Orchard Street, Bettina clicked on her turn signal, and with no further discussion they were soon pulling up beside Wilfred's ancient but lovingly cared-for Mercedes in the Frasers' drive-way.

The first sound they heard upon stepping through the front door was laughter, the mingled laughter of a man and a woman, with the man's laughter providing a bass accompaniment to the woman's delicate trill. The laughter was coming from the kitchen.

Pamela followed Bettina across the living room floor and through the dining room arch. Bettina halted at the kitchen doorway and Pamela nearly bumped into her. Peeking around her friend after she regained her balance, Pamela saw Adrienne sitting at the scrubbed pine table. She was leaning confidingly toward Wil-fred, who occupied a neighboring chair.

Adrienne was facing the doorway and noticed the new arrivals right away. She had obviously gone home to freshen up, as she had planned. Her makeup was flawless and the blond waves of her hair even seemed to have regained their bounce.

"Bettina!" she exclaimed. "I'm so glad you're here."

"Oh?" Bettina sounded skeptical.

"Dear wife!" Wilfred rose and stepped around the table to pull out chairs for Bettina and Pamela.

"I absolutely don't have to worry about June Pom-fret anymore," Adrienne said, "and I'm so relieved. One down and one to go."

Bettina raised her brows. The meaning of the look wasn't totally clear, but Pamela was sure Bettina was too kind to keep secret the fact that Adrienne didn't need to worry about Paulette Hodges anymore either.

Adrienne required no prompting to go on. "I was so

flustered when I left the police station this morning that I came straight back to Orchard Street without doing an errand I needed to do at the bank, so I put myself back together and went uptown again. And there at the bank, who should I run into but Brock Pomfret! We're still good friends"—she added a smile for emphasis—"despite all that happened.

"We chatted, like people do, and I asked what he and June had been up to." The smile became mischievous, and Adrienne glanced around the table, as if checking that her audience was paying attention. "Brock and June were at the theater last night, in the city, with dinner near Times Square before."

She leaned back and folded her arms. "That's an alibi for sure, I'd say. June couldn't have committed the dog park murder, so that means she's not the person who came looking for me on Halloween night either."

Bettina raised her brows again. "Paulette has an alibi too," she said.

"She does?" Adrienne inhaled, then seemed to hold her breath, with mouth and eyes open wide.

Bettina described the conversation she and Pamela had had with Kurt Hodges.

"So Paulette hasn't even been in Arborville for ages," Adrienne murmured after she exhaled. "You ladies are the best, and all I can say is that I'm very disappointed in Lucas. And we still don't know who killed my sister."

She climbed to her feet, an action that caused Bettina to turn to Pamela with a grateful look that she didn't try to disguise.

Once Adrienne was gone, escorted to the door by Wilfred, Bettina spoke. But her comment didn't relate to anything they had just learned or revealed. Rather, it was, "We still haven't had lunch."

"Bean soup," came Wilfred's voice from the dining room. "There's plenty left and I was just going to warm it up when Adrienne arrived." He stepped through the doorway and headed for the cooking area of the kitchen.

"It seems all the suspects have now been eliminated," Pamela said.

"It seems that way." Bettina nodded.

# CHAPTER 18

Forty-five minutes later, Pamela took her leave, stepping from the Frasers' welcoming house, now fragrant with ham-accented bean soup, into a bright but chilly fall afternoon. As she lingered on the porch for a minute, Bettina said, "Come for lunch tomorrow, a real lunch served at lunchtime. Wilfred is going out to Newfield famers market first thing in the morning and is sure to come back with something good."

Pamela had a food excursion on her schedule too, but not as far from Arborville. Her pantry was nearly bare and, with a few hours of light remaining, the timing seemed right for a walk uptown. At home, she collected canvas totes and the grocery list fastened to the refrigerator with a mitten magnet and then she hurried out to the Co-Op.

Once there, guiding her cart over the Co-Op's creaking wooden floors, she picked up items from the produce section, the meat and fish counters, the inner aisle where the cat food resided, the dairy section, the cheese counter, and the bread counter. Weighed down by the now bulging totes, she made her way back to Orchard Street, where the walk from the corner of Arborville Avenue headed straight into a setting sun. The bands of glowing color that streaked the horizon rivaled the shades displayed by the autumn foliage.

Catrina and Ginger greeted her in the entry, seemingly aware that part of the bounty contained in the unwieldy totes was intended for them. Pamela rested the totes on the table and extracted cucumbers, cherry tomatoes, cheese, and bread from one. From the other, she took a salmon filet, an organic chicken, and numerous cans of cat food.

"It's not dinnertime yet," she murmured to the cats as she stowed the cans in the cupboard. When the other groceries had been put away, she climbed the stairs to her office, settled at her desk, and summoned her computer to beeping and whirring life. Another push of a button illuminated her monitor's screen, and after a quick check of her email, she opened Word and pondered the titles of the two articles waiting to be evaluated, "Cat Mummies" and "Fashioning Witchcraft." She opened the file for the first.

The full title of "Cat Mummies" proved to be . . . "Cat Mummies"—unlike so many articles whose titles consisted of a catchy phrase followed by a colon and a less catchy but more informative phrase. But had Pamela still been uncertain that the article was really about . . . cat mummies, the photos that the author had included removed all doubt.

The photo credits indicated that the cat mummies could be found in numerous museums. They resembled large loaves of Italian bread that had been wrapped with variously colored bands of cloth woven together to create complex patterns. And the loaves had heads modeled to resemble the heads of cats and painted in a most realistic way. The modeled cat heads looked out on the world through eyes accented with the same cosmetics seen in Egyptian depictions of humans, but their level gaze was one that Pamela recognized from her own cats. *I may be smaller than you*, it seemed to say, *but I am your equal*. Were there dog mummies too? she wondered. Someone had asserted on Access-Arborville that the ancient Egyptians worshipped dogs.

The article itself described the process by which the ancient Egyptians came to consider cats sacred, starting with their very useful role in protecting stored grain from rats and mice. Eventually cats were considered as worthy of an afterlife as a human might be, and therefore their bodies were mummified in order to preserve them until the life force that had departed at their death returned to reanimate them.

The bands of cloth used in the mummification process were linen, sometimes dyed different colors, and linen of course was a fiber. But was the linen used in mummification different from the linen people wore in their everyday clothes? And was the linen used in cat mummification different from the linen used in human mummification?

Pamela sighed. The article was so appealing—especially the photos—but she wasn't sure that *Fiber*

*Craft* was the most suitable venue for its publication. Of course *Fiber Craft* had published articles on rag dolls and quilts and vintage clothing and all kinds of things whose relevance to the magazine's focus was simply that they were made out of cloth, which was made out of fiber. The cat mummies were really no different.

She opened her evaluations file and wrote an enthusiastic recommendation that the article be published, suggesting, though, that the author be requested to add a section on linen production in ancient Egypt and clarify whether linen of a particular grade was reserved for mummies of all sorts. If only a special grade of linen was used for human mummies and the same special linen was used for cat mummies, that would reflect all the more the esteem in which cats were held.

Night had fallen as Pamela worked, and the room in which she sat was dark except for the pool of light cast by her desk lamp. She saved her work, closed her files and Word, and made her way downstairs for dinner and a quiet evening of knitting and a BBC mystery.


Wilfred was just climbing out of his car as Pamela stepped out onto her porch en route to lunch with the Frasers the next day. She watched him head for the house carrying two large bags. He was trailed by Woofus, who had apparently accompanied him on his errand and was particularly interested in the contents of one of the bags.

She waited a few moments, enjoying the bright day

and the air that seemed golden with the glow of autumn foliage. Once Wilfred had disappeared inside, she crossed the street and rang the Frasers' doorbell.

It was Bettina who answered, dressed as if prepared for an outing rather than a simple lunch at home with a neighbor. Her ensemble contrasted slacks in a rich camel shade with the burnt-orange tunic that had been one of her knitting projects. A silky scarf that combined those colors with burgundy and coral accented the neckline and on her feet were her burgundy suede booties.

She glanced down at the outfit as Pamela seemed to stare and said, "I'm covering the battle of the bands at the high school this afternoon. Remember?" Then she reached out a hand and added, "Come on into the kitchen. Wilfred brought back sausages and he's just about to start frying them."

Bettina had already set the table, the scrubbed pine one in the kitchen, for lunch. Napkins printed with marigolds and other bright blooms sat atop place mats sewn from a quilted version of the same fabric, and knives, forks, and spoons waited on either side of sage-green plates. Wilfred had already placed his favorite skillet on the stove and was tying his apron around his ample waist. Woofus lay sprawled along the wall in the position that gave him a view out the sliding glass doors.

Arranged on the counter near the stove were two plastic bins and a bundle wrapped in white butcher paper. A bulging paper bag with a few green apples peeking out of the top sat on the high counter. It shared the counter space with a mysterious object hidden by a tent of aluminum foil.

"The bag of apples is for you, Pamela," Wilfred said by way of greeting. "Granny Smiths from Upstate New York."

"And," Bettina chimed in, "under that foil is a yellow plate holding a chocolate chip pound cake." Her expression implied a certain lack of enthusiasm. "Yes," she added, "Adrienne was here, first thing this morning in fact, and the chocolate chip pound cake is a thank-you gift."

Wilfred had already turned back to his cooking, lighting the flame under the skillet, adding a dollop of oil to it, and unwrapping the paper-wrapped bundle.

"Bratwurst," he explained, as he folded back the paper to reveal a string of plump and pale sausages. "Homemade from farm-raised pork and veal."

Soon the bratwurst were sizzling in the skillet. As they sizzled, Wilfred tended them gently with a long-handled fork and Bettina reverted to the topic of Adrienne.

"The mystery is by no means solved," she said, "even though Adrienne is relieved that she doesn't seem to have been the actual target. And now there's even a new mystery besides—who killed Trish Barfield?— though it's probably the same mystery because of the note."

Pamela listened, nodding but having no thoughts to add. Bettina went on, however, after shaking her head and tightening her lips into a meditative line. "I'm finished with it, though. I don't know why we even allowed ourselves to get pulled into it in the first place."

Pamela forbore commenting that Adrienne's flattery might have been a factor.

"Let *Lucas* figure it out"—Bettina gestured, open-handed, as if relinquishing the job—"not that *I* would ever call him that."

Wilfred, meanwhile, had been busy. The bratwurst were turning a tantalizing shade of golden brown and beginning to glisten. On the counter near the stove, the plastic bins had disappeared. In their place were an oval sage-green bowl mounded with what looked like potato salad and a small sage-green platter piled with cucumber spears whose color and texture suggested they were partly pickled.

"We're eating very soon," Wilfred announced. He picked up the bowl of potato salad and stepped to the end of the high counter, where Bettina took it and carried it to the table. Pamela did likewise when he handed her the pickles.

"We'll need three tall glasses too," he said, leaving the question of what they were to contain hanging in the air like a pleasant mystery, emphasized by a teasing but genial smile.

That question was soon answered, but not until three tall glasses from Bettina's Swedish crystal set had been added to the place settings and a platter holding six golden brown sausages, so plump they seemed ready to burst, had been placed in the middle of the table. Then, as Pamela and Bettina took their seats, Wilfred opened the refrigerator, reached inside, and advanced on the table bearing a tall bottle made of brown glass.

Making a slight ceremony of it, he flourished a bottle opener. The cap clicked off with a fizzy pop and he tilted the bottle over Pamela's glass. A tawny liquid chugged into the glass, forming a layer of bubbly foam as it rose. The spicy aroma made Pamela's nose tingle.

"Root beer," Wilfred explained with a delighted laugh. "A couple that makes artisanal soft drinks brings their wares to the farmers market." He filled the other two glasses and settled into his chair, wasting not a minute before uttering his customary, "Bon appétit!"

The beverage service had been dramatic and the meal itself was scarcely an anticlimax. Soon each plate had been provided with a sausage, a generous serving of potato salad, and a few of the pickled cucumbers. The potato salad was German potato salad, also from the farmers market, dressed with bacon drippings and vinegar rather than mayonnaise. It was flecked with bits of smoky salty bacon and shreds of cooked onion that tasted of bacon drippings. The cucumbers were barely pickled, still crisp and not too salty—a perfect complement to the rich potato salad and the mild but meaty bratwurst.

"Your drive to Newfield was well worth it," Bettina said after an enthusiastic but nonverbal reaction to her first few bites.

Pamela chimed in too, praising the food and adding that the chilled and fizzy root beer was the perfect accompaniment. The conversation drifted then to the Frasers' upcoming plans involving the Boston children, who would be coming down for Thanksgiving.

The Arborville granddaughter, Betty, would be old enough this year, they were sure, to have some kind of meaningful interaction with her older cousin, Morgan. Soon the plates and glasses were empty, even of second helpings and refills from a fresh bottle of root beer.

"I could not eat one more bite," Bettina declared, patting her stomach, "even though Adrienne's chocolate chip pound cake is sitting right there on the counter."

"I'm certainly full," Pamela agreed.

"The pound cake will wait." Wilfred nodded.

"And anyway"—Bettina leaned against the table edge and pushed herself to her feet—"I've got to get going. I want to interview Nadine, and I'm sure she'll be busy once the student musicians start showing up."

Wilfred was on his feet then too. "I'm coming later," he said. "Live music is live music, even if high school kids these days have different tastes than a classic rock guy like me."

Bettina went on her way, and Pamela stayed behind to help Wilfred tidy up, a process that included giving Woofus several bits of sausage. She took the farmers market apples with her when she left.

Sitting at her computer, Pamela opened the last article remaining from the batch Celine Bramley had sent the previous Wednesday. Its full title was "Fashioning Witchcraft: What Witches Wore," and the author was a professor in the folklore department at a college in Salem, Massachusetts.

Witches, it appeared, sometimes wore nothing at

all—at least in the imaginations of those who feared their power. More likely, though, they dressed like other sixteenth- and seventeenth-century women. Why, the author inquired, would they want to call attention to themselves in an era when being accused of witchcraft could result in excruciating torture and death?

Women spinners, weavers, and knitters were particularly suspect—and on this point the article overlapped interestingly with "Fiber Arts and the Dark Arts," which she had earlier read and rejected. The ability to turn an amorphous mass of fiber into a length of cloth and then a garment must have been seen as somehow beyond human—especially female—capability, unless some supernatural force was brought in to assist.

Pamela's mind wandered back to Mel's condemnation of domestic fiber arts and crafts—"You weave the web that is your prison." So illogical, when in earlier times these arts and crafts were considered manifestations of a frightening power.

She returned to the article, scrolling down as she read. With a topic like this, it would seem almost obligatory to quote from the witches' scene in *Macbeth*, and so the author had: "When shall we three meet again,/ In thunder, lightning, or in rain?/ When the hurly-burly's done,/ When the battle's lost and won."

She stopped scrolling and stared at the words. The notes associated with the murders of Mel and Trish had quoted the first line, and Wilfred had even pointed out that the night Mel was killed certainly fit the next: "In thunder, lightning, or in rain." But maybe the circumstances of the second murder were described by the next line. A hurly-burly, she believed, was something like a rumpus, like what had happened at the dog park protest.

Pamela minimized the page she had been reading and opened her browser. The day she joined the Frasers for bean soup, Bettina had consulted her phone for details on the long-ago Halloween tragedy involving the girl struck by lightning, but Pamela had been more interested in Wilfred's progress with his bean and ham bone soup. Now she did her own Googling.

There had been four girls, daring the storm to do its worst, but only one of the girls had been killed. Pamela leaned close to the computer monitor. The article had appeared twenty-five years ago, before everything was digital, and she was reading a scan of a printed page. The four girls were named, but they had been *girls*, and their last names had been their birth names, Melissa Wilson . . . Trish Unger . . . Nadine Barnes . . . and Heather Cotton. Who were they now? Things became so confusing when women got married and changed their names.

Bettina had declared she was through with the mystery, but somehow Pamela felt she had made a breakthrough that Bettina should know about. Bettina was at the battle of the bands though.

Battle! When the battle's lost and won!


Without even bothering to close the page still glowing on her monitor's screen, Pamela rolled back her chair and jumped to her feet. She bounded down the stairs, grabbed her purse and keys, pulled the front door open, and hopped across the threshold. A few minutes later, she was speeding down Orchard Street toward County Road.

Waiting for a break in the traffic to make her turn at the corner, she felt herself panting, as if she'd run the half block rather than driving. Her heart, usually so unobtrusive in its labors, had begun to throb with a steady, speedy pulse. A large delivery truck passed, momentarily blotting out the reddening sky to the west. Once the truck cleared the intersection, Pamela swung the steering wheel to the right and joined the stream of vehicles heading north.

The high school lay to the west of County Road, not far from the Timberley border. The turnoff was marked by an impressive sign announcing that Arborville High was the home of the mighty Aardvarks and featuring a cartoon aardvark rendered in the school colors of turquoise and gold. The road marked by the sign meandered down a slight hill and ended in a vast parking lot bounded to the west by a football field.

A few cars were already leaving the parking lot, suggesting that the battle of the bands had ended. Pamela sped up, pressing hard on the gas pedal and feeling the car lurch ahead. Instead of easing into one of the marked spots as she pulled closer to the high school's main entrance—heavy glass doors in a bland façade of buff-colored bricks—she simply came to a halt a few yards from the short flight of steps that led to the doors.

The doors were open as a stream of people flowed through them, students in jeans or sweatpants or leggings topped with fleece or down jackets, and parents and grandparents in outfits not that much different. A few students carried instrument cases or had gig bags slung over their shoulders. Laughter and chatter filled the air. A few people noticed as Pamela sprang from her casually parked car and slammed the door behind her, but most continued on their route down the steps and across the asphalt.

She was the only one entering the building rather than exiting, and the process of edging upstream among people heading downstream who were themselves crowded by other people heading downstream left her panting even more intensely. Once she was through the doorway, the crowd thinned and she found herself in a wide hall that smelled of floor wax.

Reasoning that the people she passed were coming from the auditorium where the battle of the bands had taken place, she continued her upstream progress, turning a corner and then another until—like a most welcome vision—she spied a familiar figure. Wilfred was ambling along, chatting with a man of similar grandfatherly mien, surrounded by other apparent stragglers as the concert venue emptied out.

"Pamela!" he exclaimed. "What are you doing here?"

"Looking for Bettina!" Pamela imagined she must seem quite frantic, to judge by the startled reaction she had elicited from Wilfred's companion. "She's all right, I'm sure, but someone else isn't!"

"What on earth?" Wilfred darted forward, dodging around a cluster of giggling young women. He peered into Pamela's face, then stepped back. "She's talking to Nadine, the woman who organized the event—checking on some details for her article. What's wrong?"

"Where are they?" Pamela nearly screamed it, and the startled man drew back. "We have to find them!" She grabbed Wilfred's arm and pulled him around in the direction he had come from. "Are they in the auditorium? Is it this way?"

# CHAPTER 19

Wilfred kept pace with Pamela as they hurried toward a pair of double doors at the end of the hallway. They were within several yards of reaching the doors when, with the metallic clang of a latch being disengaged, one of them sprang open and Bettina stepped forth.

"Bettina!" Pamela's voice overlapped with Wilfred's, and both added, in chorus, "We were looking for you," but Pamela went on to say, with considerable urgency, "Where's Nadine?"

"In her office, I think." Bettina blinked a few times and reached out as if to offer a soothing pat. "She got a message that someone wanted to meet her there. Has something happened?"

"I hope not!" Pamela whirled around, surveying the hallway for a doorway that might be Nadine's office. The whirling motion, and the fact that she had become quite breathless, nearly threw her off-balance.

"It's back here." Bettina retreated toward the door

she had just come through, seized the handle, and jerked it open. "Follow me, but please tell me what's going on."

A sloping aisle led past rows of seats to the broad stage. As they jogged along, Pamela gasped out, "Nadine is the last of the three and the battle's been lost and won and the person who killed Mel and Trish is about to kill her, and I *think* I know who that person is."

They reached a T-intersection with another aisle that paralleled the stage. Bettina veered to the right and led the way to a door in the side wall of the auditorium. She pushed on the exit bar and, over the clanking of the door hardware as the door swung open, they could hear a voice.

"'Is this a dagger which I see before me,' the voice declaimed, seeming to strive for dramatic effect. Then the voice added, in more conversational tones, "Well, a kitchen knife anyway, but stabbing seemed Shakespearean and Shakespearean seemed appropriate."

A whimper interrupted briefly, but the voice went on, "And this dagger—or kitchen knife, if you want to be a spoil sport—*is* real, even though Macbeth didn't think the one in his vision was real. At least that's what Mrs. Sheridan told us in English class."

"What on earth?" Bettina whispered. "That voice sounds like Gayle Witherspoon."

"Birth name Gayle Cotton," Pamela whispered back. "Her sister was the girl struck by lightning in the Halloween storm twenty-five years ago."

A hallway stretched ahead with doors opening off each side. A door halfway down was ajar. They proceeded on tiptoes.

"Why are you doing this?" another voice, a faltering voice, inquired.

"You killed my sister," came the answer. "You and your friends. She wanted to be accepted by you because she thought you were the popular girls, the girls who were into cool things, but you were really the mean girls. You led her out to that open field during the lightning storm. I suppose you told her it was some kind of initiation to your group, some Halloween ritual."

Bettina turned to Pamela. Pamela was surprised to note that instead of looking frightened, Bettina simply looked irritated. Before she knew what was happening, Bettina sprinted the last few yards that lay between her and the office from which the voices emanated. She pushed at the partly open door, and it swung back with a clunk.

By then, Pamela had reached Bettina, standing behind her with Wilfred hovering behind them both. Gayle whirled around, her face an unbecoming shade of red and her nondescript mouth frozen in a snarl. In her hand she held a wooden-handled knife with a lethal, gleaming blade.

"I won't be back to your knitting group," she muttered. Then she raised the knife and took a step forward, adding, "But then, neither will you."

Behind her, Pamela sensed Wilfred stirring. But within the office, Gayle's potential victim had taken advantage of the interruption to bestir herself as well. Among the objects that decorated Nadine's desk was a large bust of Elvis, plaster perhaps, and painted in gaudy colors that rendered his complexion pink, his pompadour and sideburns a dramatic black, and his eyes a piercing blue. Near it was a sheet of paper, like a flyer, on which was printed in large letters, "When shall we three meet again?"

As Gayle took another step toward Bettina, Nadine seized the bust, hopped forward, and brought it down on Gayle's head with an impact that crumpled her to the floor. The knife flew from her hand and skimmed across the threshold, bouncing past Pamela's feet.

"Dear wife!" Wilfred lurched around Pamela and opened his arms for Bettina to take refuge. She seemed disinclined, however, at least for a moment. She surveyed her fallen adversary, who had landed face-first but had now rolled onto her side.

"I knew you were up to something, Gayle Witherspoon," she said. "And you had a lot of nerve letting Roland waste his time on you when you weren't even trying to 'remember' how to knit, if you ever even knew."

Pamela, meanwhile, had taken out her phone and was tapping 911 into the keypad. Nadine, a stylish woman with a pixie haircut that set off her bold hoop earrings, had sagged into her desk chair, clearly depleted by the experience she had just been through. Elvis lay in plaster fragments on the vinyl tile floor.

"We were mean," Nadine murmured, "and very young and very stupid, and I've never forgotten what we did that night. Mel had an uncanny ability to . . . almost hypnotize people, make people believe what she wanted them to believe and do what she wanted them to do. Leadership quality, I guess, but look what it led to."

\* \* \*

The front page of Sunday morning's *Register* held no surprises. Marcy Brewer and a *Register* photographer had shown up at the high school while Pamela and the Frasers were still there and in time to get a photo of Gayle Witherspoon being led from the building in handcuffs. Now that photo illustrated the lead article, under the headline ARBORVILLE WOMAN ARRESTED IN KNIFE ATTACK ON MUSIC TEACHER, CONFESSES TO TWO ARBORVILLE MURDERS.

Knowing that the article would include nothing that she wasn't already intimately familiar with, Pamela took her time grinding coffee beans, preparing her carafe's filter cone to receive them, and adding the water from the furiously boiling kettle. As the little kitchen filled with the bracing aroma of fresh-brewed coffee, she slipped a slice of whole-grain bread into the toaster and watched Ginger and Catrina track the last few bits of food around their shared bowl.

Then, settled at the table with coffee and toast at hand, she read the article that rehearsed salient details of the murders Gayle had confessed to, those of Mel Wordwoman—birth name Melissa Wilson— and Trish Barfield—birth name Trish Unger—and described the role she and the Frasers had played in the previous evening's drama. Marcy Brewer had clearly done her homework, looking up articles describing the Halloween tragedy that had launched Gayle on her murderous quest for revenge and connecting those long-ago mean girls with the murder victims. She hadn't neglected to mention that Nadine Dennis—birth name Nadine Barnes—had been the third mean girl.

Pamela's first cup of coffee had lasted exactly as long as it took to read the article. She set Part 1 aside and rose to refill her cup, but midway to the stove she was summoned by the doorbell's chime.

"Bettina, probably," she murmured, glancing down at her fleecy robe and fuzzy slippers.

But when she stepped into the entry, the view through the lace that curtained the oval window in the front door was of someone a great deal taller than Bettina, much taller even than the average man. She glanced down at the fleecy robe and fuzzy slippers again, sighed, and opened the door to greet Richard Larkin.

"I was just . . . I came by to . . ." he began, ducking his head as if anticipating that he might be invited to step through the doorway.

"Oh . . ." Pamela felt her heart thump. "It's okay. I'm finished with breakfast . . . or, there's a little coffee left. Would you . . . ?" She tipped her head toward the kitchen and made a vague gesture.

"You're all right? I saw the article . . ." He raised his head and studied her with the serious expression that emphasized the stern angularity of his features.

"Fine," Pamela said, unsure whether to maintain the eye contact that was making her a bit breathless or look away. "Perfectly fine, and it's thoughtful of you to ask." He was still standing on the porch. She took a few steps back and tipped her head toward the kitchen again. "I could make more coffee, or maybe you and your wife have already . . ."

"My wife?" A frown made his expression even more serious, if that was possible.

"Maureen?"

"Oh!" He flashed a smile that vanished as quickly as it had come. "My former wife."

"But . . . isn't she . . . back with you now?"

"Only briefly." Richard's tone became conversational. "She's relocating, or I should say, *they're* relocating, from San Francisco to Manhattan, and she's come out to look at real estate before the move. I told her she could stay here for a bit."

The original split must have been quite amicable, Pamela reflected, and Richard seemed undisturbed by the fact that Maureen had apparently moved on to a new partner.

As if he'd read her mind, Richard said, "Yes, my wife—my former wife—has moved on. She has a wife."

Pamela searched her mind for something to say. Losing a spouse to a rival would be hard, of course. But a woman of Maureen's likely generation might have married a man before she had a chance to discover her heart's true desire. Apparently Richard understood that.

Again, though she hadn't spoken, Richard responded, seemingly to her thoughts. "That's why she left me," he said, "and I understood. Laine and Sibyl weren't children anymore, and they understood too."

He smiled again, but not the smile that came and went. Rather, it was a sad smile that suited his angular features. "The heart wants what it wants, and there's no way around it."

"No," Pamela responded with her own sad smile. "There's no way around it."

Richard's focus shifted from Pamela's face to somewhere beyond her. "Do I hear a telephone?" he inquired.

He did, Pamela realized. She'd been standing in the open doorway for what seemed like an age, and his remaining on the porch despite offers of coffee suggested that he'd intended only to inquire about her well-being and go on his way. The conversation had shifted from her well-being to another topic with very interesting implications, so interesting that she wanted nothing more at the moment than to retreat and let the implications sink in.

With a courtly nod, Richard took a few steps back and said, "I'm glad you're okay." Pamela nodded in return, retreated from the doorway, and closed the door.

The phone was still ringing when she reached the kitchen. She picked up the handset and heard a familiar voice say, "I tried this number once and no one answered, so I tried your cell phone and no one answered, but I knew you were home because Bettina said she saw you talking to Richard Larkin on the porch."

"Penny?" Pamela inquired, though she knew the caller was Penny.

As if her identity was indeed a given, Penny went on. "I know all about what happened at the high school yesterday because Lorie Hopkins saw it on Access-Arborville even though she's living in Rhode Island now."

Pamela smiled to herself. When members of the Knit and Nibble group were tempted to gossip about their fellow townspeople, Nell often admonished them, saying they should tend to their own knitting—a Nell era expression for mind your own business. But it was a lost cause, Pamela knew, because most people could not resist tending to other people's knitting at the drop of a hat—like who was conversing with whose neighbor on whose porch on Sunday morning.

"Why didn't you tell me that Richard Larkin and his wife weren't actually getting back together?" she blurted out.

"What?" Penny's confusion was to be expected because the question had been asked without preamble.

"The day Sybil's mother gave me Sybil's jeans for you to take back to the city. Why didn't you tell me why she was staying next door?"

"I thought you knew." Penny laughed, a sound that over the phone, resembled static "It wasn't a big secret. Her mother and her mother's wife are moving to New York because of her mother's wife's job. It will be great for Sibyl to have both her parents so close now."

"I didn't know," Pamela said, "but I know now, and the mystery of the two Arborville murders has been solved besides."

"*Mo-om!*" Penny squealed. "That could have been dangerous, showing up just when you suspected murder number three was in progress."

"It *was* in progress, and Nadine Dennis would be dead and the police would be no closer to a solution." Pamela paused. "I hope you've put Thanksgiving in Arborville on your calendar. And maybe Sibyl and Laine will be here with their parents and Maureen's wife, and if you stay through the weekend, maybe we can all do something together."

The thought hadn't occurred to her until the words

came out of her mouth, but yes, maybe they could all do something together. And maybe later she could invite just him, by himself, to do something with her. The implications of what she had learned were beginning to sink in.

"You're trying to change the subject!" Pamela had always been amused at Penny's expression when she tried, unsuccessfully, to appear stern. She pictured that expression now and smiled.

"No, no," she murmured. "Thanksgiving is just around the corner and we really should make plans." Penny's response, to the effect that there was plenty of time to make plans for Thanksgiving, was interrupted by the doorbell's chime. Pamela rose, still holding the handset.

"Someone's here," she said when Penny finished talking. "It's Bettina," she added once she stepped into the entry and recognized the figure waiting behind the lace that curtained the oval window.

"You're still trying to change the subject." Penny sounded unconvinced.

"I have to go," Pamela insisted. "Bettina's really here."

"Tell her that showing up just when she suspected murder number three was in progress was very dangerous, and tell her to tell Wilfred that too."

Penny disconnected, and Pamela twisted the knob and pulled the door open.

"Did Penny call?" Bettina inquired brightly as she lifted a foot, shod in a red sneaker, over the threshold.

"You know perfectly well she did." Pamela laughed.

Bettina surveyed her friend for a long moment and then commented, "You look awfully happy."

"I *am* happy." Pamela waved Bettina toward the kitchen and followed her through the doorway, speaking to her back. "The when-shall-we-three-meet-again killer is in police custody."

Bettina turned when she reached the table. "You look happier than that, though." She glanced down at the table, where a half-eaten piece of toast sat forlornly on a small rose-garlanded plate. "I guess Richard Larkin interrupted your breakfast."

"As a matter of fact, he did," Pamela said, "and I only drank one cup of coffee. Shall I warm up what's left in the carafe and we can share it?"

"I can't really stay because Maxie is bringing Betty over." Bettina lowered herself into her accustomed chair as if she hadn't been listening to her own words. "This leftover bit of toast doesn't look very appealing. If you're going to make a fresh piece, I wouldn't mind one too."

"There's boysenberry jam in the refrigerator. Heavy cream too."

Pamela lit the burner under the carafe, fetched another cup, saucer, and plate from the cupboard, and slipped two slices of whole-grain bread into the toaster.

"I was surprised that the killer turned out to be Gayle," Bettina said as she bent into the refrigerator in search of the jam. "Did you know that was who you were going to find when you came dashing to the high school?"

"I wasn't sure." Pamela was standing at the stove.

She glanced up from watching for the small bubbles that would indicate the coffee was ready to serve. "But I knew the killer was going to strike again because I remembered you had said someone named Nadine was organizing the battle of the bands. I Googled one of the articles about the long-ago Halloween tragedy and recognized the name, though Nadine had a different last name then. And we'd have figured things out a lot sooner if Gayle didn't have a married name now instead of her birth name, Cotton, like the last name of Heather Cotton, the girl struck by lightning."

A *ka-chunk* as the toast popped up interrupted her then, and the coffee was ready to pour as well. Discussion didn't resume until coffee and toast were served, Pamela and Bettina were both seated at the table, and Bettina had transformed the dark liquid in her cup into the sweet and creamy concoction she preferred.

"Gayle never really wanted to learn to knit, did she?" Bettina commented after she had sampled her coffee. "She wasn't even trying, despite Roland's efforts. She just wanted to get to know us so she could steer us on that wild goose chase involving Adrienne's indiscretions."

She opened the jar of boysenberry jam and scooped out a glistening purple dollop, which she spread on her toast.

"I just remembered the other thing I wanted to tell you," she said after taking a bite of toast and following it with another sip of coffee. "I had a call from Roxanne Ballard. The bicycle fish grapevine has been buzzing with the news that Mel's killer has been identified and arrested, of course. She also wanted to let me know that despite what I told her colleague at the Little Corner Bookshop, she and her mother are on great terms and the scheme I came up with to track down Graham Tuttle was very underhanded."

Pamela nodded. "It *was* underhanded, and you didn't need to dwell on the fact that Roxanne isn't getting any younger." She nibbled on her fresh piece of toast and took a swallow of coffee.

Bettina winked. "It worked, though. We found out what we wanted, and anyway, Roxanne said she didn't mind because she and Graham are back together again and she couldn't be happier."

"People *do* get back together," Pamela said. "The heart wants what it wants, but not *every* heart can have what it wants. That neighbor of Graham's was head over heels in love with him and now he's back with Roxanne." Pamela felt a sudden pang of sympathy. The woman's eyes had been so large and hopeful behind her glasses.

"Pamela!" Bettina had been about to take a sip of coffee, but she returned the cup to its saucer with a clunk. "Are you seeing yourself in that poor neighbor—with Pete and his ex-wife reconciling and Richard's ex-wife moving in with him?"

"Not exactly." Pamela suppressed the beginnings of a smile. "Things aren't always what they seem."

"They're not?" Bettina's open-mouthed expression mingled amazement and delight. She leaned across the table, ignoring the sticky peril represented by the remains of her jam-covered toast on the plate before her. "What did Richard Larkin come over to tell you?"

"He came to ask me something."

"He did?" Bettina half-rose. "What?"

Pamela struggled against the smile. "If I was okay after yesterday. He had just read Marcy Brewer's article in the *Register*."

"Oh, you're hopeless!" Bettina sat back down. "What are the things that aren't what they seem?"

Taking pity on her friend, Pamela explained what Richard had told her about the reason for his former wife's presence.

"And so," Bettina summarized when Pamela had finished, "his former wife is still his former wife and will always be his former wife, and that means that he's . . ."

Bettina's voice trailed off. Had she seen something in Pamela's face that reflected a disinclination to count chickens before they were hatched?

"We'll see." Pamela shrugged and picked up her coffee cup.

Several minutes later, Pamela and Bettina stepped out onto Pamela's porch, just in time to see a baby stroller approaching the Frasers' house. Pushing the stroller was Bettina's daughter-in-law, Maxie. Bettina hurried down the porch steps, waving and calling hello, and Pamela followed.

By the time Pamela crossed Orchard Street, Bettina was already stooping toward the occupant of the stroller, one-year-old Betty Fraser. *It's really Bettina*, Bettina had explained when the name was chosen, *but we're going to call her Betty so people don't get confused*.

Betty was wearing a zip-up jumpsuit in pink fleece, with the hood pushed back to reveal tendrils of reddish hair framing chubby pink cheeks. She was pointing at Bettina and smiling delightedly, two tiny teeth visible in her lower jaw. Her gaze shifted then and she said "Dog" quite audibly—and there was Wilfred hurrying down the driveway with Woofus at his side.

Pamela greeted Maxie, and Wilfred and Woofus, and then bade her farewells and crossed the street to her own house.

# CHAPTER 20

It was Tuesday morning, and the Knit and Nibblers were meeting at Pamela's that evening. The cats had been fed, breakfast had been eaten, the newspaper had been perused, and Pamela was standing in the middle of her kitchen, staring at a wooden bowl nearly overflowing with the Granny Smith apples that had been a gift from the Frasers.

The obvious thing to do with them would be to make a pie, but Wilfred had made a pie—a sweet potato pie—when Bettina hosted the knitting group just a few weeks ago. Something with apples that wasn't a pie would be fun, but what?

She stepped over to the shelf where she kept her cookbooks and browsed the titles, pausing to extract a very thin one from between two very fat ones. It was little more than a pamphlet, and she had bought it on a recent outing to a restored village in Massachusetts. One of the restored buildings was a mill, and one of the products of the mill had anciently been buckwheat flour. Now, the docent had explained, the mill was producing buckwheat flour once again.

She had come away with a small cloth bag of buckwheat flour and this cookbook, which featured recipes involving buckwheat flour. She lowered herself into a chair and opened the cookbook to the section labeled DESSERTS.

One of the desserts was an apple galette, identified as a traditional recipe from the Normandy region in northwestern France, where apples grow in abundance and baking projects often combine buckwheat with wheat flour. A little sketch of the apple galette showed a pizzalike creation with a ridge of crust around the edge and a low mound of sliced apples in the center.

Pamela laid the cookbook on the counter open to the recipe and set to work. The first step was to make the apple filling, which required four Granny Smith–type apples. She took four apples from the wooden bowl, cut them into quarters and cored and peeled the quarters, adding the thin green peels to the small compost bin at the end of the counter. Then she sliced each quarter into horizontal slices about a quarter-inch thick, transferring the slices to a one-quart measuring cup just to make sure she ended up with at least the four cups of sliced apples the recipe called for.

Unlike a typical apple pie recipe, in which raw apple slices softened as the crust that enclosed them baked, the galette recipe cooked the apple slices with butter, brown sugar, and heavy cream in advance. The process began by melting the butter in a skillet, then adding the sugar and cream and stirring to blend. The color, as Pamela stirred, deepened into a rich caramel as an intoxicatingly sugary aroma rose from the thickening syrup.

She reached for the measuring cup full of apple slices and tipped them into the skillet, prodding them with her wooden spoon to spread them out and coat them with the caramel syrup. This step in the recipe, which involved cooking the apples until they were tender, invited daydreaming. They couldn't be left to themselves lest they burn, but the only intervention required from the cook was to rearrange the syrup-coated apple slices with a twirl of the wooden spoon as they added their sweet fruitiness to the aroma of the caramel and their color changed from pale to golden.

Pamela found herself contemplating Richard Larkin's kitchen window. She had often seen him at work in his kitchen, or at least bending over his sink, which she knew gave him a clear view of her at her own sink, though the sinks weren't visible. But there was no sign of activity in his kitchen now. He was doubtless at work, and Maureen was perhaps in the city too, touring condominiums with a Realtor.

She took a fork from the silverware drawer and poked an apple slice. The fork slipped in easily, and she declared the galette filling nearly done. All that remained was to mix in a dollop of vanilla, a sprinkling of cinnamon, and a pinch of salt. That done, as the perfume and spice of those additions blended with the caramelized apples, she turned off the stove and applied herself to making the galette crust.

The buckwheat flour was pale but not white, and it had a nutty smell. The recipe required only a third of a cup of buckwheat flour together with a whole cup of wheat flour. Pamela sifted the flours together with a bit of salt into her favorite vintage mixing bowl, the buff-colored one with three white stripes circling it near the rim.

The shortening that the recipe called for was butter. She added the butter, chopped into small pieces, to the bowl and cut it into the dry ingredients with her pastry blender until the mixture resembled pebbly sand. She sprinkled ice water over the mixture, tossing with a fork, until the dough clumped together, and then began kneading with her fingers. Finally, she turned the dough out onto a square of plastic wrap, and used the plastic wrap to shape the dough lump into a flat disk. The dough was sticky and her hands needed a good washing at that point.

From there, it was simple, with the aid of generous dustings of flour to roll the dough into a large circle. She folded the circle in half and in half again for ease in transferring it to the large round pizza pan that was perfectly suited to the size and shape of the galette. Unfolded, the dough reached nearly to the edges of the pan. Once the caramelized apples had been scooped onto it, however, and smoothed to within a few inches of the circle's edge, that dough border was folded inward in a way that made the creation truly resemble a pizza. The final touch was to brush beaten egg over the folded border and sprinkle it with granulated sugar.

The oven had been heating while Pamela worked on the crust, and the light that signaled it was hot enough had just clicked off. She opened the oven door, picked up the pizza pan with its delicately assembled cargo, and leaned into the oven's heat to place the pizza pan on the upper rack. The galette would be done in thirty-five or forty minutes, enough time to clean up the kitchen and set out the cups and saucers and plates and all else that would be needed to serve the refreshments that evening.

"Something certainly smells good!" Bettina exclaimed even before she began to unbutton her coat. The day had been blustery, as the pleasant autumn weather gave way to winter. "Apples, I think," she added after she had slipped out of the coat to reveal a jersey wrap dress in a shade of violet as dramatic as the scarlet of her hair, with violet kitten heels to match.

"Not a pie, though," Pamela said. "You can take a peek if you like. It's on the dining room table."

Bettina left her coat on the entry's sole chair and veered off into the living room and the dining room beyond. There, the antique chandelier cast its soft light on a table covered with a lacy cloth. On it were six rose-garlanded cup-and-saucer sets, a stack of six rose-garlanded plates, six white linen napkins, and six forks and six spoons. In their midst, a circular serving platter held the galette, apple slices glistening with sugary syrup and bordered by a wide crust burnished golden brown.

Bettina's high-pitched sigh of delight was echoed by the doorbell's chime, and Pamela backtracked to the entry. She opened the door to admit Holly and Karen, closing it quickly to interrupt the gust of chilly wind that had accompanied them. Holly began speaking before removing her coat, fake leopard styled in a flaring

1950s mode. But her topic was not the aroma that gave a preview of the evening's nibble.

"Gayle Witherspoon!" she exclaimed. "Who on earth would have suspected?"

The doorbell chimed again before Pamela could respond, and a moment later, she was greeting Nell and Roland.

"He intercepted me at the corner of Orchard," Nell explained. "I was doing fine on foot."

"Quite a surprise we had in the news on Sunday morning," Roland commented as he unbuttoned his trim wool topcoat and laid it carefully atop the other coats that had accumulated on the chair.

"Very sad." Nell shook her head, and her halo of white hair, already disarranged by the wind, shivered. "For twenty-five years, Gayle brooded over that long-ago tragedy, and then she finally decided to avenge her sister."

"Mean girls." Holly's head shake mirrored Nell's. "I don't know if they called them that back then, but Mel and her friends were definitely mean girls, with their clique. Gayle's little sister was desperate to be accepted by them, to the point of doing any mean thing they suggested."

Bettina had joined them from the dining room and finished the thought. "Even standing in an open field in the midst of a lightning storm. *Duh!*"

"Gayle mentioned her sister one of the nights she was here," Holly said. "She even mentioned that her sister was long gone, and that she had loved Halloween. I suppose that was a clue, but none of us connected it with Mel's murder."

As they talked, the group had begun moving toward the living room and settling into their usual spots. In no time at all, Nell was seated in the comfortable armchair at one end of the hearth, with Roland on the hassock at the other end. Nell was already at work on another Christmas stocking, this one using an ombré yarn that shaded from yellow through chartreuse all the way to deep forest green. Roland's briefcase sat open on the hearth as he checked a detail in a printed knitting pattern.

Holly, Bettina, and Karen were lined up on the sofa, with Holly at the end closest to Pamela, who was perched on the rummage sale chair with the carved wooden back and needlepoint seat.

No one said anything for a bit as projects were extracted from knitting bags and knitters pondered where they had left off and what the next steps would be. One leg of Holly's chartreuse leggings sprawled nearly to the floor, suggesting she had found extra time to knit during the previous week.

"You're really making progress," Bettina commented, leaning past Karen, who sat in the middle.

"This is just the first leg, though," Holly said. "Each leg gets knitted separately, like two long cable-knit stockings without feet but with half a panty section at the top. Then the tops get sewn together."

She shifted her attention from Bettina to Roland. "You were *amazing* to help Gayle with her knitting," she said, accompanying her comment with a smile that revealed her perfect teeth. "And it turned out she didn't even really want to learn."

"She didn't?" Roland's astonishment appeared genuine. "I certainly wouldn't waste time trying to learn something I didn't really want to learn. I'm busy enough as it is."

"Not everyone is you, Roland," Bettina said. "Gayle sat in with the group because she wanted to get to know Pamela and me so she could tell us why she thought Adrienne was actually the intended target."

"Why on earth would someone want to kill Adrienne?" Karen inquired.

"There were reasons"—Bettina smiled and glanced toward Nell—"but I'd best not reveal them."

"You'll tell us later?" Holly whispered.

"Maybe," Bettina whispered back. "And anyway," she went on in a louder voice, "it turned out Adrienne wasn't the intended target, and Mel's murder didn't have anything to do with her feminist activities in the city either."

"I was glad about that," Holly said, "though the feminist angle seems to have struck a nerve. A follow-up article in the *Register* included some quotes from members of that group Mel was involved with. I guess the world she inhabited seems very exotic to suburbanites."

"Mel was apparently very charismatic"—Nell spoke up from the depths of her armchair—"which made it possible for her to convert the members of Shakespeare's Rib to her views about men."

"But then there was that boyfriend," Holly said, "and she was fighting her attraction. I was surprised he was willing to be interviewed."

"I'm certainly glad things have progressed beyond what women could expect from their lives when I was growing up," Nell said.

Roland had been focused on his knitting, peering at his complicated four-needle project as his fingers moved busily. But he looked up, his expression even more intense than usual. He glanced around the group and said, "You don't all think men are superfluous, do you?"

"Of course not." Nell turned toward where Roland was sitting, at the other end of the hearth. Her gaze was almost tender. "I can't see that it's necessary to renounce men—especially in this day and age, when so many are so enlightened."

"But how did they get so enlightened?" Holly asked, her knitting forgotten in her lap. "Who enlightened them?" There was no immediate answer, but it seemed the question was rhetorical. Holly answered it herself. "Women like you, Nell!"

"Yes!" Bettina exclaimed. "I'm certainly happy that my Wilfred sees cooking as a worthy outlet for his energies. And here's Roland knitting, even though the Womanifesto apparently warns women 'You weave the web that is your prison.' Of course, Roland is a man."

Roland looked up again, puzzled. "I don't think it's a prison, but I really am trying to concentrate. I talk all day at work and when I come here, I want to knit."

There was much more to say, Pamela thought, about women's work and weaving webs—and even the many clues that had come together before she went dashing out to warn Nadine that she was about to become the third victim referred to in the "When shall we three meet again?" notes.

But Holly, at the end of the sofa nearest to the rummage-sale chair, was bent industriously over the half legging currently nearing completion. Next to her, Bettina, smiling a bit—perhaps at the thought of her good fortune in having a husband who cooked—was hard at work, and Karen's fingers were plying her needles as the sweater intended for her husband grew.

Pamela relaxed into her project as well, feeling her breathing slow, enjoying the yarn's caress against her fingers. Time passed. She recalled the last time she had handled this kelly-green yarn, purchased for a sweater she'd made for Michael Paterson long ago. No, men weren't superfluous. They were necessary—though at the moment in her own life . . .

She was relieved when that train of thought was interrupted. Roland set his knitting on the hearth, pushed back his immaculate cuff to consult his impressive watch, and intoned, "It's just eight o'clock." She'd been so caught up in her thoughts that she hadn't noticed when Bettina slipped from the room, and she hadn't noticed the aroma of coffee drifting in from the kitchen. Now, as she rose, Bettina appeared in the arch that separated the dining room from the living room.

"Pamela has prepared a wonderful treat for us," Bettina announced.

Some minutes later, the knitters were back in their seats, but holding plates that bore slices of the apple galette garnished with scoops of vanilla ice cream. Steaming cups of coffee, or tea in the case of Karen and Nell, waited on the coffee table and hearth as bites of galette were sampled and enthusiastically approved.

"What is it?" was the question, and Pamela was happy to explain, even describing the trip to the restored village where she had acquired the buckwheat flour. In sampling her own piece, she was happy to note that the Granny Smith apples, with their slight sourness, were crucial to the recipe's success, the intense apple flavor coming through despite the sweetness of the caramel syrup. And the dusting of granulated sugar added the perfect finish to the wide crust with its nutty hint of buckwheat.

"Pamela, you have outdone yourself," Holly declared as she leaned forward to set her empty plate on the coffee table. "This *amazing* recipe, and you solved the Halloween mystery too."

"And the dog park mystery," Karen added.

"And all's well in our little town once more." Nell turned her benevolent gaze on the women lined up across from her and then shifted that gaze to Roland at the end of the hearth.

Apparently feeling a need to contribute, Roland added, "As Wilfred might say, 'All's well that ends well.'"

Nell laughed and observed, "I think Shakespeare said it first."

# KNIT

## Cozy Scarf Hood with Optional Ears

This scarf hood idea is a way to make sure that a scarf draped over the head for warmth stays in place. Ears are optional for a fun touch, and a smaller version can be made for a child by adjusting the width and length of the scarf that forms the basis of the scarf hood.

For a picture of the completed scarf hood, as well as some in-progress photos, visit the Knit & Nibble Mysteries page at PeggyEhrhart.com. Click on the cover for *A Dark and Stormy Knit* and scroll down on the page that opens. References in the directions below to photos on my website are to this page.

Use yarn identified on the label as Medium and/or #4, and use size 7 needles (though size 6 or 8 is fine if that's what you have). With this yarn and these needles you will average about four stitches to the inch. The scarf hood requires about 560 yards of yarn. This amount will allow plenty for the ears if you want them.

If you've never knitted anything at all, it's easier to learn the basics by watching than by reading. The internet abounds with tutorials that show the process clearly, including casting on and off. Just search on "How to knit," "Casting on," and "Casting off." You only need to learn the basic knitting stitch. Don't worry about purl. That's used in alternating rows to create the stockinette stitch, the stitch you see, for example, in a typical sweater. If you use knit on every row, you will end up with the stitch called the garter stitch. That's the stitch used for the scarf hood. With this stitch, there's no wrong side because both sides of the knitting are the same, which works well for this project.

**Make the scarf**

Cast on 40 stitches, using either the simple slipknot process or the long tail process. Casting on is often included in internet "How to knit" tutorials, or you can search specifically for "Casting on." After you've cast on, keep knitting, using the garter stitch, until your piece of knitting is 60 inches long (5 feet). Cast off and hide your tails. To hide a tail, thread a yarn needle—a large needle with a large eye and a blunt tip—with the tail, work the needle in and out of the edge or bottom of the scarf for half an inch or so, and clip the small tail that remains. There is a photo of this step on my website.

**Make the ears (make 2)**

Cast on 8 stitches, using either the simple slipknot process or the long tail process. Knit 2 rows. Increase 2 stitches on row 3 by casting on 1 stitch after the first stitch in the row and 1 stitch before the last stitch in the row. Increasing this way makes for a neater edge than adding a stitch at the very beginning or end of a row. There are photos of this process on my website. Use the same process on all subsequent rows that require increasing. Knit 3 rows. Increase 2 stitches on row 7. Knit 3 rows. Increase 2 stitches on row 11. Knit 9 rows.

Decrease 2 stitches on row 21 by knitting 1 stitch, knitting the next 2 stitches together, continuing until 3 stitches are left, knitting 2 stitches together, and knitting the last stitch. Decreasing this way makes for a neater edge than decreasing by knitting the first and last 2 stitches together. There is a photo of this process on my website. Use the same process on all subsequent rows that require decreasing. Knit 3 rows. Decrease 2 stitches on row 25. Knit 3 rows. Decrease 2 stitches on row 29. Knit 3 rows. Decrease 2 stitches on row 33. Knit 3 rows.

Now you will have 6 stitches. Knit 1 stitch, knit the next 2 stitches together and the next 2 stitches together, and knit the last stitch in the row. Now you will have 4 stitches. Knit 1 row. On the next row, knit the first 2 stitches together and the next 2 stitches together. Now you will have 2 stitches. Knit them together and slip the 1 remaining stitch off the needle. Clip your yarn, leaving a tail of about 3 inches, thread the tail through the loop, and pull tight. To hide this tail, thread your yarn needle with it, work the needle in and out of the edge of the ear for half an inch or so, and clip the small tail that remains. There are photos of this step on my website. Leave the tails from casting on and use them to attach the ears.

**Assemble the scarf hood**

Fold the scarf in half crosswise and, starting at the fold, pin the two sides together for about 10 inches along one edge. There is a photo of this step on my website. Thread a yarn needle with your yarn and sew this seam, using a whip stitch and catching only the outer loops along each side. Pin the ears, closer to the open edge and pointing up, into position as shown in the photo on my website. They will flop down realistically when sewn. Thread your yarn needle with the tails and sew the ears into place.

# NIBBLE

## Pamela's Apple Galette

In *A Dark and Stormy Knit*, Pamela makes an apple galette when she hosts the Knit and Nibble group. For the crust, she combines wheat flour with some buckwheat flour from a visit to a restored village where an old flour mill had been put back in operation.

Buckwheat actually isn't a type of wheat at all but rather the seed of a plant in the rhubarb family. It's been cultivated by humans for millennia and was a very common crop in North America in the eighteenth and nineteenth centuries—thus the mill in the restored village. Buckwheat flour is also used in France, where crêpes and galettes made with it are traditional in Normandy and Brittany.

Buckwheat flour adds an interesting, slightly nutty flavor to pancakes, pastries, and breads. It is easy to find online, if not locally.

For a picture of Pamela's Apple Galette, as well as some in-progress photos, visit the Knit & Nibble Mysteries page at PeggyEhrhart.com. Click on the cover for *A Dark and Stormy Knit* and scroll down on the page that opens. References in the recipe below to photos on my website are to this page.

## Ingredients
*For the crust:*
1 cup flour
$\frac{1}{3}$ cup buckwheat flour
1 tsp. salt
$\frac{1}{2}$ cup (4 oz.) butter, not room temperature
$\frac{1}{4}$ cup ice water, or more as needed
You can also substitute pie crust made with your usual pie crust recipe (for a single-crust pie).

*For the filling:*
2 tbsp. butter
$\frac{1}{4}$ cup heavy cream
$\frac{1}{2}$ cup brown sugar
4 apples, Granny Smiths preferred, peeled, cored, and sliced (about 4 cups)
1 tsp. vanilla
Pinch of cinnamon
Pinch of salt

*For the assembly:*
1 egg beaten with a bit of water
2 tbsp. granulated sugar

## Make the apple filling
There are photos of this process on my website.
Melt the 2 tbsp. butter in a skillet over medium heat.

Add the heavy cream and brown sugar and stir to blend. Add the apples. Cook over medium heat, stirring occasionally, until the apples are tender and the liquid has thickened into a heavy syrup. You might have to turn the heat up at the end to accomplish this. The process of cooking the apples will take 10 to 15 minutes.

Add the vanilla, cinnamon, and salt and stir to blend.

Let the filling cool while you make the dough for your crust.

## Make the dough for your crust

There are photos of this process on my website.

Sift the flour, buckwheat flour, and salt into a medium-sized bowl. Cut the butter into little pieces and add it to the flour mixture. Using two knives, a pastry blender, or your hands, work the butter into the flour mixture until only pebble-sized pieces of flour-covered butter remain.

Sprinkle the ice water over the flour and butter mixture and, using your hands, work the contents of the bowl into a stiff dough, kneading until there are no dry bits and the texture is fairly uniform. Add a little more ice water if necessary. Turn the contents of the bowl out onto a work surface covered with a piece of plastic wrap.

Bring the edges of the plastic wrap up over the dough and, with the plastic wrap between your hands and the dough, use your hands to make the dough cohere into a ball and then shape it into a round disk about an inch thick.

(You can make the dough way in advance and refrigerate it for a few days. If you do this, let it return to room temperature before proceeding further.)

**Assemble the galette**

There are photos of this process on my website.

Set the dough on a floured surface large enough to accommodate a 14-inch circle. Flour a rolling pin, sprinkle a bit of flour on top of the dough, and start rolling. Lift the dough from time to time and sprinkle more flour under it. Roll until you have a circle that's 14 inches in diameter.

Before you assemble your galette, transfer the rolled-out pastry to the pan you will use to bake the galette. I used a pizza pan, but you can use a rectangular cookie sheet. It's okay if the pastry flops over the edges at this stage. The baking pan only has to accommodate the finished galette, which will be about 11 inches in diameter.

Grease the pan with a tiny bit of oil or soft butter. To transfer the pastry easily, use the same technique you'd use for a pie: fold it gently into quarters, move it to the baking pan, and unfold it.

Mound the filling in the middle of the pastry, then distribute it so it comes within an inch and a half of the pastry edge. Don't worry if there's a bit of liquid. Now fold an inch or so of the dough inward all the way around to make a raised rim. Brush this rim with the beaten egg and sprinkle it with the granulated sugar.

Bake the galette at 400 degrees for 35 to 40 minutes.

The pastry should be attractively browned. Let it cool a bit before transferring it to the serving plate. Two spatulas can be useful, or loosen it with a spatula and slide it onto the serving plate.

It's good served slightly warm with ice cream.